6/20

D0054330

The Sullivan Sisters

Also by

KATHRYN ORMSBEE

The Water and the Wild

The Doorway and the Deep

The Current and the Cure

The House in Poplar Wood

Midnight on Strange Street

Lucky Few

Tash Hearts Tolstoy

The Great Unknowable End

The Sullivan Sisters

KATHRYN ORMSBEE

SIMON & SCHUSTER BFYR

NEW YORK   LONDON   TORONTO   SYDNEY   NEW DELHI

SIMON & SCHUSTER BFYR

An imprint of Simon & Schuster Children's Publishing Division
1230 Avenue of the Americas, New York, New York 10020
This book is a work of fiction. Any references to historical events, real people,
or real places are used fictitiously. Other names, characters, places, and events
are products of the author's imagination, and any resemblance to actual events or
places or persons, living or dead, is entirely coincidental.

Text copyright © 2020 by Kathryn Ormsbee
Jacket illustration copyright © 2020 by Pedro Tapa
All rights reserved, including the right of reproduction in whole or in part in any form.
SIMON & SCHUSTER BFYR is a trademark of Simon & Schuster, Inc.

For information about special discounts for bulk purchases, please contact
Simon & Schuster Special Sales at 1-866-506-1949 or business@simonandschuster.com.
The Simon & Schuster Speakers Bureau can bring authors to your live event.
For more information or to book an event, contact the Simon & Schuster Speakers Bureau
at 1-866-248-3049 or visit our website at www.simonspeakers.com.
Jacket design by Chloë Foglia
Interior design by Hilary Zarycky
The text for this book was set in Electra.
Manufactured in the United States of America
First Edition
2 4 6 8 10 9 7 5 3 1
Library of Congress Cataloging-in-Publication Data
Names: Ormsbee, Kathryn, author.
Title: The Sullivan sisters / Kathryn Ormsbee.
Description: First edition. | New York : Simon & Schuster Books for Young Readers, [2020] |
Audience: Ages 12 and up. | Audience: Grades 7–9. |
Summary: The once tight bond among three sisters, ages fourteen to eighteen, disappears as
each deals with a personal setback; but when a letter arrives informing the sisters of a dead uncle
and an inheritance they knew nothing about, the news forces them to band together in the face
of a sinister family mystery, and possible murder.
Identifiers: LCCN 2019035014 (print) | LCCN 2019035015 (eBook) |
ISBN 9781534420533 (hardcover) | ISBN 9781534420557 (eBook)
Subjects: CYAC: Sisters—Fiction. | Inheritance and succession—Fiction. | Families—Fiction. |
Secrets—Fiction.
Classification: LCC PZ7.O637 Su 2020 (print) | LCC PZ7.O637 (eBook) | DDC
[Fic]—dc23
LC record available at https://lccn.loc.gov/2019035014
LC eBook record available at https://lccn.loc.gov/2019035015

To Annie and Matt Snow—
my favorite Oregonians
and the best siblings a girl could ask for

Today is far from Childhood,
But up and down the hills,
I held her hand the tighter—
Which shortened all the miles.

—EMILY DICKINSON, "One Sister have I in our house"

The Sullivan Sisters

SEVEN YEARS
BEFORE

CAYENNE CASTLE

The castle was Claire's idea, to begin with.

It came to her in drizzly December, four days before Christmas, when she, Eileen, and Murphy were cooped up inside the house.

Claire was full of plans and, more than that, good ideas for how to see them through.

"Leenie," she said, waking her older sister, "let's build something with *all* the blankets and *all* the sheets in the house."

Eileen didn't take time to reply. She threw the comforter off her twin bed, lightning zigzagging across her dark eyes. She was full of vision—a painter of colors and words and feelings. She knew which blankets to pair: Mom's fuzzy goldenrod quilt next to an evergreen U of O fleece, powder blue sheets knotted atop a peach duvet.

That morning the castle began to rise, and during its construction, Murphy, the youngest sister, appeared in the den.

"Whoa," she said reverently as she beheld the fabric battlements drawn over the sofa, armchairs, and TV. She found an opening between clothespinned sheets and poked her freckled face through.

"Ta-da!" she cried. "It's a stage!"

"Castle," Claire corrected.

"It could be both," said Eileen. She was busy taking out colored ribbons from her craft kit—a birthday gift from Mom—and tying them to blanket tassels for a pop of color.

Claire, meantime, was tapping her chin, squinting at a blueprint she'd drawn up on notebook paper. "There's enough material to make it to the hall and still have enough blankets for walls."

"Walls?" said Murphy. "Or . . . *stage curtains.*"

She grabbed the Magic Marker from Claire's hand and, using it as a microphone, announced, "Welcome to the main eveeent!"

Murphy was full of energy—performing for anyone who would listen and applaud.

The name of the castle came later that day, when Mom called and said she'd have to work late again. She'd been doing that recently: picking up extra shifts at Walgreens and, in her absence, leaving Eileen officially in charge.

"I wanted to show off the castle," Murphy pouted, once Eileen was off the phone. "Now Mom won't be back till after bedtime."

"It's Christmastime," Claire reminded Murphy, with a sagacious arch of her brow. "You like presents, don't you? Well, Mom has to work to afford them."

Murphy made a face. "I'd rather have Mom."

That made Eileen's insides twist. When Eileen had been Murphy's age, Leslie Sullivan had spent more time at home, reading books aloud and leading impromptu radio dance parties. Once, when Eileen had been five, Mom had helped her and Claire build a blanket fort like this one. It sucked that Murphy wasn't old enough to have those memories. Just like it sucked that she had no memories whatsoever of Dad. He'd died before Murphy had been born.

Dad seemed far away these days, but Eileen liked to think he would approve of the castle. Mom definitely would, when she finally got home from work.

That morning's breakfast had been easy to make on their own: bowls of cereal drenched in whole milk. Lunch was trickier, though. Claire stared into the fridge, determining that their best bet was five-day leftover chili. She tugged out the Tupperware, slopped its contents into bowls, and heated the meal in the microwave.

"It tastes funny," said Murphy, trying the chili. "Like . . . swamp!"

Murphy was a picky eater—she *was* only seven—and tended to make grandiose statements. When Claire tasted the chili for herself, though, she also made a face. It *did* taste funny. That wouldn't do. This crisis required another plan of action.

From the fridge, Claire tugged out a bag of old shredded cheese. "Toppings," she said. "That's the solution."

Eileen, meantime, crossed to the pantry. She reached straight for the spice rack, taking down a jar marked CAYENNE PEPPER. A bold choice—one that suited her.

The new additions made the meal better. Sprinkled on the chili in a low dose, mixed through with old kidney beans and chunky tomatoes, the spice covered the off-ness and brought out the flavors left to be enjoyed. The Sullivan sisters contentedly slurped their chili in the kitchen while, outside, rain pattered against the windows.

Claire reflected as they ate that they wouldn't need cheese and spices if Mom were here. Once upon a not-too-distant time, Mom had been just around the corner—in her bedroom, or the kitchen—helping Claire with long division or watching movies, the whole family snug on the couch. Claire could still taste Mom's signature chicken potpie, a mouthful of crisp peas, tender carrots, flaky crust.

Mom hadn't made that pie in months. There hadn't been time, with the extra night shifts she'd taken on. Rent on the house had gone up last year, and Dad's medical bills were bigger than ever, thanks to "accrued interest"—two words Claire couldn't make sense of but knew to be bad. They hung over the house, souring into a fetid smell. As though they were . . . a curse.

Curses. They were the dark stuff of fairy tales. But a castle? That was a fairy tale at its finest.

When the sisters returned to the den, surveying their handiwork, Claire said, businesslike, "It needs a name."

And the name had been Murphy's idea.

"Cayenne Castle!" she shouted with confidence.

When her sisters agreed to it, Murphy spun a circle and sang an impromptu song: *"Cayenne Castle, where dreams come true! If you eat our spice, it'll make you poo."*

6

"Weirdo," Eileen said, mussing Murphy's mess of red curls.

Murphy grinned wide. She liked when her sisters paid attention, even if it was to call her "weirdo." Mom was usually better about noticing Murphy, though lately she'd nodded distractedly at Murphy's original songs, saying, "That's nice, sweetie," as though she'd heard but hadn't *listened*.

Murphy sure hoped once Christmas was over, and their presents paid for, that Mom would go back to listening.

The sisters piled into their christened castle, diving into blankets and body pillows. Claire and Eileen shared salacious secrets from fifth and sixth grade, and Murphy watched them admiringly, chin on knees, eating a pudding cup dessert.

"Hey," she said, chocolate gloop coating her mouth. "Let's make Cayenne Castle every year. No matter what, we put up our castle on December twenty-first."

Claire and Eileen shared a smirk—an older sister thing. When they nodded at Murphy, she knew they were on her side.

"Deal," Eileen said, winking.

"Deal," Claire chimed in.

"Deal," Murphy concluded, with a pudding-stained grin.

So, the walls of Cayenne Castle were raised for the first time by a planner, a visionary, and a performer. It was an auspicious beginning, but as is the case with many agreements made in youth, the pact would break.

If, seven years later, you were to ask the Sullivan sisters why it broke . . .

Well, you would get three different answers.

DECEMBER
TWENTY-FIRST

ONE

Eileen

The letter arrived the morning of December twenty-first.

Eileen wasn't expecting mail addressed to her. No packages, because she hadn't ordered art supplies for two years. No Christmas cards, because who the hell sent those anymore? Extended family members, maybe—grandparents and great-aunts—but Eileen didn't have those. She definitely wasn't expecting a press-and-seal business envelope with a law office for a return address and a red-ink note on the flap that read, OPEN IMMEDIATELY.

Eileen was affronted. She didn't take orders, especially not from goddamn attorneys and their red-ink pens. She had a bad history with letters, and she didn't want to know what this one had to say—whether she opened it *immediately* or in ten years. So she threw the envelope out, dropping it in the trash can beneath her desk. Then she left the house for her Safeway shift.

Soon, she'd forgotten about the letter.

She forgot about a lot of things when she worked, and especially when she drank.

That was the point of both full-time occupations.

That night, back at home, Eileen was filled throat-high with Jack Daniel's. She'd ended up horizontal on the floor of her converted-garage bedroom, and that's how she found herself facing the trash can beneath her desk.

Music was playing on her boom box, fuzzy through the ancient speakers. "Christmas Wrapping" by the Waitresses had been on repeat for half an hour. It was a terrible song. It was the *best* song. Eileen hummed along.

Her mouth tasted like regurgitated milk. It was gloomy outside—typical Oregon. Mom had left that afternoon for the Bahamas. But none of this bothered Eileen. She was numb to every bad thing. She wiggled her ankles to the beat of the music and, through blurry eyes, read the address of the trashed envelope.

Ms. Eileen Sullivan.

The "Ms." really got to her. *Ms.* Eileen Sullivan. If those fancy attorneys could see her now.

Eileen pawed at the rim of the trash can, tipping it over and grabbing the envelope.

It was already opened, and Eileen didn't remember doing that. Then again, she did a lot of unmemorable stuff when she was drinking.

She laughed at the envelope—at the "Ms."—while tugging the letter out of its torn top.

Pretty soon, the laughing stopped.

TWO

Claire

At the same time Eileen was reading the letter, Claire was being rejected from her dream college.

She stared at her phone and the ugly words written on the admissions portal homepage.

Maybe my thumb slipped, she thought, *or I entered someone else's password.*

She'd been telling herself that for six days.

Delusional.

Ms. Hopkins, Claire's guidance counselor, had said Yale would be a long shot. But Ms. Hopkins wasn't familiar with Harper Everly's YouTube videos. She didn't know what it meant to be an Exceller. If she did, she wouldn't be working for the Emmet, Oregon, school district, and she wouldn't say, "Good grades and letters of rec aren't enough for places like this." She wouldn't bring such negativity into Claire's life.

That was what Claire had been telling herself from October

to November to December fifteenth, when she'd received the e-mail from Yale, instructing her to check the Internet portal. She'd been so nervous, she'd messed up the password entry twice. That's why, when she'd finally logged in, she'd thought the rejection was a mistake. She'd told herself it had to be wrong, even the second time she'd checked, and the third.

And the fiftieth.

The official letter had arrived in the mail the next day, telling Claire what the Internet had: *You're not good enough.*

Still, Claire logged in to the portal every day, hoping for a change in reality, a discovery that it had been a technical error.

Doing the same thing over and over, expecting different results—that was the definition of insanity, right?

Or of perseverance.

It only took one yes. Harper Everly said that, and Harper's word was gold.

She also said, "Don't plan for failure, or failure is what you'll get."

Harper was confident making that pronouncement, with her glistening teeth and jewel-toned statement necklace. She was confident for a reason: She'd *succeeded.* She was only twenty, and she had over two million subscribers, plus the resultant commercial sponsorships. She'd been named a "Young Entrepreneur to Watch" by *Cosmopolitan*, and to top it off, she'd grown up without anything, in a nowheresville town that may as well have been Emmet.

Harper knew what she was talking about.

So why was Claire staring at a rejection?

No.

Not even waitlisted. A sturdy, solid *no*.

How did you reject someone with a perfect 800 on her SAT reading and writing section *and* a 4.0 GPA? A saint with hundreds of hours of community service and letters of recommendation from her AP teachers, saying what a natural-born leader she was? How did Yale reject *Claire Sullivan*, a brilliant, well-rounded, blue-collar girl who was also gay? Didn't they understand she needed a way out? She had to be in a beautiful, broad-minded, intellectually stimulating place. Everything Emmet was not.

"Fuck you, Yale," Claire said, hurling her phone from the bed onto the pink shag rug.

Immediately, she regretted it.

"Fuck" was an ugly word, used only by Settlers.

It felt wrong to say, a betrayal.

But Yale had betrayed Claire first.

She'd been so sure. If Mom, a Settler, could win a Bahamian cruise through sheer luck, then Claire, a tried-and-true Exceller, would absolutely make it to New England.

Now there was no New England.

No snow-blanketed winters or historic gray-stone archways.

No Socratic dialogues around a crackling fire.

No Ainsley St. John, and no perfect first kiss.

Claire lay on the bed, at last allowing the heavy truth to leech into her body, slog through her veins, thunk against her heart.

She should have seen this coming a month ago. That was when Claire's perfect facade of a future had started to crack. She had opened Instagram to find a new post by Ainsley, her arm slung around the shoulder of a beaming blond girl in a baseball cap. The caption read, "♥ my girlfriend."

Girlfriend.

A girlfriend who wasn't Claire.

That wasn't in the plan.

Still, Claire had told herself, girlfriends were only *girlfriends*. Not fiancées. Not wives. They would last a few months, or mere days, and Claire could wait that out.

She'd done what Harper had said and not planned for failure. She'd ignored the Instagram post, because she refused to be worried. She hadn't applied to a "safety" school, because what was the point? It was single-choice early admission to Yale, or bust. She wouldn't be caught dead with her name on an application to U of O.

And now?

It was too late.

She wasn't going to get the girl.

She wasn't going to Yale.

She wasn't going to college, period.

Everything Claire had worked for these two years was gone — specks of snow that lived for one moment in her imagination, now dissolved into a useless puddle.

Claire was a planner, and her plan had failed.

Not even Harper Everly, with her two million subscribers, could change that.

THREE

Murphy

At the same time Claire was not getting into college, Murphy was discovering the dead body.

Unlike, say, hamsters or hedgehogs, pet turtles have remarkably long lifespans; the average is forty years. Siegfried had lived to be thirty, so really, he'd had a decent turtle life. He hadn't died of natural causes, though. He'd died—Murphy was convinced—because she'd forgotten to feed him.

She'd been busy lately, with school and drama club.

She simply hadn't been thinking.

She couldn't remember *not* feeding him. Only, that was the trouble with turtles: They didn't remind you when you'd forgotten to fix them dinner. They couldn't bark or meow or claw at their cages. They simply stayed in their shells, chilling. Hungry. Hungrier. Dead.

Murphy had read once that turtles could survive for months, even years, without food. That's why she'd grown lax with feeding in the first place: Siegfried was cold-blooded, so he could handle a few skipped days. He could deal with dirty, months-old tank water and a blown heat bulb that Murphy hadn't gotten around to replacing.

Now, though, it seemed that even the cold-blooded had their limit.

Murphy wasn't sure she'd ever forgive herself.

To make matters worse, she had a dead body on her hands. What was she supposed to do about that? In her fourteen years of life, no one had prepared Murphy for this. Who did she even ask about turtle burials?

Not Mom. Leslie Sullivan had left that morning for her all-inclusive sweepstakes Bahamian cruise, and she'd told her daughters that once the boat hit the open sea, she'd have no cell phone service and only limited access to expensive Internet.

Even if Mom had been around to hear the news, would it have bothered her much? Six years ago, when Murphy had asked to take care of the family turtle, Mom had happily moved his tank into Murphy's room like it was a big relief. She hadn't even realized that Murphy had changed his old name of "Tortue" until months later, when Murphy had asked her to stop by Petco for Siegfried A. Roy's food pellets. Mom was always busy working long hours at Walgreens. She didn't have time to worry about Murphy's schoolwork, let alone an old turtle.

That left Eileen and Claire, Murphy's older sisters, as possible advisors on turtle funeral matters. Eileen, who locked herself in her bedroom, playing loud music and emerging only to sway and slur her words. Claire, who locked herself in her bedroom, emerging only to lecture Murphy about leaving dried oatmeal bowls in the kitchen sink.

Like Murphy would ask *them* for help.

Maybe four years ago, when they'd been nicer and hadn't shut their doors.

Not now.

In Siegfried's burial, Murphy was alone.

Tonight, the house was silent, both of Murphy's sisters barricaded in their rooms. Murphy sat at the family computer in the den. It was a behemoth from the twentieth century, with a broken fan that juddered like a bullet-riddled fighter jet every time it started. As Murphy waited for the hunk of machinery to boot up—*ri-tat-tat-tat-ti-tat*—she pulled her newest rope trick from her jeans pocket.

She was trying to master this one:

Over, under, tug through and out.

The instructions from the *Magic Today* booklet made it sound easy enough. Currently, though, the rope lay limp in Murphy's hands, forming the shape of a loose *M*.

M for Murphy.

M for Murderer.

At last, the computer lurched to life. Murphy put away the accusatory rope, opened the Internet, and clicked on the search bar.

She typed in "How to dispose of a dead turtle."

She winced.

She hit enter.

She avoided the images tab, because this wasn't her first gross search engine rodeo. Instead, she clicked on a forum result from a website called Pet Savvy. Most forum users suggested a shoebox burial.

Murphy couldn't remember the last time she'd bought shoes.

Having two older sisters made her the hand-me-down queen.

She kept scrolling through comments.

"SparksandDarts" said:

> I'll tell you what my dad did when our turtle kicked
> it. He pretended our turtle had "powers" and had
> "disappeared" overnight. Then he claimed he'd
> "reappeared" inside our TV, and he was now one of
> the Teenage Mutant Ninja Turtles. I spent half my
> childhood believing Michelangelo was my old pet.

Murphy snorted and muttered, "Sick."

Still, she filed away the information. Not for real life. For an act.

Magicians made rabbits disappear on the regular, but Murphy had never seen a disappearing turtle act. That could be new. Fresh. Fun. Murphy's big break. She could go down in the books as "Turtle Girl."

Murphy made a face.

Not a great name.

Turtle Empress Supreme?

Better. She'd workshop that, once she made it to Vegas.

Scrolling deeper into the forum replies, Murphy discovered posts about using Clorox to prevent bacterial growth.

That's when she began to feel nauseated.

Murphy had realized something: She was going to have to move Siegfried. *Touch* dead Siegfried.

She modified her search to "How to dispose of a dead turtle *without throwing up.*"

DECEMBER
TWENTY-SECOND

FOUR

Eileen

The Law Offices of Knutsen & Crowley | 218 Avenue B #5

December 18, 2020

Dear Ms. Sullivan,

    I represented your uncle, Patrick Enright, in life, and as of his passing one week ago, I serve as the executor of his will. Mr. Enright has informed me that this will come as a surprise, but he left behind the majority of his estate to you and your sisters. This estate is to be divided in equal thirds and bequeathed to each of you upon your respective eighteenth birthdays.

    Since you are the first Sullivan sister to reach the age of majority, I am writing to request you make an appointment at my office, during which time I will go over the terms of the late Mr. Enright's will and address any questions you may have. You are welcome to bring your own attorney, should you desire. I look forward to making your acquaintance.

Sincerely,
William J. Knutsen

Eileen looked up from the letter in her hand. She was facing 218 Avenue B, listening to Mariah Carey on holiday radio. Vigorously, she chewed four pieces of Dubble Bubble.

She hated this song.

But she wasn't sure she could get out of the van.

"Shit," she said to the steering wheel.

She welcomed the gum's ephemeral sugar rush. Not alcohol, maybe, but like it—necessary for short-time existence, detrimental to long-term well-being.

It was misting outside, and rain had puddled in the parking lot, iridescent with gasoline and who knew what other crap. Eileen hadn't known what to expect from William J. Knutsen. This eyesore of an office sure wasn't it. A town as small as Emmet didn't exactly have right and wrong sides of the track; nearly every house was run-down, the strip malls grimy. This place was especially both those things: a tan-brick shopping center that hadn't been updated since the start of the new millennium. Half the storefronts were empty, their windows papered up, with FOR LEASE signs left on the doors like despairing afterthoughts. Wedged between two of these storefronts were the law offices of Knutsen and Crowley. A rusted plaque by the glass double doors told Eileen so, and in case she had any remaining doubts, a banner strung overhead shouted, TROUBLE WITH THE LAW? BILL CAN HELP. Beside the words was an illustration of a green bird breaking free from a birdcage prison cell.

It seemed like a scam.

But then, scams weren't supposed to seem like scams. This place was *so* scammy, it had to be legitimate.

Wasn't that how it worked?

Eileen hadn't known there was a law office in Emmet, period. She'd assumed that town residents in need of legal assistance looked for it farther afield, in an actual city, like Eugene. This place was a shock.

As was the fact that she had inherited a third of her uncle's estate.

As was the fact that she had an uncle.

Patrick Enright.

What the hell.

Eileen ran her thumb along the letter's edge, studying its very fibers for signs of fraud.

Meanwhile, Mariah crooned about what she wanted for Christmas.

Eileen knew the responsible thing to do: wait until Mom was back from the cruise, show her the letter, and ask point-blank about its contents. Who said Eileen was responsible, though? And who said Mom was up for a heart-to-heart? Eileen hadn't had a real talk with her mother for the past four, maybe five years. These days Mom was in one of two places: the Walgreens on Fourth Avenue or inside her locked bedroom, the television's murmur at war with her snores. One place she was not: Eileen's life.

No. After last night's revelation, Eileen had decided the best thing to do was go straight to the source: Mr. Knutsen himself. She wanted to see the man in person. First, to be sure this law office *existed*. Second, because she wanted immediate answers, to her face. Worst-case scenario, this was a scam, and she'd bolt. But best-case?

Goddamn. Best-case, she had family—albeit dead family. And maybe that family had an explanation—a *different* explanation for the letters she'd uncovered two years ago. That could change everything.

Eileen sure as hell wanted things to change.

The gum had lost its flavor. Eileen spat it into her hand and formed a glistening ball, which she dropped into the cup holder. Claire would call her disgusting, but this wasn't Claire's car. And this wasn't Claire's letter to deal with. The task fell solely to Eileen.

So, she'd better do something about it.

Enough was enough. Eileen cut the engine and got out of the van. Avoiding the deeper rain puddles, she crossed the parking lot, opened the door to the office, and stepped inside.

The place was nice in an outdated, seventies kind of way, with wood-paneled walls and shiny gold fixtures. A receptionist sat at the front desk, typing on a keyboard. Three heavy lines cut across her forehead—permanent ridges, it seemed.

Eileen cleared her throat.

"Appointment time?" the receptionist asked, keeping her eyes on the screen.

"Uh. I didn't make one. Was I supposed to?"

Eileen knew she was supposed to. She'd read the letter five hundred times.

The receptionist stopped typing. Her face reminded Eileen of

26

her fourth-grade teacher, Ms. Larson. And since this was Emmet, there was a big chance the two of them were related.

"We don't take walk-ins anymore," said Ms. Larson's probably-sister. "You'll have to make an appointment with either Mr. Crowley or Mr. Knutsen."

"Yeah, Mr. Knutsen sent me this."

Eileen held out the letter. The lines on the receptionist's forehead bulged.

"That may be," she said after a pause, "but you still have to make an appointment. It'll have to be after the holiday sea—"

"Send her on in, Tonya."

Eileen glanced up. There were three doors leading off the reception area. One of those doors was open. The one marked WILLIAM J. KNUTSEN, ATTORNEY-AT-LAW.

"Bill," Tonya called back, "I don't think—"

"I said, send her in."

Tonya looked helpless and pissed. She glared at Eileen, who was considering that maybe she should've washed and/or styled her hair for this occasion. Maybe not worn the usual leather jacket, combat boots, and heavy eyeliner. Too late for that, though. Tonya was motioning for Eileen to do as the voice of Bill commanded. Eileen stepped into his room.

William J. Knutsen, like his law office, was not what Eileen had expected. For one thing, he had a head of hair; she'd been picturing him as bald. For another, that hair was white; she'd pictured a young, upstart grifter. The guy before her was more of a Santa Claus. His chin was sagging and his stature straight—a striking combo. One that, once upon a time, Eileen would've loved to have painted.

From a leather chair behind his desk, he said, "Please have a seat, Ms. Sullivan."

Mr. Knutsen spoke the way Eileen thought Santa might: jolly. Down-to-earth. She eyed the chair opposite him and said, "I'm cool where I am, thanks."

Mr. Knutsen didn't put up a fight. He tented his fingers in front of his whisker-bordered lips.

Eileen frowned at him. "How do you know who I am?"

"Well, my usual clientele is over the age of thirty."

"Deduction." Eileen tapped her temple. "You're one clever bastard, Billy."

Mr. Knutsen appeared unruffled. If Eileen had addressed any of her teachers that way, they would've given her detention. In fact, Eileen *had* addressed them that way, and she *had* gotten detention. But she wasn't sure exactly why she was mouthing off now. Was it nerves? Possibly. Maybe she was more anxious about this than she'd planned to be, and maybe the only way to cope was to be an asshole.

She dropped the letter on the table. "So, what is this? I have an uncle?"

At last she got a reaction out of the guy: Mr. Knutsen's eyelids fluttered, and he sat straighter in his chair. He said, "I'm sorry, I thought you knew."

"My mom was a foster kid. Doesn't have family. And my dad was an only child."

She was telling him what she'd thought had been true—what she'd believed until yesterday. Inside, she was begging Mr. Knutsen to prove her wrong. She needed this change.

Change. Her heart thumped with the word: *Ch-change, ch-change.*

28

Mr. Knutsen fluttered his eyelids again. "Your father *wasn't* an only child, according to my records. Or, I should say, Patrick Enright's."

Eileen said, "There's no one in my family named Enright."

At that Mr. Knutsen rose from his chair, and for a moment, Eileen feared he might fling her from the room, shouting, "YOU'RE RIGHT, I'VE MADE A HUGE MISTAKE!"

Instead, he crossed the office to a tall filing cabinet and, using a key, opened the topmost drawer. He riffled through the folders and removed one, thick with papers, setting it on the table before Eileen.

"Have you considered, Ms. Sullivan, that your parents changed their name?"

Eileen made no move to touch the folder. "Yeah, when my mom got married. She was a Clark, though. Not an Enright."

"I'm not talking about maiden names. It was your father who made the change."

"You know that's the weirdest term? 'Maiden name.' Like, okay, do you want a dowry and a side of cattle with that?"

Mr. Knutsen stared, blank-faced, at Eileen. She'd gone a step too far, maybe.

"Fine," said Eileen. "Why would my dad change his name?"

"That's for him to say, not me. Go on, open the folder."

Eileen didn't take orders. She crossed her arms and studied the wall behind Mr. Knutsen's head. His diploma was huge, set in tomato-red matting. University of Phoenix. Definitely not Harvard. Eileen got a scratchy feeling at the back of her neck. *Was* this a scam? She'd heard of elder fraud, but what was this? Recently-graduated-teenager fraud? If so, the joke was on Bill.

Eileen was flat broke. And if Eileen thought of it that way, she was invincible to scams, and therefore to whatever was in that folder.

Still, something inside Eileen wouldn't allow her to open it.

Instead, she focused on something Mr. Knutsen had said: *That's for him to say.* This guy couldn't know much if he didn't know John Sullivan had been dead for fourteen years. For all that time, he'd said nothing to Eileen from beyond the grave. Why would he start today?

Silence passed, eventually turning obscene. Mr. Knutsen caught on. He slid the folder away from Eileen and opened it himself. He unhooked something from a paper clip—a photograph—and held it out to her.

Eileen took the photo. It seemed a bitch too far not to.

She was looking at a man in his midtwenties standing in front of a wire fence. She knew who this was. Soft jaw. Ruddy cheeks. Strawberry-blond hair. Close-set eyes, colored cornflower blue. Traits Eileen had not inherited but recognized easily enough from other photographs of her father.

"So?" She flapped the photo at Mr. Knutsen.

"So, that's Patrick Enright."

Eileen stopped flapping. She held the photo close and looked. Really looked. Traits *similar* to John Sullivan's, but it wasn't him. There were differences. The turn of his nose. The hunch of his shoulders. The gauntness.

A long-nailed claw dug into Eileen's gut. It was familiar, though she hadn't felt it in a while—the pain of not knowing a dad who'd died young. There were vague memories of him left in her head: arms swinging her high in the kitchen, bangs that drooped over his eyes. Still, she didn't know him well enough. Not enough to distinguish him from a stranger.

A real daughter would've noticed the difference.

Eileen needed a drink.

"It's an older photo, of course," said Mr. Knutsen. "Hadn't taken anything recent before his death last week. Cirrhosis of the liver, complications thereof. Nasty way to go, I hear. Now, Ms. Sullivan, do you know much about your father's upbringing? Where he lived before he moved to Emmet?"

You couldn't imagine the things I know, thought Eileen.

What she said was, "Some other shit town. Why does that matter?"

"It's really not my place to tell you that."

Eileen gave Mr. Knutsen a long, hard look. What was this dude playing at? She'd come here for answers, and all she was getting were hems and haws and hedging. It was time to play hardball.

"Right!" she said, slapping her knees. "Thanks, Bill. This has been super enlightening."

She headed for the door, still holding the photo.

"He gave you a house."

Eileen stopped. Slowly, she turned around.

Finally they were getting somewhere.

"Beg your pardon," said Mr. Knutsen. "I've been skirting around the point. My job is to tell you about the inheritance, not its history."

"A . . . house?" The question dropped from Eileen's mouth like crusted glue.

"A third of the proceeds from its sale, to be precise. That's your portion of the estate. Your sisters will inherit the remaining thirds."

"Uh-uuuh." Eileen had stopped feeling things right. Her face was numb, or maybe not there. She *really* needed a drink.

"Please, Ms. Sullivan, take a seat. We have a lot to discuss."

Eileen obeyed Mr. Knutsen's order, just this once.

FIVE

Claire

I t was mailing day, and Claire wished she were anywhere but here, at the post office, three days before Christmas.

"Delusional," she muttered—to herself, and to the nine customers on her Etsy shop who had placed orders after the Christmas cutoff date. It didn't matter how clearly Claire had laid out the shipping guidelines; shoppers would disregard them, holding on to false hope that their last-minute gifts would reach them in time.

Some people had no regard for scheduling, let alone logic.

That didn't mean Claire wouldn't take their money, though.

As she stood in line, a dozen people away from the mailing counter, Claire copied and pasted a message into the Etsy app, tapping out the previous customer's name and replacing it with the next:

Hey Rebecca,
One last reminder that this gift will arrive AFTER

Christmas, as indicated by my Holiday Shipping
Guidelines. I hope you or your recipient enjoy this one-of-
a-kind, handmade piece. Thank you for your business!
    xo Claire @ Silver Lining Boutique

She hit the send button and moved on to the next:

Hey Madison,

Lance,

Zoe,

Finally, she reached number nine. The ninth last-minute, frazzle-brained customer who'd bought an online boutique gift less than a week before Christmas. Based on experience, Claire expected six of the people to not respond, two to send back a chipper *I understand, thanks!*, and one Unenlightened Settler to write that she was *affronted*, and what *terrible customer service*, and she had *no idea*.

Before Claire had started watching Harper Everly, she would have straight-up called that last person a bitch. But Harper had taught her that "bitch" was a Settler's word—a cheap stand-in for how you actually felt about another woman, and certainly not helpful in the grand scheme of things. "Bitch," said Harper Everly, was decidedly antifeminist.

So Claire called bitchy customers Unenlightened Settlers instead, and she used intelligent words to describe their actions: entitled, oblivious, ignorant. Maybe those weren't as satisfying to say, but they were true, and ultimately, those customers rarely requested a refund. It simply wasn't worth the effort at Claire's price point. They could write their nasty messages, but Claire was the one who ended up with their money. The joke was on them.

That's how it worked, Harper had taught her. "Settlers shout loudest. Excellers *live* loudest. It's a long game, and Excellers win out."

That had been true of Claire's business, a dainty jewelry shop she'd set up at fourteen using only her phone and cheap supplies from Michael's. Since that time she'd made good money—more than she could ever make at a minimum wage job like Eileen's or Mom's. Thousands of dollars and counting, which she was saving up for college. Thus far, she'd been a success.

All that success . . . to what end?

What was the point of a modestly successful Etsy shop if its profits had nowhere to go? Of succeeding as a budding entrepreneur if, in the end, you failed at the one thing that mattered most?

Ahead at the counter a woman with two screaming toddlers was screaming herself, telling a beleaguered worker how a post-Christmas delivery was "unacceptable."

An Unenlightened Settler, indeed.

Claire's eyes drifted from the drama to the limp, green tinsel garlands draped on the walls. Overhead, a near-dead fluorescent flickered. Behind Claire a man hacked a phlegmy cough. If hell was real, then it was a post office on December twenty-second.

Normally, Claire didn't spend much time here. She had a system: pack and weigh mailers at home, print labels from the family computer, and ship packages weekly, on mailing day—a simple drop-off with no waiting, no hassle. Yesterday, though, on printing day, she'd discovered the printer was out of black ink.

Claire had her suspicions. She was sure Murphy was to

blame. Excellers didn't blame, though; they rose above. So here she was, rising above in the ninth circle of hell.

"Delusional," she whispered again.

Delusional to come here today.

To think these bubble mailers of twenty-dollar infinity bracelets and threader earrings could one day save her.

To presume she could get in to Yale.

To imagine a life outside her dumpy town.

This didn't feel like rising above. It felt like sinking down.

Down.

Down.

Claire had to focus. Her thoughts were spiraling, getting her nowhere. She opened her phone again, tapping on a familiar text thread labeled "Ainsley Internet."

Claire knew her full name now: Ainsley St. John. Seven months ago, when the two of them had first met on an online Harper Everly group, she'd simply been username "AinsAGoGo." She and Claire had connected over—what else?—their love for Harper Everly, both of them self-professed "Harperettes."

Ainsley had commented on a post of Claire's about good consignment shops in the Portland area.

> I lived in Portland for fourteen years! Hopefully,
> these gems are still there:

Then Ainsley had listed those gems, and she and Claire had got to talking, tangent turning to tangent, and posts leading to DMs. That was how it had begun. They'd discovered their shared obsession with thrifting, *The Great British Baking Show,* and Bette Midler. They'd talked about growing up in Oregon, and how Claire was living in Nowheresville and Ainsley's family had moved cross-country to Cleveland, which, according to her, wasn't much livelier. They'd discovered they were both stressing about the SATs, and *then* they'd shared with each other that they were gay.

And that had been it. Claire, accustomed to crushing on unavailable girls at Emmet Middle and High, finally had a crush that could go somewhere. Sure, she and Ainsley had met on the Internet, but didn't most people these days? And when *no one* at her high school was out, and simple statistics gave Claire slim odds for finding love in real life, meeting Ainsley felt . . . meant to be.

Ainsley was an Exceller, like her, bound for the same fate. They'd compared notes on the schools they meant to apply to, and when Ainsley had announced she was going to risk it by applying early action to Yale, Claire had decided she would too.

Delusional.

Temporary madness.

Claire had known how near-impossible it was to get into the Ivy League. Before meeting Ainsley, she'd planned on applying to state schools in big cities closer to home: PSU, UW, Cal State LA. Schools where she could get a scholarship, but she could also get *out*. Into a progressive city where she could be herself. Where she wouldn't be a queer fish in a small, straight pond.

She wanted a new start. A haven.

A *New Haven*.

She hadn't considered the East Coast before. It had seemed far-fetched. Ainsley had made it seem possible, though, and the

37

more she and Claire had chatted, the more Claire had believed it was possible. Why not go all out, and take the risk? Yale could give her everything a big city could.

She'd thought she was being brave, not irrational. This was what Harper had promised: "Take the right steps, and your life will fall into place." Claire had taken the right steps, from building a lucrative small business to working her butt off in school to slaying her SATs to bolstering her résumé with weekends at the soup kitchen. She only got five hours max of sleep per night, but that was how Excellers lived. Ainsley understood that in a way no one else had—a way that Eileen, for instance, never could.

And though, over the months of texting, Ainsley and Claire had remained in decidedly nonromantic territory, Claire felt sure Ainsley was thinking the same thing she was: Once they got to New Haven and met for the first time, sparks would fly.

So, okay, Ainsley had been posting for the last month about her girlfriend, Bri—selfies of the two of them in front of concert venues and food trucks. But that was only a momentary setback. A senior year fling. It'd be over by the time college began.

Claire had been holding on for that late August day when she'd show up on campus and say to herself, "All the work, it's paid off." She'd be getting an education *and* her first girlfriend, and she'd finally be free from the toxic stagnation that was Emmet, Oregon. She wouldn't be dealing with sisters who asked annoying questions or gave her two years of the silent treatment. She wouldn't be bitter about a Mom too busy with work to take Claire on college visits. Those bad parts of life would be over for good.

That had been the plan. Life had been all buoyant hopes and adrenaline, even throughout the nerve-wracking autumn months. When her spirits faltered, Claire told herself that Yale *was* going to happen. It had to, because she'd put in the work. She hadn't lost faith.

Not until a week ago when she'd read her online rejection and ten minutes later gotten a text from Ainsley saying, YALE, BABY!

Claire hadn't responded, because what was there to say?

A week later, she still couldn't reply.

And what was she even doing, looking at the text?

Claire pocketed her phone.

"Delusional," she said a third time.

Maybe she was.

Maybe college wasn't happening, and Ainsley was another dream girl, out of reach, but the wait in this post office line had given Claire time to think. She'd made a decision: She would die before staying in Emmet another year.

In fact, she'd do a lot of desperate things.

SIX

Murphy

Digging a grave was more difficult than the Internet made it seem. And this wasn't even a regular grave.

Murphy had meant to get two feet down, but now she'd be happy to make it six inches. She looked to the sealed Tupperware container in which Siegfried lay wrapped in a holiday-printed napkin.

"Wanna pull a Lazarus for me?" she asked. "It'd make this easier."

Siegfried remained dead.

He wasn't the performer Murphy aspired to be. He was just a turtle who deserved better, and there was no magic trick that would bring him forth from his napkin burial shroud.

Murphy jabbed at the cold, hard earth. Maybe this would be easier if she had an actual shovel, instead of a garden spade. Maybe it'd be better if it were summer, and the ground weren't caked in frost.

Maybe this wouldn't be happening if she'd remembered to feed Siegfried like a good, responsible person.

When it came to choosing a burial site, Murphy had decided against her own yard. Neighbors might see and ask questions. Instead, she'd taken Siegfried off-site, walking a few street corners down to a place where no one would be: Morris Park. Here, a few yards into the tree line, down a loose gravel path, was a thick copse of evergreen trees.

Murphy figured it was symbolic: evergreen, the way Siegfried would remain evergreen . . . in her heart?

Yeah. Poignant. Siegfried deserved freaking poignancy.

The grave-digging was taking so *long*, though. Murphy had been here over half an hour and had hacked out only the barest outline of a square. It was getting dark. Dusk rested on the trees, and cold slithered beneath Murphy's puffer coat, prickling gooseflesh from her skin.

It was silent.

Too silent.

In the summer the park was filled with joggers, barbecuers, yelling kids. Families gathered here for the Fourth of July, celebrating past midnight with sparklers and Bud Lights. In December, the park was a different place. A deserted chunk of icy ground.

Shadows gathered around the spruces and pines, forming deepening pockets of darkness where unknown figures could hide. Murphy hadn't considered safety before. She'd only been thinking that the park was the nearest deserted, concealed plot of land.

Murderers and kidnappers probably thought that too.

Murphy staggered to her feet, wiping the dirty spade on her jean leg and picking up Siegfried's coffin.

"Later," she said. "When there's more light."

She set out from the copse in a nervous jog, keeping to the path, following it to the parking lot.

If someone were to kidnap her out here, Murphy wondered, how long would it take Eileen and Claire to notice? Hours? *Days?* Until Mom returned from the cruise?

Even then, they'd probably get over it fast. Mom had two whole other daughters. Claire and Eileen had each other for sisters. Murphy wasn't essential.

I'm the spare tire of the family, Murphy thought, crossing the parking lot. *No one notices me when I'm around. Who would notice if I were gone?*

The lot was empty. There were no cars here. No one to see if gloved hands reached out, wrapped around Murphy's mouth, and dragged her into the gathering shadows. A shudder drove through her spine like a metal stake.

It was a bad idea to dig out here.

A very bad idea.

In this deserted place Murphy's jokes were pallid, powerless things. Her illusions were silly tricks, learned from library books titled *Magic for All* and *The Art of the Con*. Murphy wasn't meant for deserted places. A magician couldn't perform without a lively audience. Murphy was going to find that crowd eventually. It would require years of work to make it on stage, but she had what it took. The drama club advisor, Ms. Stubbs, had even confided in Murphy that she was the most talented kid in the group. One day Murphy would make it big.

In the meantime, though, she had to be careful about not getting randomly murdered. What a waste of fourteen years—the book reading, diagram studying, rope-trick solving—that'd be.

As Murphy headed for the poorly lit street, it began to mist. Raindrops stuck to her gloves. They lived for a second, visible droplets, before seeping into black knit. Murphy tucked her hands into her coat, where her turtle's coffin sat snug between her ribcage and the coat zipper. She patted the Tupperware and sighed.

"Siegfried," she said, "this is one screwy Christmas."

DECEMBER
TWENTY-THIRD

SEVEN

Eileen

I t was two in the morning and Eileen was eating a day-old donut, leftover from her most recent Safeway shift. She chewed while sprawled on her frameless mattress, raining sugar flakes on the wrinkled sheets. Her own private blizzard. And people said it barely snowed in the Willamette Valley.

It was pretty in a way, this everyday snowstorm. Two years ago Eileen would have chosen Titanium White and Pewter Gray from her acrylic set to do the scene justice.

Beside her rested a manila folder filled with several important-looking documents, which Mr. Knutsen had asked Eileen to look over carefully. The only document Eileen cared about was the paper with the address:

2270 Laramie Court, Rockport, OR

Patrick Enright's house. Her inheritance. The way Mr. Knutsen had explained it, the house would truly be Eileen's once Murphy turned eighteen. That's when she and her sisters could jointly decide what to do: keep the house, or sell it. Until then, Patrick Enright had left behind enough money for Mr. Knutsen to manage the estate.

Mr. Knutsen had descended into legalese after that—mumbo jumbo about capital gains and property taxes. Eileen had stopped listening. She'd heard what mattered most.

Maybe it was the donut sugar blasting through her veins or the fading buzz of two shots' worth of Jack Daniel's. Maybe it was Christmas delirium, but there, on her bed, Eileen Sullivan was hatching a plan. Mr. Knutsen had scheduled a follow-up appointment with her, for after the holidays, but Eileen wasn't one for appointments. Or waiting.

What she had was tonight. And tonight? She was going to Rockport.

She couldn't shake what Mr. Knutsen had said, right before she'd left his office:

"Who knows what he's kept locked away in there."

"Sorry," Eileen had said. "What?"

Mr. Knutsen had patted his sides and chuckled. "Patrick . . . well, he's been the oddest of my clients, by far. Do you know, he found out about you by way of a private investigator? The PI's findings brought Patrick down here, where he sought out my services. I've never had such a client: insisting on secrecy, informing me of his impending death—and I believed it, the man looked like hell. Directing me to not breathe a word to your mother and only send the letters out to you girls individually, when you were eighteen. Funeral? None. And a private burial. No relations or friends to speak of. Quite the eccentric."

"Yeah, reminds me of someone."

Eileen had been thinking of herself.

"As I was saying," Mr. Knutsen had said, "it's a mystery what's in that house. Documents, photographs, antiques, maybe. Could be piles of junk. But he's shut it all up. No estate sale. Left it waiting for you girls."

On her bed, Eileen squinted in thought.

Documents.

Why would Mr. Knutsen have used that word? Not "knick-knacks," not "possessions." He'd distinctly said "documents."

Documents could mean answers.

Hadn't Eileen's troubles begun with documents? With the letters she'd found in the linen closet two years ago?

Documents could mean *change.*

The word pumped through Eileen's heart, filling the ventricles, rushing in from veins and out through arteries: *Ch-change, ch-change, ch-change.*

She'd known the secret for two years. It had messed with Eileen's head, fucking up everything—her art, her life at home, her will to do anything but drink in this drafty garage.

All because Eileen believed the secret to be true.

But *what if.*

What if Eileen didn't have all the facts?

Patrick Enright. Her uncle. He had to have known the secret too.

And there were documents.

What if those documents told a different story from the ones she'd read?

Eileen hadn't considered the possibility before. Now she craved it: a diary entry. A written confession. A letter to Eileen herself, left for her to discover—an inheritance of a different kind.

That was another thing: She'd inherited a *house*. So, best-case scenario, she got an answer to the question that had eaten her alive for two years. Worst-case? She was richer than she'd been a week ago. Either way, things were looking up.

This was *ch-change, ch-change, ch-change*.

It was after two o'clock when Eileen got up and filled a back-pack with supplies: a blanket, socks, a thermal shirt, a refillable water bottle, Dubble Bubble, her flask of Jack Daniel's, and lastly, the manila folder Mr. Knutsen had given her.

Not a creature was stirring, not even a mouse, and that was when Eileen crept out of the house.

Eileen owned a 1989 Dodge Caravan. It was equipped with wood paneling, a red interior, and a finicky alternator. Eileen hated the Caravan with her whole heart. It sucked that you could work hard for three years and in the end all you could afford was something you hated with your whole heart. In fact, Eileen con-sidered this reality the running theme of her life.

For the Caravan's engine to start up, you had to turn the key in the ignition *just so*. Eileen had mostly mastered the trick of it, but every once in a while she had to try a second or third time through a primordial sputtering under the hood. Tonight she needed stealth on her side, so with one hand she crossed her fingers and with the other she turned the key.

The engine started.

Her lucky night.

Eileen drew her seat belt snug across her chest and shifted the van into drive.

This was it. She was leaving.

Fuck Emmet.

Fuck everything.

But first—one deep, long breath.

THUMP.

The sound came from the passenger window. On instinct, Eileen shrieked.

Then she saw who it was.

Claire.

Before Eileen could reach for the lock, Claire had climbed inside. She settled into the passenger seat, primly crossing her legs and facing Eileen.

"Get out," Eileen ordered.

"No," Claire replied. She jangled a foot, clad in a gold glitter Keds shoe. It sparkled up at Eileen. Actually *sparkled.* "What are you doing? Running away from home?"

"I'm an adult," said Eileen. "It's not running away, it's leaving."

"Sure."

"Get out of my car."

"If you're road tripping, I'm coming with."

"Why do you—"

Claire leaned in, revealing the painted contours of her cheeks. "Okay, Leenie, think. Think super hard. Who does the chores in the house?"

"No one. That's why it's a shithole."

"Who does. The chores."

Eileen growled. "You, I guess."

"Who empties the trash?"

Eileen was quiet. She had the sudden urge to puke.

"I read the letter," Claire said.

51

"What . . . the *hell*."

It came together as Eileen remembered the envelope's torn top. She thought she'd made that tear in a drunken stupor. She'd been wrong.

"I called Mr. Knutsen myself," Claire said, with utmost composure. "He wouldn't tell me details, since I'm not eighteen, which I guess is fair. *You* have the details, though. So we're going to do this."

Eileen couldn't remember ever being this surprised. It felt kind of nice to feel something this much. But that didn't mean she was okay with it.

"*We're* not doing anything," she said.

"Sure we are. We're going to our dead Uncle Patrick's house. I know you visited Knutsen this afternoon." Claire tapped the manila folder resting on the dash. "You left that on the kitchen counter when you came home and peed. I saw the address. Rockport, right? That's where we're headed."

Eileen narrowed her eyes. "When did I invite you?"

Claire's lips curled upward. Another thing Eileen couldn't remember: the last time Claire had smiled at her.

"I've got money," Claire said.

Eileen was quiet.

"Unlike you, I didn't blow mine on a van. I've got thousands. *Thousands*, Leenie."

Eileen studied Claire, incredulous. "Are you . . . bribing me?"

"One hundred dollars," Claire answered, "for the use of your vehicle. I looked up the address, and it's a three-hour drive north. You're the only one with a car, and no Lyft is that cheap. It makes perfect sense."

Eileen shook her head at Claire. "You're unbelievable."

"Well?" Claire pressed. "One hundred. I bet that's twice the money you've got to your name."

Eileen stayed quiet. There was a crumpled dollar in her back jeans pocket.

One dollar.

That was it.

"Why do you care?" Eileen asked. "Why's it worth a hundred bucks to you?"

Claire looked at Eileen like she was dense. "Because it's my inheritance too. I want to know what I'm working with. Anyway, I've made you a fair offer."

"Three hundred," Eileen said tonelessly.

Claire looked surprised for only a moment. She countered, "Two."

"Two-fifty."

Claire screwed up her eyes. "You know, I already wrote down the address. That's your leverage."

"I've got the van," said Eileen. "That's plenty of leverage still. Two-fifty, you ride. Any less, and I drag you out of this van by your goddamn messy hair bun."

This time Claire didn't miss a beat. "Two-fifty, fine. We drive, we check out the place, and we get home by morning. Murphy won't even notice we're gone."

Though it was technically Eileen's victory, she didn't feel triumphant. Instead, she got a twinge of guilt thinking of leaving Murphy home alone overnight. But Murphy was fourteen, a high schooler. She could take care of herself. And nothing bad ever happened on their street.

Unless you counted Dad's death.

Or Eileen's everyday life.

This was a perfect example: Eileen had won the argument, but in the end she felt screwed over. Claire had still gotten what she'd wanted. She'd known she was going to get it from the beginning. She had the money. The *real* leverage.

That's why she was smiling.

"You freak," said Eileen. "Reading my goddamn mail."

Claire's smile opened wide, revealing two rows of crooked, ultrawhite teeth. "I'll be back with my things."

Eileen waited, watching Claire open the kitchen door with laughable slowness, clearly afraid a single creak might wake Murphy.

God. She was going to turn this trip into a downright ordeal.

Eileen eyed her keys, dangling in the ignition. She could still leave. What was $250 to her, really? Then she eyed the gas gauge, where the red arrow sat tauntingly close to empty. She could probably make it to Rockport on fumes, but one dollar wouldn't buy her the gas to get home.

What exactly had been her master plan?

How had she intended to get that money? By robbing a bank?

Eileen hadn't thought this through. She'd never been a big-picture person.

But Claire sure as hell was. She was the planner.

Eileen needed a drink.

Not too much. A shot. Sure, she'd already taken two tonight, but she could handle that much fine without risk of driving impaired. Eileen opened her backpack and removed the flask. She pulled a swig and let the liquid rest for a moment, sitting cold on her teeth, burning hot on her tongue. She remembered again what Mr. Knutsen had said: *documents.*

She stowed the flask in the glove compartment and, for the second time that night, she crossed her fingers.

Only then did she swallow.

EIGHT

Claire

Claire had reached her limit. Christmas radio had been piping from the minivan speakers for two hours, and in that space of time the station had broadcast not one, not two, but *three* variations of "The Twelve Days of Christmas." It was enough to drive anyone up the wall—even a patient Exceller like Claire.

She had said nothing for a long time. In fact, Eileen and Claire hadn't spoken since Claire had returned to the van with her packed Vera Bradley tote, and they'd driven into the silent night.

If they spoke to each other, they would fight. That was inevitable. So the sisters had wordlessly agreed to keep the peace. Eileen drove and Claire sat scrolling through Instagram, avoiding the urge to double-tap any of Ainsley St. John's posts from the last week. Occasionally, she glanced out at the green-gray landscape of I-5: fields and mist and overpasses, illuminated by streetlights, and beneath it all, the music of Christmas.

When Claire had first found Mr. Knutsen's letter in Eileen's room two days ago, she'd been stunned. She wasn't a scavenger; she didn't normally snoop through Eileen's things while taking out trash. But the words OPEN IMMEDIATELY in bold red had been conspicuous. They'd caused Claire's fingers to itch. So much so that, for the first time in years, Claire did something rash. Unplanned. She'd opened the envelope, she'd read the letter, and she'd promptly called Mr. Knutsen, attorney-at-law.

The lawyer had been hopelessly vague, informing Claire that his client had given him strict instructions: Claire would get her own letter and explanation when she turned eighteen, not before. Meantime, she could calm any expectations she had about earning fast money; the house could not be sold until Claire's little sister inherited. Only then could the siblings decide what to do.

The phone call had deflated some of Claire's hopes. Though Claire earned a decent wage from her Etsy shop, her current college fund was barely enough for moving costs and maybe books. For the rest of her expenses, she'd been counting on student loans. And student loans were for *students*, not for college rejects who simply wanted to flee their awful hometown. Claire needed actual money if she was going to get out of Emmet. For one moment, she'd hoped the inheritance would be that: a direct answer to her problem. But as it turned out, whatever money was to be made wouldn't come her way for another four years.

That night Claire had gone to bed as she had the six nights before—bitter and helplessly confused. None of her plans had come to fruition, and not even this mysterious inheritance could help her achieve them.

Then, yesterday morning, Eileen had walked into the house

and left that folder in the kitchen while she used the bathroom. It had been pure chance: Claire had heard the kitchen door slam, which reminded her she was hungry, and she'd abandoned her Etsy work for a snack. That's when she'd found the folder, and she hadn't been able to resist. She'd grabbed it, looking through its contents, taking quick photos on her phone, like a trained spy. Then she'd returned to her room to reflect.

Her plans hadn't worked. And this house? She didn't see how it could help her in the here and now. But Claire reached a conclusion—one that had been brewing inside her since her time in that purgatorial post office: This situation was precisely what Harper Everly called a "golden moment."

You only got so many golden moments in your life. They might strike you as nonsensical, or even as distractions on your path. But golden moments were where true growth and personal innovation occurred. Take, for example, Abraham Lincoln, who lost his senate race before becoming president. Or Bill Gates, whose first business flopped before he went on to found Microsoft. Or Michael Jordan, who'd been cut from his high school basketball team before becoming . . . well, *Michael Jordan*.

If any of those successful people hadn't persevered, where would they be? You had to recognize your golden moment, and you had to seize it and squeeze it dry of every good thing. This wasn't the time for Claire to despair, to stay home for a dreary holiday, bemoaning what she'd lost. This was the time to move forward. To be—did Claire dare think the word?—*impulsive*.

Just this once, Claire wasn't going to plan. She was going to pack a bag and go along with Eileen on a harebrained, midnight trip. Because maybe this—the mysterious 2270 Laramie Court—was her golden moment.

Claire had done what sleuthing she could at home, searching the address online. There had been no listings, though; nothing on Zillow or other realty sites. When she'd tried to glimpse the property on Google Maps, there'd been nothing but blue check-in dots scattered throughout the coastal town. No street view. No clue as to what her inheritance looked like. And then there was the matter of an uncle Claire had never known. A family secret her mother hadn't told. Claire would be lying if she said she wasn't curious. There were so many reasons to go on this trip.

She wanted a distraction from her bad news.

She wanted a way forward, to better things.

She wanted her golden moment.

So, planning be damned, she was taking it.

Here was a hitch, though: Harper Everly hadn't warned Claire about the trials preceding golden moments. Like two hours' worth of insipid Christmas tunes.

Claire kept thinking Eileen would get annoyed and change stations, but as the songs played on, she seemed impervious. Claire chose her words carefully. This didn't have to be a *big* argument.

"You know," she said, "they sell cassette converters. Like, for your iPhone. You could use one to play your own music in the car."

Eileen flinched, like the sound of Claire's voice had been a bullhorn. She looked at Claire with glazed eyes, uncomprehending. "My *iPhone?*"

Right. How could Claire have forgotten? Eileen didn't have a

59

phone. She'd foresworn them two years ago, when she'd read an article about the working conditions of smart phone manufacturers.

"You could always get one secondhand," Claire said, not sure where she was going. "Then you wouldn't be . . . you know, directly contributing to . . . whatever."

"I'm acquit—" Eileen frowned, correcting herself: "*acquainted* with eBay."

Yes. Claire knew that, too. She still remembered the best gift she'd ever received. A lot had changed since that Christmas four years ago.

"Sure," she said. "Yeah, okay."

Eileen breathed heavily out her nose. Her profile was eerie and shadowed—severe cheekbones, knife-sharp nose. The heat from the vents was warming her jacket, filling the van with the scent of leather . . . and something else. A biting scent. Sharp, like vinegar, or—

The truth sucker punched Claire.

"Oh my God," she said, sitting up straight. "Have you been *drinking?*"

Eileen didn't answer. She kept her lips shut tight. That had been her mistake: She'd spoken to Claire, thereby letting out the damning stench of whiskey.

"Pull over," Claire ordered.

Eileen's body was tense, shoulders drawn too tight—*trying* to act sober. She wasn't, though. Claire got it: the flinching, the stumbling speech, the glaze in her eyes that Claire had mistaken for tiredness.

Thirty-six days of Christmas could be endured. This could not.

"Did you hear me?" Claire raised her voice. "Pull over. NOW."

"I took a *shot*, okay?" Eileen groused. "I'm fine. You don't know my toler—"

"Uh, I know you drank, and now you're driving. Which means you're *drinking and driving*. So pull over the car, or so help me—"

The car juddered, swerving violently onto the shoulder. Tires screeched beneath them as Eileen pumped her foot on the brake, bringing the Caravan to a graceless stop.

Claire breathed out rapid breaths, staring at Eileen through the dim light. She could believe that Eileen would drink and drive; she'd known her sister's not-so-secret habit for a while. She *couldn't* believe Eileen would actually pull over.

And who knew how long that rationality would last? Claire had to act now. She threw off her seat belt, pointing to the driver's seat.

"I'm taking over," she announced. "Switch out."

Eileen ran her tongue over her teeth for a languid, thoughtful moment. Then, shrugging, she unbuckled her seat belt.

"Yeah, whatever. I'm sick of driving anyway."

Claire stared, disbelievingly. What was happening? Was Eileen *listening* to her? Or did Eileen know she was buzzed? Was she . . . acknowledging defeat?

Whatever the reason, Claire didn't hesitate.

She'd taken her golden moment, and now she was taking the wheel.

Claire gripped the steering wheel, squinting at I-5 through swishing wipers.

> *God rest ye merry gentlemen*
> *Let nothing you dismay*

She hadn't bothered changing the Christmas station. She was too bewildered by what had gone down. Yes, she'd known Eileen drank, but this was a new low. Driving like that, with Claire in the car—did she have no respect? And then switching out with Claire on demand, only to shut up and sulk? Claire glanced at Eileen, who was glaring out at the road, head rammed against the passenger window. What was *with* her? Claire didn't want to know. She focused instead on the music:

> O *tidings of comfort and joy*
> *comfort and joy*
> O *tidings of comfort and joy*

Those weren't even close to the tidings Claire had received from Yale.

Suddenly, thoughts of Eileen were gone, the rejection back on Claire's brain. How could it not be? For months Yale had been the only thing Claire thought about. She'd pictured her New Haven future, pumped with living color the way it had been in the admissions brochures. She'd envisioned it, done the work.

Where had she gone wrong?

Where had Ainsley St. John gone right?

And how could Claire ever respond to Ainsley's text?

The pain was fresh, a knife twisted into a vital artery, so deep that Claire was afraid to move.

She took in the view in her periphery: wide open fields, dotted by grand firs. Her mind strayed, unexpectedly, to the subject of Murphy. Claire did feel bad, leaving her home alone without warning, or even a note. She couldn't send a text, either, since

Murphy didn't have a phone. Then again, Murphy practically lived home alone, as it was. Claire barely saw her, too busy these days with Etsy and schoolwork. And God knew Eileen rarely emerged from her garage cave. Mom was almost always working a late shift. Tonight wouldn't be unlike any other, would it?

Claire didn't need to feel guilty. This was a six-, maybe seven-hour roundtrip. She wasn't abandoning Murphy for a five-day Bahamian cruise, like Mom.

Mom.

Claire remembered nights when Mom hadn't worked late, when she'd fixed them Hamburger Helper dinners in the Crock-Pot, and they'd eaten together and talked about their day. She remembered school field days when Mom had shown up and cheered Claire on in a three-legged race, afterward telling her what a good job she'd done over cups of lemonade.

Once, Mom had been *Mom.* The older Claire had grown, though, the more removed her mother had become—an untethered kite drifting higher, toward the sun. Claire knew, from TV shows and friends at school, that teenage girls weren't exactly supposed to get along with their mothers. It wasn't that Claire didn't get on with Mom; it was that they didn't get *anywhere.* They didn't even fight, because Mom wasn't around to do the fighting. The closest Claire had gotten to that had been two days ago, when Mom had left for her cruise, and Claire had yelled for her to *just go.*

Mom had tried hard to make this year's Christmas special, but didn't she get it? December twenty-first wasn't *Christmas.* It was a difficult date, an open wound. Mom had given them presents like she cared, but didn't she understand? The presents were a giveaway that she didn't know her daughters anymore.

She'd given Claire a backpack for college, colored bright pink. "Your favorite color," she'd said brightly.

As though Claire were seven, not seventeen.

If Mom was a mom who *knew* her daughter, she would have asked Claire about early admission a week ago. Maybe Claire would have even told her about not getting into Yale, and Mom would've realized that a backpack for a nonexistent future was the worst possible gift.

She hadn't known, though, and Claire had lost her calm—a very un-Exceller thing to do. She'd *yelled* at Mom.

The hard truth was, the Yale rejection was driving her mad. She was having a breakdown. Was that possible, at seventeen? What was this, a fifth-life crisis? She *was* acting way out of character, getting in this van without a plan.

All she could tell herself was, *golden moment*.

This was her golden moment. And maybe, when she arrived at the house she'd inherited, it'd all fall into place.

Claire had wedged her phone into the console cupholder after plugging 2270 Laramie Court into the GPS. Now, according to the app, her exit was coming up soon. The path that would take her to Uncle Patrick's house.

Did *that* sound strange: Uncle Patrick. Uncle *Anything*.

An uncle she'd never known, who'd died and left an inheritance, like Claire was a Dickensian orphan.

This is your golden moment, Claire reminded herself. Riding in a junk van and enduring an endless barrage of carols—blasé as it was, the moment was *happening*. She had to focus on that— her unknown future—and not the past.

She glanced at her phone, following the inexorable route of the pulsing blue dot northward, toward Rockport.

Exceller mindset, she instructed herself. *Keep moving forward.*

"I gotta pee."

Claire frowned at the glowing map. "You can't hold it?"

That was when she realized Eileen hadn't spoken the words.

She and Eileen jerked their gazes together. From the back seat a shadowy figure emerged.

"Holy crap!" shrieked Claire.

While Eileen shouted, "Look-at-the-look-at-the-look-at-the road!"

A semi blared its horn and Claire swerved onto the highway's right shoulder.

From the back of the Caravan Murphy howled with laughter.

NINE

Murphy

I t wasn't funny, but it *was*.

If Murphy's biological needs hadn't forced her to ruin the surprise, it could've been even funnier.

She'd meant to wait it out in the back of the van the whole way to wherever her sisters were headed, all furtive, in the middle of the night. Then, once they'd arrived, she'd sneak out and climb onto the roof of the Caravan, sprawl herself on its hood, and begin to sob hysterically. She'd draw their attention and then she'd cry out, "I had to hold on the whole way heeere!"

It was too ridiculous to believe, but that wasn't the point. The real punch of magic was in the curtain rise—that first glance. Eileen and Claire could think better of it after, could even get angry. In that first instant, though, they'd believe the preposterous, and they would be *amazed*.

A magical twist with a punch line to boot. The aim of any true magician.

Claire and Eileen would have to pay attention to her then.

Murphy's grand plan was shot to pieces now. She'd really, *really* tried to hold it. If only she hadn't drunk a bottle of Dr Pepper a mere fifteen minutes before sneaking into the van.

She'd been staying up late, taking full advantage of Christmas break and reading through her library copy of *The Art of the Con*. The plan had only occurred to her *after* she'd sipped the last dregs of soda. She'd heard Eileen emerge from her bedroom and head to the carport, Claire following immediately after.

She'd snuck after them, leaning into the carport from the kitchen, listening to her sisters argue through the minivan's open passenger door. At the end of it she'd heard Claire say, "Murphy won't even notice we're gone."

Claire had been wrong about that. She only thought Murphy wouldn't notice because *they* wouldn't notice if *she* were gone.

Murphy, the spare tire.

All she wanted was a little road time. Claire and Eileen could be going to Medford, to Los Angeles, to Tokyo—that didn't matter. What mattered was coming along, making them *see* her, whether they liked it or not.

That's why, while Claire had been gathering her things, Murphy had devised the ingenious plan. She'd pulled on her coat, stuffing the right pocket with the new rope trick she hadn't mastered. And of course she'd brought Siegfried's coffin. She wasn't letting go of him until she found a proper burial spot. She may have failed Siegfried in life, but she was going to make it up posthumously.

Sneaking into the back of the Caravan as Eileen drank and

Claire packed a bag—that had required utmost stealth and concentration. There hadn't been time to pee.

For the first half hour of the trip Murphy had kept perfectly still, lying on the back floorboard with her arms crossed mummystyle. She was wearing her purple puffer coat, and if she moved an inch, she'd crinkle. So she hadn't moved.

At first, it was awesome. Murphy was a legit stowaway, and Eileen and Claire's fight had served her piping fresh info to digest:

I read the letter.

Uncle Patrick.

Inheritance.

This stuff didn't happen in the real world; not Murphy's real world, anyway. Murphy's reality was not like life on TV. There were no FBI investigations or car chases or life-altering secrets. Murphy's reality was SpaghettiOs that cooked too long on the stove. It was a string of Bs on her report card and Cs, *always Cs*, in science. Her reality was a turtle dying on her for Christmas.

But *this* was prime-time TV. From what Murphy had gathered, the facts of her new reality were:

1) She had an uncle

2) Who was dead

3) And whose death involved a house

4) Which Eileen and Claire were going to inherit

5) And maybe she was, too???

Murphy wasn't sure what points one through five added up to, but she'd figure out the details later. What was important was this: *Drama* was unfolding, and Murphy was going to be part of it. The stage was set for the performance of a lifetime. Murphy was waiting in the wings.

That's how it had been for the first couple minutes.

Then Murphy's bladder had begun to fill. She could practically see it expanding beneath her puffer coat, inflating like a balloon. Little stings shot through her body, making Murphy want to squirm. She couldn't though. If she did, they might hear. She tried to focus on something else. Something solid, outside her body.

The music was a good distraction, even when the same songs began to play over and over again:

Eight maids a-milking
Seven swans a-swimming
Six geese a-laying
Five
golden
rings

As she listened, Murphy got to thinking. Deeply. Really, what kind of sicko Christmas presents were these? Who had room in their house for six geese, let alone the a-laying kind? And what newborn baby enjoyed a little boy drumming? Wouldn't that keep him up, screaming through the night? Mary probably loathed that drummer kid.

But even Murphy's song-scrutinizing was interrupted by incoming signals that bladder bursting was imminent. Eileen—and then Claire, after *that* incident—had been driving for hours, and who knew how much longer there was to go. At last Murphy decided it was better to ruin the surprise than to pull her stunt in pee-soaked jeans.

So she'd spoken up.

And everyone had gone totally crazy.

Murphy lost her balance when Claire swerved the van. She fell in an awkward squat, conking her head against an armrest.

"Holy *shit!*" shouted Eileen, looking at Murphy as though she were one of the undead.

They'd pulled off on the shoulder, and the van shuddered with every high-speed pass of a car on the highway.

Murphy rubbed her head and decided to try the *No, I'm affronted!* approach.

"What?" she demanded. "I wasn't going to let you have all the fun without me."

"You've been in here *the whole time?*" Claire choked. She'd undone her seat belt and was up on her knees, staring at Murphy over the driver's seat.

It was time for the *Shock them with what I know!* approach.

"This trip's about an Uncle Patrick." Murphy's face heated up. "Well, if he's your uncle, then he's mine too. I'm your sister, and I deserve to know what's going on."

Claire looked at Eileen. Eileen looked back. They were silent, both of them panting. Claire slammed an open palm to her face.

"This is the last thing we need," she groaned.

Music played on, a crooner singing about Jack Frost nipping at your nose. Eileen cut him off midsentence by way of the volume knob and turned on Murphy with heavy-lidded eyes.

Murphy gulped. Why had she thought this plan was ingenuous? Eileen had been driving buzzed, apparently, but what about Murphy? Had she been drunk on Dr Pepper?

"You're right, Murph," Eileen said. "You deserve to know."

Claire, who was tapping frantically on her phone, jolted to attention. "*What?* Are you kidding me? You don't *give in* to her. That's not how discipline works."

"Who the hell is disciplining her? She's our sister, not our kid."

"I'm not a kid, I'm fourteen," said Murphy.

It was dark in the van, but not so dark that Murphy missed Claire's glower as she said, "I seriously can't believe you."

Murphy scoffed. "Me? *You* were going to leave me home alone! Overnight! Like, wow, how considerate."

Her sisters didn't answer. No doubt because "being considerate to Murphy" hadn't been at the top of their to-do list for years.

Eileen leaned over the console and shifted the car into drive.

"WHOA!" shouted Claire, pumping the brake. "What are you doing? We haven't decided—"

"We can decide when we're not on the side of the road at four in the morning." Looking to the rearview mirror, Eileen added, "Sit down and put your seat belt on."

Murphy wondered if Eileen was talking to her or to Claire. They both obeyed. Claire craned her neck to make out the oncoming traffic. When her path was clear, she revved onto the interstate.

"Where are we going?" Murphy asked, because maybe this time she'd get actual answers.

"What do you think, genius?" said Eileen. "We're finding you a piss pot."

FOUR YEARS
BEFORE

CAYENNE CASTLE

B y its third year the castle had grown. Its blanket walls and quilted parapets stretched past the den, down the hallway, and into the kitchen, where snacks of chips and kettle corn—luckily, no bad chili—could be easily obtained.

This year Claire went by an alias: Princess Paprika. She sat on her throne, a white-and-green lawn chair, tapping away at her brand-new phone.

Well, not *brand*-new. The iPhone was used, purchased from eBay, and yes, it was four whole versions behind the latest model. Still, it was the best Christmas gift Claire had ever received.

The sisters had decided two years ago to add a new tradition to the twenty-first: Once Cayenne Castle had been constructed in all its glory, they would exchange presents. It was Christmas before Christmas, and it was better, really, than the twenty-fifth itself, when Mom tried to be cheery but ended up dozing off on the couch by noon. Last year she'd napped so hard she'd forgotten the pecan pie in the oven. Only the fire alarm had woken her, and by then the kitchen was filled with smoke and the stench of burnt sugar.

December twenty-first, though? That was just for the Sullivan sisters. A sacred celebration. For this round of gift-giving Claire had presented Murphy with a deck of trick cards. Murphy had given Claire a hot-pink day planner. Eileen had given Murphy a DVD of Penn & Teller, who she'd declared were "dope as hell." Murphy had given Eileen a postcard book, each card a famous work of art, from Van Gogh's "Sunflowers" to Jackson Pollock's splatters.

Then there had been Claire's gift to Eileen: a set of watercolors made by a pricey brand that Eileen had told Claire she couldn't afford. It had taken a lot of babysitting, but Claire had managed to save enough for the paints. She'd thought that no other present could beat them.

And then she'd opened Eileen's gift to her.

Claire was going into high school next year; she *needed* a phone. Mom was stressed with work, though, and making ends meet, and an iPhone seemed so extravagant an ask. So Claire hadn't asked, and she'd known, with dejected certainty, there was no phone in her future.

But *now*.

Now, she had freedom. Now, she could plan with ease, using a digital calendar. She could finally start an Instagram account. Maybe even look into an Etsy shop for her jewelry.

"It's old," Eileen had told her, "and you'll have to pay for the plan from here on out. But it's something to get you started."

A start was all Claire needed. She'd find a way to make the payments. There were bright things ahead for this princess.

Eileen had been dubbed Sir Sage by Murphy, who'd doled out both sisters' titles wielding a remote-control scepter. Then there was Murphy herself: Prince Pepper, ruler of all she surveyed and master-in-training of a folding-paper quarter trick. She'd been working on the magic act for a week but hadn't gotten the method down. It involved folding the green corner, then the blue, and—

Murphy squeaked as the quarter flew from her hand and rolled into the kitchen, disappearing beneath the oven.

"Crap," she said.

Murphy really wanted to get this right. On the twenty-first her sisters were a captive audience. They were busy with school and work other days, but December twenty-first was for hanging out: Murphy's time to shine. A few years back Mom would have stopped for Murphy's songs or speeches and tricks. Now? Murphy was lucky if she got a "hello" after school. Mom wasn't . . . *here*. She worked longer hours than ever before, and most nights when she got home, she was too tired for Murphy. No time to talk about school or how Murphy wanted to join drama club, and *definitely* no time for a performance. Once, Mom had paid full attention. Then she'd heard without listening. These days, she didn't even *hear*.

Those were the gloomy thoughts on Murphy's mind as she watched the quarter roll out of reach. So much for a magical beginning. Sighing, she returned to the castle, ducking under the U of O fleece.

A moment later Eileen flung open a quilted flap, revealing a canvas the size of a textbook, painted with magentas, grays, and blues.

"I call it *Masque of the Red Death*," she said. "It's based on a short story by Poe."

The announcement drew Claire out of her Instagram daze. She looked up from the phone and gasped, "Leenie, it's a *revelation*."

"Super cool," said Murphy. "Looks like blood splattered on walls."

"Murphy, gross." Claire wrinkled her nose.

"Well, it does."

"I guess," admitted Eileen. "Anyway, where should we hang it?"

"Over the dais, of course!" Murphy produced the boisterous laugh of a royal, as though to say, *What a preposterous question, oh peasant!*

"Agreed," said Claire. "It'll be impressive there."

Together the sisters crouch-walked deeper into the den until they reached the fireplace. Stockings had been hung with care — Claire's doing, not Mom's, and it was Claire who removed the small wreath from the brick mantle and motioned for Eileen to hang the painting in its place.

"Your work is welcome within our court, Sir Sage," she said.

Eileen nodded gravely and stepped forward, situating the canvas on the nail.

The sisters scooted back admiringly.

Murphy sighed. "I wish we could keep the castle up year-round."

"No," said Claire. "It's better to have a set date. The twenty-first forever, like a birthday. It's the once-a-year part that makes it special."

"Dunno," said Murphy, "I think life would be pretty special if every day was my birthday."

Eileen snorted and said, "You're not wrong, Murph."

"My name is *Prince Pepper*," Murphy corrected, pridefully raising her chin. "Or perhaps you didn't recognize me without the crown."

Eileen wrapped an arm around Murphy's shoulder. She wrapped the other around Claire's. Some days, like today, Eileen noticed a sore spot in her gut—a realization, growing little by little. Mom wasn't around anymore. Even when she walked through this house, she was more ghost than human, pale and vacant-eyed. Once, she'd bought Eileen craft kits and put her art on display in the kitchen. Not anymore.

It wasn't that Mom had grown cold; there were moments— glimmers—of her old smiling self. Eileen would probably get a glimpse of that in four days' time, when Mom would try to arrange the best Christmas celebration she could.

But that didn't change the fact that Leslie Sullivan was distant, and Eileen didn't know how to draw her back. Not when Mom was talking constantly about bills and rent hikes and debts that hadn't been repaid since their father's death—debts that never seemed to go down, but only up with interest. That's what happened, Mom had told Eileen once, when you got a bad cancer and had no insurance. She and Dad hadn't been able to afford it at the time.

Now, Mom wouldn't be able to afford Dad's bills in perpetuity.

Soon, though, Eileen planned to get a bagging job at Safeway. Maybe the extra money would help. Maybe that would bring Mom back to the land of the living.

Until then, at least Eileen had sisters by her side. Nobility, the three of them. Constructors of an impermeable fortress.

"We made a good castle," said Sir Sage.

"We *did*," Princess Paprika agreed.

"And," said Prince Pepper, "we'll make an even better one next year."

DECEMBER
TWENTY-THIRD

TEN

Eileen

I f we'd gone to the Dairy Queen bathroom, we could've gotten cheese curds."

"Dairy Queen isn't open this early, and we needed gas. Wash your hands."

Eileen leaned against the tile wall, eyeing Murphy with annoyance.

This trip was supposed to be about *her*. Eileen's life, her family, her past, her secret. When she'd snuck into the Caravan, she'd envisioned a solo trip. A transformative journey. Just her and an old house, filled with memories she desperately needed to uncover. *Documents*, even a mere slip of paper, that could either confirm or deny what she'd suspected since she was sixteen.

This was *her* goddamn self-revelatory journey.

So how the hell were her sisters here? Claire, a briber, and Murphy, a stowaway? Eileen was pissed. But she needed the gas money, and there was no way they were driving Murphy the two hours back to Emmet. This was reality: She was stuck with her sisters. The only thing Eileen could control now was the damage. Whatever documents were in that house for her to find, she'd keep them out of her sisters' hands. Whether or not the secret was true, they couldn't know about it. She'd kept it from them for two years, and she could go on doing so for one more night.

"I want cheese curds." Murphy's whining pierced through Eileen's thoughts.

"You're fourteen," Eileen said flatly. "Get the hell over it."

"But *cheese*. Cheese that's *fried*."

Eileen couldn't tell if Murphy was genuinely whining or trying to be funny. Probably both. She was always putting on a show.

As Murphy lathered her hands with soap, Eileen glanced in the mirror. Black liner was smudged at the edges of her eyes, and she made quick work of wiping away the excess. That didn't help her face much. It remained gaunt, cheekbones sharp as a metal frame. Her gaze was dark, shoulders slouched.

Did she know this version of herself? The one who threw back whiskey before driving her sisters up I-5?

Was this the face of a goddamn alcoholic?

Eileen snapped her gaze from the mirror to the sticky tile floor. No. That wasn't the word for it. Claire's charge had been bogus. Eileen had been buzzed, *maybe*, but she hadn't been driving drunk. And she wasn't *a* drunk. Even now, as the need for booze turned her throat to a gaping vortex of liquor-lust, she wasn't going to call it *that*.

But then . . . why had she pulled off the interstate? Why had she let Claire take the wheel?

Because she was tired. She hadn't been up for a fight.

It wasn't because she was drunk.

She was *fucking tired*. Wouldn't anyone be at four in the morning?

Murphy shut off the sink faucet with the back of her wrist, then searched around the bathroom, presumably for a paper towel dispenser. Eileen tapped the dryer she was leaning beside—a white, rusted clunker. In response Murphy wiped her hands on her jeans.

"What's the point of those things?" she sighed.

Then she stopped in front of the bathroom door, looking expectantly at Eileen.

"What?" Eileen asked.

Murphy said primly, "My hands are clean."

Eileen rolled her eyes and jerked open the door. Murphy could be a real princess—a trait she shared with Claire. Eileen followed Murphy down a convenience store aisle stacked with jerky out to the Caravan. In their absence an attendant had filled the tank using Claire's dirty bribery money.

Once everyone was in the van, doors slammed shut, Claire turned to Murphy and asked, "How much do you know?"

Murphy told them how much, which was basically everything: Uncle Patrick, their inheritance, and the deal Claire had struck with Eileen. Snooping—another thing Eileen's sisters had in common.

Claire was pink in the face by the end of it. "You're staying in this van the rest of the trip," she commanded.

Murphy scoffed. "What, do you think bandits are going to drag me off or something?"

"Maybe I do," Claire snapped. "We're going to a town no

one's heard of to see a dead man's house. We don't know what to expect, and what we especially don't need is a little sister to worry about."

"I'm *fourteen*," said Murphy. "I'm three years younger than you. You always act like it's a decade."

"Maybe because you *act* like you're four."

"Okay," Eileen said, dispassionately. "Can we not? Murph, you do whatever the hell you want. Claire, chill out. This is my car, and you're both here thanks to my mercy, or whatever."

"I'm here thanks to my money," Claire sniffed. "Murphy is deadweight."

"Oh my God," groaned Eileen. "This isn't the zombie apocalypse. We're not fording raging rivers, we're checking out a house. That's it, okay? And Murph's right, it kind of sucked that we were going to leave her alone overnight."

It *did* suck. Eileen was realizing that. She'd been so set on going to Rockport, she hadn't considered the fact that leaving Murphy behind was exactly what Mom had done to the three of them with her cruise. Big surprise: Eileen sucked as a sister. She hadn't planned on receiving the Best Older Sibling award anytime soon.

"Yeah," Murphy piped up. "What's with that?"

"You chill out too." Eileen pointed to Murphy in the rearview mirror. "You got what you wanted: You're in the goddamn car."

Murphy had no reply for that. She sniffed and shrugged.

"Keys," Claire said from the driver's seat. She extended a hand to Eileen, who'd grabbed the keys when they'd parked.

"I'm fine to drive," Eileen muttered, not putting her heart into it.

She was too tired to argue. And that's what had impaired her driving: tiredness. That had been *it*.

Claire clicked her seat belt in place and repeated, *"Keys."*

Rolling her eyes, Eileen produced the keys from her pocket. Rather than hand them over, though, she jammed the car key into the ignition herself. Then, crossing her fingers out of sight, she turned the key *just so*.

The car started on the first go, with a full tank of gas.

One hour till they reached Rockport.

"So, our first sister road trip, huh? Go-see-our-new-house-we-didn't-know-existed road trip. And after we see the house, we can get cheese curds for breakfast. Claire, you like cheese curds, right?"

"Those have gluten."

"Well, what about Blizzards?"

"They clog your arteries."

"Yeah, that's why they're good."

"We don't have time for Dairy Queen."

"It's a road trip. We gotta eat sometime."

"It's not a road trip. It's . . . reconnaissance."

"What's the Renaissance got to do with anything?"

Eileen turned up the radio, chewing viciously on two new pieces of Dubble Bubble. She and Claire fought, sure, but at least they knew how to stay quiet. Murphy? The kid didn't have a filter. And Claire? She always rose to the occasion.

"Murph," Eileen shouted over the music. "You were better as a stowaway."

The rearview mirror reflected Murphy's grin—crooked teeth,

no orthodontic intervention. Like Claire's. Eileen's were perfectly straight. A waste, since out of the three of them, she smiled the least.

Eileen glanced at the GPS on Claire's phone and muttered, "You don't need that. I know the way."

Claire looked at her funny. "What, you have a photographic memory?"

"Yeah, Claire, maybe I fucking do."

"Don't say 'fuck' in front of Murphy."

Murphy laughed. The kid had a weird sense of humor.

"Anyway," Claire went on, "the phone is more reliable. I'm not risking taking wrong turns in a small town. We could end up someplace bad. It could be like Hawkins, Indiana, for all we know."

"Hawkins?" Eileen asked.

"Indiana. From *Stranger Things*."

"*Stranger Things*?"

"Oh my God, Leenie."

"What?"

"You know what *Stranger Things* is."

"Yeah."

"So, you know what Hawkins is."

"Sheesh, Claire, who doesn't know what Hawkins is?"

Claire slammed a hand on the wheel, releasing a sharp honk. "You *ass*!"

"Hey," Murphy said. "Don't say 'ass' in front of me."

Eileen snorted. Maybe Murphy's sense of humor was okay.

Claire appeared to be taking deep breaths. Steadying herself. Calming down. Probably a technique that god-awful YouTube girl had taught her. Eileen didn't press her. As always, it wasn't worth the effort.

"It's raining," Murphy said a half hour later.

It was. Featherlight rain was misting the windshield, accumulating enough to warrant the lowest wiper setting. The moon shone on the highway, spilling silver light outward, toward a field of evergreens on the right—a whole forest of Christmas trees.

"It's beautiful," Murphy murmured, dreamily.

Eileen wondered what it was like to be that person: an Oregonian still in love with the rain. After all the muddy, sunless winters. After so many too-damp springs. To be a person who could say, "It's beautiful." Murphy's age was probably to blame. Give her five winters more and maybe, like Eileen, she'd be sick to death of it. Claire was sick of it too, Eileen knew—desperate to get to Yale. They were both over this place.

It hadn't always been that way, though. Once, Eileen had been as excited about a new pastel set as Murphy was about her magic tricks. Eileen couldn't remember a time she hadn't liked to make art. There were even memories, lodged deep in her mind, of finger painting with Dad. He'd squirted greens and blues on a Styrofoam plate in the kitchen, and together they'd dipped their hands and drawn a school of fish on a flattened Amazon box.

For her birthdays Eileen had asked only for paints and pencils, cardstock and crayons. Mom had hardly ever bought the right kind. The crayons were waxy, and faint on paper. The paint was cheap, filled with gloopy chunks. The pencils had bad erasers that left behind pink streaks, or worse, tore through paper. Still, they'd been supplies, and Eileen has used them all up. She'd traced animals from old magazines, and she'd filled in every free space of her Dollar Tree watercolor books. She'd mastered the art of outlining and checkering in crayon drawings.

As she'd grown Eileen had advanced to freestyle. She'd started with little things in the house like tape dispensers and tumblers of orange juice, and then, eventually, moved on to people, like Claire. She'd found tutorials on YouTube, she'd made As in Ms. Kletter's sixth-grade art class. She'd gotten good at technique.

Then she'd grown up more, and it was no longer about technique, but *expression*. Mr. Lee had taught her that freshman year: A piece of art was about more than technical perfection; it was about how it made a person *feel*. So Eileen had nurtured an obsession with color wheels and spectrums, with the impressionists and modernists, and the *umph* you felt, like a kick in the throat, when certain colors and shapes grabbed your eye.

She'd been a true artist—curious since birth, devoted since she could hold a brush. Back then the world had been colored in rainbow hues, the saturation ticked up to the max with optimism. The future had seemed clear: an arts program—maybe even the Myrtle Waugh Fellowship in Eugene—and after that, teaching, and as a side gig, an art shop. And *maybe* she'd get lucky, and someone important would notice her work, and she'd find herself lauded in galleries in New York.

It was possible. Anything had been possible then, when she was fourteen. Back then, like Murphy, she'd been in love with the rain.

The letters had changed that. The letters first, and then the junior art exhibit.

Now rain was . . . rain.

The wipers sliced through it, violently flinging every offending droplet aside.

The clock on the dash read 4:53 a.m.

Sleep in heavenly peace,
Sleep in heavenly peace.

Frank Sinatra crooned the carol as Claire took the exit for Rockport. The empty countryside turned to rows of weather-worn bungalows. A sign appeared, its letters caught in the Caravan's headlights:

WELCOME TO ROCKPORT

POP. 4,572

WE MAKE YOU KINDLY WELCOME

Eileen grimaced as Claire slowed the van.

"The hell," she muttered.

The carved wooden creatures on the sign were bad enough—a mermaid, gesturing toward the town name, a seahorse set among bubbles, a row of shells at the sign's base. Each was carved with cartoonish proportions, and wind, rain, and salt had worn the paint away to a thin, chipped base. It was the slogan that got under Eileen's skin: *We make you kindly welcome.*

Maybe the greeting was meant to be nice, but to Eileen's ears it was sinister. Like the townspeople who'd written it had left off the tail end: *We make you kindly welcome, and you'll never leave.*

A chill passed through Eileen.

"What?" Claire said, glancing over.

"Nothing."

She shook it off as they moved on, kindly welcomed into

the town of Rockport. The coastline had become visible, peeking through a line of ocean-facing bungalows. The road sloped upward, forcing Claire to push harder on the gas. The houses grew farther apart, allowing wider views of the water, and then the rocky ground grew so steep the bungalows disappeared altogether. Still, Shoreline Road continued upward. Eileen realized they were making their way up a bluff. The rain was spitting against the van, and Claire notched up the wipers and turned on the Caravan's brights. At last the incline flattened out, and in the gathering rain, Eileen squinted to make out the street sign ahead: LARAMIE COURT. She scratched through the last of her mental directions: *Turn right on Laramie, and the destination will be on your left.*

The destination.

2270 Laramie Court.

Claire cut the Caravan's engine, and the sisters stared ahead.

The house was bigger than Eileen had imagined. Way bigger than any of the places on the coastline below. It was built in the Victorian style, complete with gables and a wraparound porch. Its two stories were fitted with rows of wide windows, set in splintering, baby blue wood. On the house's far right side, a domed turret poked out. The house backed up to the coast, its rear windows overlooking the Pacific. The place was dark, deserted. No sign of life. There were no neighbors. This was the only home at the top of the bluff, built amid a small wilderness of rocks and evergreens.

I had an uncle, Eileen thought.

For the first time that thought seemed real. Because here she was, in front of a real house. Eileen had an uncle her mom had never told her about.

Had Mom not told her for a good reason?

And the secret—had Mom had a reason for keeping that, too?

Eileen could stop right now. She could force herself into the driver's seat and head south, away from the coast, back to Emmet. Murphy would whine and Claire would raise holy hell, but Eileen was eighteen and the only one who could inherit. In the end heading home affected her alone.

Heading inside this house? That affected them all.

What was waiting for them in there? What had Mr. Knutsen meant by *documents*? What if Claire or Murphy found something that clued them in to what Eileen had known for two years? The secret. Mom's secret. A secret that had ruined everything.

Head back, said a voice in her head. Eileen wasn't sure if it belonged to fear or better judgment. Some days those two sounded exactly alike.

Head back to what? said another, sturdier voice. *Your drafty bedroom. Your boozy nights. Your empty drawing desk.*

The thumping began anew in Eileen's chest, beating beneath her leather jacket:

Ch-change, ch-change, ch-change.

Eileen yanked the keys from the ignition. She pocketed them and opened the passenger door, resolved.

She had an uncle named Patrick Enright, and she was about to break into his house.

ELEVEN

Claire

L eenie. Leenie . . . *Eileen!*"
    Now that Claire was here, parked in front of her inheri-
tance, her insides were turning graceless pirouettes. The
sight of the house had cemented Claire to the seat, causing her jaw
to unhinge like a Halloween skeleton's.

Claire wasn't sure what she'd expected from 2270 Laramie
Court. A weathered farmhouse, maybe, or a slipshod starter
home. A double-wide with a chicken wire fence. What else could
you expect from a house in small-town Oregon? Those were the
everyday homes Claire saw in Emmet.

Not here, though.

Rockport wasn't a mere small town, but a coastal one, bordered by vast ocean. And this house, while it wasn't Downton
Abbey, certainly wasn't slipshod. It was two stories of imposing
bulk, outfitted with a glimmering, domed turret. This house inti-
mated history, money, and class.

One might say it was an Exceller of homes.

The overwhelming revelation of the place—that's why Claire had first been insensible to the fact that Eileen had taken the keys and was out of the car, approaching the front door. Then clarity had struck Claire across the face.

This house wasn't theirs yet. Eileen would have to square away legal matters with Mr. Knutsen. There were papers to be signed, no doubt, and important conversations to be had. Claire herself wouldn't inherit until next September. So what on earth had she meant to do here?

Claire always had a plan. *Always.* But tonight she'd acted on impulse, desperate for a scrap of hope: lemonade that would make sense of the lemons. Her *golden moment.* Now, what were they supposed to do next? They couldn't just break into the house.

Though that seemed to be exactly what Eileen had in mind.

"Eileen, *stop!*" Claire yelled through the open passenger door.

Claire knew Eileen heard her. She didn't stop, though, and she didn't turn around. She kept walking ahead. *Is she in a trance?* Claire thought irritably, ignoring the fact that she'd recently been in one herself.

Then she heard a noise from the back of the van: another door opening, shoes hitting gravel. A moment later Murphy was passing in front of the windshield, a jogging blob of a purple puffer coat.

"Murphy!" Claire shouted. "I told you to stay in the van!"

Murphy waved without looking back. She might as well have been giving Claire the finger.

"Unbelievable," muttered Claire, throwing open her door and stepping into the night.

Eileen had reached the front porch and was taking the steps slowly, studying her feet as she moved, as though inspecting the wood's integrity.

Could be rotting, Claire thought. *Magnificent as it is, the entire house could come crashing down.*

Sudden panic burst in Claire's chest, and she broke into a run, moving fast enough to catch up with Murphy and grab her by the arm.

"Hey—ow!" Murphy yelped, tugging away.

Claire held firm. "What do you think you're doing?"

"Uh, checking out the house. What are *you* doing?"

Murphy's intonation could only be classified as sassy. Claire ignored her, looking ahead.

"*Leenie*," she whisper-shouted.

Eileen, still unresponsive, had moved her inspection of the porch to the front door. Claire stomped up the steps, hauling Murphy along. There, she got a good look at the situation. Eileen was turning the door handle left, then right. When it didn't give, she shook it violently.

"Would you stop that?" Claire hissed. "You can't break in."

"I'm not," Eileen said, fiddling. "You can't break into a house you own."

"*We* own," Claire corrected. "And you don't own it yet."

"I'm eighteen, aren't I?" Eileen countered.

"Yes, but there's paperwork that—"

"If I can vote for the president and fight in a goddamn war, then I can enter my new house."

"We can't risk it," said Claire, realizing with dawning horror the position she'd put herself in. "What if the police come out here? They could *arrest* us. We can't afford to get arrested. We don't have that kind of money."

"Sure we do," said Eileen, smiling placidly. "You have *thousands*, Claire. Isn't that what you said? The people of the Internet have paid you well."

Claire threw Eileen a dirty look, then felt instantly ashamed. Was this the kind of person she was? Making faces, like a child? Claire couldn't imagine Harper Everly—with her perfectly contoured face, radiant hair, poise, and grace—even *thinking* of such behavior.

Being impulsive had been a terrible idea. Claire wondered how nonplanners did this, day after day—running where the wind took you until you landed flat on your face. It put you in precarious positions, led you to throw dirty looks.

Claire had to rise above. This had been a bad idea from the start, but she could turn it around. She could devise a way to get out of here.

"Think about it," she told Eileen, her thoughts leaping one step ahead of her words. "We get arrested here—just set aside the implications of *that*. It'd get back to Mr. Knutsen, and you don't know what kind of trouble that could put us in. You haven't seen Uncle Patrick's will for yourself. What if there's a clause saying he disinherits us if we break in?"

Eileen squinted. "Yeah, Claire. I'm sure there's a clause that says exactly that."

"You don't know!"

"You're goddamn paranoid."

"Fine," Claire snapped, grasping for a different approach.

"It'll get back to Mom, though. You want her hearing about this?"

Eileen grew very still. Even though the sisters barely spoke anymore, in this moment Claire knew what Eileen was thinking. She had to be wondering, like Claire, why Mom would lie about this. Why had she told them, all their lives, that they had no family?

These days Claire thought of Mom as plenty of things: frazzled, distant, out of touch. She'd never thought of her as a liar, though. Never malicious. So should Claire and Eileen have taken Mr. Knutsen's letter to Mom directly? Was it right, keeping this a secret from her? Maybe, maybe not. It was pointless asking the question when Mom was currently worlds away, in the Bahamas.

Still, Claire's words had an effect on Eileen. She stopped fiddling with the door and rose from her crouch.

Claire forgot sometimes how tall her sister was—a good six inches above her, supermodel height. She wondered where Eileen had gotten those good genes, and why the universe in its infinite irony had given them to *her* and not Claire. Eileen didn't do herself justice with those black, baggy clothes and constant slouch.

Claire shook her head. *Concentrate.* She could judge Eileen's fashion at a more convenient time.

Eileen, meantime, was frowning into the distance. "Where's Murph?"

Claire looked around. In the heat of her fight with Eileen, she had released Murphy's arm. Now her little sister was gone. She wasn't on the porch or in the front yard.

"I GOT IT."

The shout came from the back of the house.

Claire and Eileen exchanged wide-eyed looks before clambering toward the sound.

They had followed the deck around to a set of French doors. The left door was open, swinging in a sea-born breeze, and Murphy was nowhere in sight. Claire drew closer, trying to peer inside, but the house was utterly dark.

"*Murphy!*" It was getting harder to whisper her shouts.

Claire pulled out her phone and switched on its flashlight, directing the beam inside the house. She didn't step inside, though. Somehow, she couldn't.

It was Eileen who charged ahead, boots stomping across the old, hardwood floor.

"Murphy!" she bellowed into the house.

Cautiously, Claire followed Eileen, casting light in every direction, trying to calm her thudding heart.

"Murphy," she squeaked. "Not funny!"

"Jesus," Eileen said, snatching the phone from Claire. "This isn't a rave."

A protest bulged, then died in Claire's throat. She was behaving frenetically, she knew, but how could she help it? She didn't like dark, open spaces—the thought of who, or *what*, could be ahead, masked by shadows.

Eileen, by contrast, steadily shone the light ahead. There wasn't a whiff of fear coming from her. That's the way it had been growing up: Eileen was the one to remove spiders from the bathroom, the one to tell Claire that there was nothing in her closet at night save sweaters and shoes. She'd been the brave one. It seemed she still was.

"Murphy!" Eileen called again.

They passed through a narrow hallway that turned into a larger room—a kind of parlor. As the flashlight cut through the darkness, Claire took in the room piecemeal: a green velvet sofa, a mantle, crown molding, a grand piano, a pile of filing boxes.

Boxes. There were lots of those, stacked four high and many across, running along a wall.

Eileen stepped deeper into the room and slowly slid the beam upward, illuminating a grand staircase nearly as wide across as the parlor itself.

There, a few steps up, stood a motionless figure.

"AAAH!" Claire screeched.

"Fucking fuck!" Eileen added.

The figure, all purple and puffy, said, "Calm down, do you want the police to show up?"

"*Murphy. Maureen. Sullivan.*" Claire spat every one of her sister's names.

In an instant she'd gone from terrified child to the worst maternal version of herself.

"What do you think you're doing?" she barked, and had to stop herself from adding "young lady."

"You keep asking that," said Murphy, blithely hopping down the stairs. "Maybe you should spend more time asking *yourself* what you're doing. You and Eileen waste time fighting. You weren't getting anything done. Me, on the other hand—"

"Are a criminal!"

Claire's whisper-shouts had completely lost their whisper.

"Whoa, whoa." Murphy brought down her hands in a calming gesture. "Who's breaking the law?"

"What do you think that is?" Claire shrieked, motioning

toward the French doors. "That is *literal* breaking and entering."

"No, it's not." Murphy grinned as wide as the Cheshire Cat.

Was there something *wrong* with this girl? Claire hadn't paid much attention to Murphy lately . . . as in the past couple years. Had she hit her head at some point? Become feral from lack of parental oversight?

"How did you get in?" Claire demanded.

"Magicians. We're good at locks." Murphy beamed. *"Ta-da."*

Claire put a hand to her head and whispered, "Oh my God."

"It's our house," Murphy said, indignant. "We split it three ways, right? So, I'm scouting it out for my third. Isn't that the whole point of our sister road trip?"

"No," Claire said coldly.

"Then what?"

"Yeah, Claire," Eileen turned to her, shining the flashlight directly in her face. "Why are we here?"

Claire angrily shielded her eyes until Eileen relented and lowered the beam. Then, and only then, did she answer. She'd been given a chance to lay out a plan. Eileen hadn't meant it that way, with her snarky question, but Claire was going to seize the opportunity. Impulse had brought her here, but planning was going to get her out.

"We came to see the house for ourselves," she said, addressing Eileen with a steady glare. "All right, we've seen it. We didn't have to break in, but we did. Now we leave, before anyone finds out, and we proceed the *legal* way."

"You can leave if you want," said Murphy. "No one's stopping you."

Claire ignored Murphy, intensifying her glare at Eileen. "We had a deal. You're here because of my money."

Eileen's lips twitched. "The deal didn't involve me taking orders from you."

In one rabid swipe Claire grabbed her phone out of Eileen's hand. "*Fine.* You have fun exploring a pitch-black house. I'll be in the van, waiting for you. And if the police show up? Have fun getting back to Emmet on your own."

Claire stalked toward the double doors, leaving behind the two most infuriating sisters known to earth.

"You're not curious?"

Claire stopped. She turned slowly to Eileen. "Excuse me?"

Eileen said, "You don't wonder why Mom didn't tell us we had an uncle?"

Claire wasn't going to admit that she'd been asking herself that question minutes ago. She folded her arms and said, "I'm sure she had a good reason."

"You're *sure* about that?"

Eileen's words were sour with sarcasm, and Claire couldn't think of a rebuttal. Mom *had* to know about Uncle Patrick, didn't she? Mom didn't talk much about Dad, and Claire had understood that, at least: The memory of him was too painful to revisit.

But why had Mom hidden the fact that Dad had a brother? She'd told the sisters they had no extended family. Mom had been in the foster system since she was two, handed from house to house, never remaining in one long. She'd emancipated herself at seventeen, and that's when she'd met Dad. He'd been an only child, and both his parents had died when he was a teenager. Car accident. Claire hadn't ever asked questions, because the stories of her parents' pasts had made her sad, and because . . . well, who lied about something like that?

As it turned out, some people did.

"Do you know how Uncle Patrick found out about us?" said Eileen. "Knutsen said he used a private investigator to track us down. He left instructions, too, for Knutsen not to tell Mom about any of this."

A prickly feeling spindled up Claire's arms. She couldn't help herself from responding, "But . . . why? Did she do something wrong? Was there, like, a falling out?"

"Who knows," Eileen shrugged. "The way Knutsen talked, the guy was batshit."

"Then he's *got* to be our real uncle," Murphy said, guffawing.

No one else laughed.

"All I'm saying," Eileen said to Claire, "is there's a chance we could find some answers here, if we stick around. Knutsen said this place could be chock-full of stuff. Documents, photographs, antiques."

"So, what?" said Claire. "You've broken and entered, and now you want to *steal*?"

"I didn't say that." Eileen threw out a hand. "I don't need this crap. I *do* want some time to see if there's a clue about who Patrick Enright was, and, you know, what the hell is going on. And *you* want to know what the place is worth, right? How much you could get for the shit, to pay for Yale."

Claire was wavering. Eileen had it partly wrong, of course. Claire didn't need the money for Yale, but she *did* need it to start a new life. Even if this house was unsellable for four years, it was money for the future. Money she could plan on, down the line.

She *was* curious. About the house, but also—unexpectedly—about family.

She hadn't let herself think about who Uncle Patrick could be, or how this could have anything to do with her father, long dead of a bad cancer. Those things weren't part of her golden moment. Now, Claire was thinking better of it. This house wasn't merely money-in-waiting. It could've touched her dad in some way.

Claire had only a handful of memories of her father. He'd passed when she was three. She didn't even remember the funeral, and she wondered sometimes how her mind could have failed to hold on to something as big as that. What it held on to instead was him by her bedside, reading *Harold and the Purple Crayon*. And another memory, when she'd skinned a knee and come in the house sobbing, and he'd stuck a Band-Aid on the damage before handing her a Reese's cup, saying, "These make the pain go away."

He'd been a good father, Claire was certain of that. He'd just been gone for so long. Occasionally, when she told people her dad was dead, they got a serious look on their face and said, "I'm sorry." When that happened, Claire felt guilty, because she *was* sad that her dad had died young. But the truth was, she didn't think about him most days. She didn't miss him, exactly, because there were so few memories of him to miss.

She'd made do without a dad, just like she'd made do without much of a mom. Like she'd made do without an older sister, once Eileen had abandoned her for the garage bedroom two years ago. She'd made her own new family, with Harper Everly as its head and fellow online Harperettes as siblings. She'd more than made do. She'd *excelled*.

But now, what was waiting for her at home? A rejection from Yale and an unanswered text from Ainsley St. John.

Claire was scared to be here. She didn't like recklessness, not knowing what came next. But maybe she was supposed to work through this fear. Maybe that was *part* of the golden moment. Maybe she could give this one more try.

Claire narrowed her eyes at Eileen. "You don't plan on taking anything?"

Eileen raised two fingers in a mock salute. "Scout's honor."

This wasn't how Excellers behaved. They played by the rules, worked hard, and got their just reward. But then, Claire had done all that work, and there was no reward to be had. No Ivy League for her, and no breathless romance with Ainsley. No escape from Emmet.

They were already here, inside the house, the worst of the damage done. As long as they didn't steal, they wouldn't be breaking additional laws.

Maybe they could stay. For an hour. Two, tops.

"Look at her, Leenie," said Murphy. "I can tell: You've got her convinced."

TWELVE

Murphy

M urphy had never set foot in a house this big, not even when she'd made friends with Zoe Colvis in fifth grade and been out to her pool party in Chester Heights, the one nice neighborhood in Emmet. There, bedrooms had their own bathrooms and the kitchens had fancy spigots over the stoves, and there were, of course, in-ground pools.

But even Zoe's house hadn't been *this*. Her place had been so new that the trees in the front yard were saplings supported by wooden stakes. The house on Laramie Court was *ancient*. Murphy could tell by the crystal doorknobs and giant staircase. She'd seen houses like this on TV, in movies set in the 1800s and shows about rich teenage vampires. Maybe that's why, walking around, she felt she was on a Hollywood set, and at any minute a director might call, "Cut!"

One day I'll know what that's like, Murphy thought. *When I have my own Netflix magic series.*

"WHOA!"

Murphy staggered, knocked clean out of her thoughts. Light had flooded the room where she and her sisters stood.

"How about that," said Eileen, hand resting on the light switch. "These still work."

Claire looked aghast. "What are you doing? Leenie, turn those off!"

"Why?"

"Someone could see!"

"The place is deserted. It's on top of a goddamn cliff."

"Exactly. Someone could see the lights from below."

"Like I said, paranoid." Eileen yawned, squinting above their heads at the parlor's brass chandelier.

Loaded, thought Murphy. That's what Uncle Patrick had been. Zoe Colvis sure hadn't had a chandelier.

With the parlor illuminated, Murphy took in the scene in gulps, staring first at the shiny black grand piano, then a circle of plush sofas and chairs, then the artwork on the wall—oil paintings of farmland landscapes. It was impressive, but Murphy wanted more.

She ran from the room, up the grand staircase—the route she'd wanted to take before her sisters had interrupted. With electricity at her command, there was no stopping her. Murphy flicked light switches as she passed them, running up the stairs and then down an arcing hallway. She popped into one room and took a look: a four-poster bed, grated fireplace, and massive armoire.

She let out a squeal and carried on to the next room: a canopy king-size bed, vaulted ceiling, and writing desk. Another squeal and Murphy was off, continuing her mission. She was going to drink in this whole house, lighting its rooms as she went.

She made quick work of it, too. Within a minute Murphy had poked her head into every room on the floor. There were four bedrooms, two bathrooms, and one office. *Office*. Who the heck had enough rooms in their house for an *office*? Murphy was vaguely aware of Claire calling her name from downstairs, but something more exciting had caught her attention: the spiral staircase at the end of the hall. Murphy sprinted toward it, then stopped to gawk up at its spindling, metal form. The staircase completed three full spirals before it led into a hidden place.

Murphy charged the stairs. There was no door blocking her way at the top. The landing led straight to a small, round room with a domed ceiling. A large window at the room's center overlooked the front yard and, beyond it, the sea. But the very best part were the shelves hewn into the walls, crammed with books.

"Magic," Murphy whispered—and she didn't use that word lightly.

She approached the window, surveying the darkened bluffs and the Pacific Ocean—wide and restless on the horizon. She breathed in deep as she spun a circle and took in the room's treasures: hardcovers of all sizes and colors stacked in the floor-to-ceiling bookshelves.

"Yeah, Uncle Pat!" she yelled, punching the air. "Way to share the wealth."

"Murphy?"

Claire's voice came from the bottom of the stairs. Murphy leaned over the banister, looking down.

"Oh, hey," she said to Claire's supremely annoyed face.

"The entire town's going to know we're here," Claire chided. "It's like a lighthouse up there."

Murphy gasped. "It *is* a lighthouse. Come see!"

Murphy could see that, despite her annoyance, Claire was intrigued too. She stomped up each step, trying to look stern, but once she reached Murphy, her face turned traitor.

"Whoa," she said.

"Right?" Murphy agreed. She pulled a book from the shelf— *The Three Musketeers* by Alexandre Dumas—and raised it over her head like a sacred tome, spinning more giddy circles. "A secret library! A castle turret!"

Then, feeling serious, she turned to Claire. "Do you think Uncle Patrick lived in this place by himself? I would get creeped out. Too many places for intruders to hide."

"Guess I'm not the only paranoid one," Claire muttered, pulling a book from the shelf and opening it. "Wow," she said, splaying a hand on a page. "First edition. This could be worth a lot."

"Hey!" came a shout from downstairs. Eileen.

"Up *heeere!*" Murphy sang. She felt ecstatic, or maybe delirious; she *had* stayed up all night. She couldn't shake the feeling, though, that something magical was going on. She was in a grand house, with her sisters. They were sharing this moment together, making a memory. Eileen and Claire were paying *attention* to her. It was their first sister road trip, and the best one yet.

Eileen appeared, black-lined eyes popping the way Claire's had.

"It's ours," Murphy whispered. "All ours."

"It won't be yours for another four years," Claire said helpfully.

"Yeah, but Eileen will share, won't you, Leenie? We can fake our death, blow up the Caravan, and come live here. No one will have to know."

"Sure," Eileen said distantly. "We'll fake our deaths."

"What's that?" Claire asked Eileen, who was holding something to her chest.

"I, uh, found it one of the bedrooms." Eileen turned the object for them to see.

It was a picture frame, containing a color photograph. In it, three boys faced the camera, a fierce swath of sun on their faces. Two had fair hair—one blond, one tinged red. Freckles clustered on their noses, and their blue eyes seemed to shine. The third had dark eyes and darker hair. He wasn't smiling like his brothers. Because they *had* to be brothers, Murphy decided.

"It's us," Murphy said reverently, tapping the centermost brother—the one who looked the youngest.

"It's Dad," Claire said. "Can't you see? And Uncle Patrick, I guess. And . . . I don't know who the other one is."

Murphy was in the midst of a revelation: If Mom had lied about Uncle Patrick, what else could she have kept hidden?

"We could have *ten* uncles," she whispered. "Or fifty aunts. Maybe Mom wasn't even a foster kid. She could have a secret family too!"

"Don't be silly, Murph," said Claire, though she sounded less certain when she asked, "Could Dad really have two brothers?"

"Dunno," said Eileen, drawing the frame back to her chest. She was wearing a weird expression. Almost like she was . . . *scared*? But that couldn't be right. Eileen didn't get scared about anything.

The expression faded as Eileen shrugged and added, "We're not here for a history lesson."

At that moment Murphy's stomach growled. Only, it was bigger than a growl. More like a roar.

"Shit, Murph," said Eileen, arching a brow.

"I told you I was hungry."

She really was, and now that Murphy was thinking about food, an undeniable, ravenous hunger took over. A body wasn't meant to stay up through the night, she guessed, with only Dr Pepper for nourishment.

As though confessing, Claire said, "I'm kind of hungry too."

"What time is it, anyway?" said Eileen.

Claire pulled out her phone. "Almost six. That's early enough for some places to start serving breakfast, right? Starbucks opens at four on weekdays."

"You *would* know that," said Eileen.

Murphy winced, expecting a fight, but it seemed Claire was too busy with her phone. She tapped at the screen, brow creased, and after a few moments resurfaced to say, "Here's a place. A diner. They opened at five. It's only"—she checked the screen—"a two-minute drive from here."

Eileen shrugged. "So we're doing this?"

"Why not, I guess," said Claire. "I'm not riding three hours home on an empty stomach."

"You know you're treating though, right?" Eileen smirked.

Claire rolled her eyes and said nothing as she pushed past Eileen and headed downstairs.

"Is there a website menu?" Murphy called, following them to the first floor. "Does it say they have cheese curds?"

"A two-minute drive, Murph," Eileen said. "We'll find out soon enough."

The sisters reached the parlor, where Murphy realized she was still holding *The Three Musketeers*. She set it on a sideboard and joined her sisters at the French doors. That's where Claire stopped, fists on hips, and asked, "What do we do about this?"

"How do you mean?" asked Murphy.

Claire narrowed her eyes. "I *mean*, if you broke in, there's no good way to lock up."

Murphy snorted. "I don't think you understand the concept of picking a lock."

"Why does it matter?" Eileen said, looking bored.

"It matters," said Claire, "because if Murphy could sneak in, then *anyone* could."

"And the chances of that are . . . ?"

"Doesn't matter what the chances are. It's *possible*, and I'm not risking anyone's safety."

"Stop using that as an excuse," groaned Murphy.

Then, because she could see where this was headed, she did the unthinkable. She broke the code of magicians: She revealed the *how* of her trick.

"What's that?" Claire asked, squinting at the small object Murphy had removed from her coat pocket.

It was, in fact, a latchkey.

"I found it under the doormat," Murphy explained.

"You didn't break in?" said Eileen. "You used a fucking key?"

They really had to rub it in, didn't they?

"Yeah, whatever." Murphy pushed past them, out to the porch.

"Then what was all that 'magician' talk?" Claire demanded shrilly.

Eileen, by contrast, was grinning. "Nice," she said, nudging Murphy's shoulder.

That mollified Murphy a little. Eileen hardly noticed anything Murphy did, let alone called it "nice."

"You are ridiculous," Claire told Murphy, joining the sisters outside. "Why didn't you tell us the truth to begin with?"

Because it wouldn't be magical. That's what Murphy wanted to say but didn't. It would sound too silly aloud, even if it was true. She closed the double doors and, using her key, locked the dead bolt from the outside.

"There," she said, turning haughtily to Claire. "We're *safe.* And we didn't even break the law. Feel better?"

Claire muttered something about how they had still, technically, broken in. Murphy rolled her eyes, secretly grateful Claire hadn't demanded to have the key. That would've been such a Claire thing to do. Anyway, Murphy had to concentrate on her goal. It was a resolution that had been forming throughout her house tour: She was going to use this stuff—the road trip, the house, the diner. They were the wand, the top hat, and the glitter in her magician's toolbox.

Murphy wasn't naive. She knew that, sooner or later, Eileen would leave the garage for her own place, and Claire would head to college, and Murphy would remain behind.

She had nice memories of Claire and Eileen from when they were younger. Memories like Cayenne Castle. She wanted more of those to hold on to when they left home.

Operation Memory Making—from here on out, that was

Murphy's task. One that required magic to the highest degree.

"Come on," Eileen said, with the house secure. "Let's get some food."

The sisters clambered down the back porch, rounding the house.

And that's when they made the discovery:

The Caravan was gone.

THIRTEEN

Eileen

D amn," said Eileen. "They told me that emergency brake was faulty."

The sisters stood staring at the place where the van had been parked on the bluff's asphalt incline. Now, it wasn't there.

A real vanishing act. One that Murphy, with her bizarro magic obsession, could appreciate.

Claire, however, was making a choked-up sound, like she'd gone into anaphylactic shock. *"How,"* she wheezed. "How could it be gone?"

"I told you," Eileen said, "the brake is messed up. Van must've rolled down the hill."

"B-b-but—" Claire sputtered.

Eileen didn't wait for an end to that sentence. She headed down the hill, calling back to the others, "It had to have stopped somewhere!"

Eileen would be lying if she were to claim, right then, that she wasn't worried. Of course she was. The Caravan was a piece of shit that she hated wholeheartedly, but it was also (a) the sum of her life savings, and (b) their only way back to Emmet. It couldn't be simply *gone*, and worse than that, it couldn't have crashed. It had to be okay.

Eileen wouldn't show that she was freaking out, though. Claire was clearly losing her goddamn mind, and only *one* Sullivan sister could lose it at a time. She had to keep it together for Murphy, and for herself.

It was slow going down the bluff—an effort that strained Eileen's calves and nearly sent her tripping—but at last she reached the base of the hill. That's where she found the Caravan.

The old junker was okay. From the looks of it, the van had slid all the way down the road, but it had curved inward, away from the cliffside, and ended up perched on a grassy embankment. Beyond that was a row of foreboding hemlock trees, a reminder of what could have been a sorrier end.

"Oh, thank God," cried Claire, joining Eileen. "It's okay, right? It'll still run, won't it?"

That was when Eileen got the idea.

Yes, she knew her Caravan would run. *Claire* didn't know that, though. Claire, who seemed obnoxiously determined to get them back to Emmet today, before Eileen had the chance to do what she'd come here to do. Claire didn't know the trick of turning the key in the ignition *just so*.

In an instant, Eileen made her decision.

Turning to Claire, she said, "Of course it'll work. Come on, get inside."

They piled into the van, Eileen in the driver's seat, Claire on the passenger side, and Murphy in the back.

Eileen slid the key in the ignition.

She turned it. Not the right way.

The engine sputtered, then died.

Eileen turned the key again.

The engine whirred. Then silence.

"What's wrong?" demanded Claire.

"Hang on," Eileen said. "This happens sometimes."

She removed the key, making a big show of inspecting it. Then she jammed it in again and turned.

A guttural groan. No success.

"Fuck," Eileen said, convincingly.

"W-w-wait," said Claire. "*What?* All it did was roll down a hill. Why would that kill the battery? How could it be dead?"

"It's a thirty-year-old dinosaur." Eileen shrugged. "That's how. Maybe the engine dropped out on the way down."

"Don't *joke.*"

"I'm not. That's Murphy's job."

From the back seat, Murphy said, "Good one, Leenie."

"Well, what are we supposed to do?"

Eileen detected a new surge of panic in Claire's question. It almost made her feel guilty.

Almost.

"It's fine," she said. "The battery's not dead. This just happens sometimes."

"It just *happens?*"

"Yeah, Claire. In case you hadn't noticed, it's not a Tesla."

"But . . . how do you get it to *not* happen?"

"The engine has to rest," Eileen lied, with maximum smoothness. "That's what the guys at the shop told me: You gotta let it rest for a while, after it's been running for long periods of time."

"For how long?"

Eileen squinted. "A few hours."

"*What?*"

"Maybe longer."

Maybe, her mind added smugly, *until I get what I want from this house.*

Claire was openmouthed. "How do you even know that's the issue? How do you know it's not the battery, or the . . . the . . . you know, the thing that starts the engine? Or *the engine*? How do you know we don't need a mechanic?"

"Because I know my van."

"What does that even mean? It's not a *person*, it's a *machine*. Are we supposed to wait until —"

"WOULD YOU TWO SHUT UP?"

Eileen started.

Fights with Claire were predictable. They had been for two years, ever since their shared bedroom had begun to feel too tight, and Eileen had moved into the garage, and Claire had begun watching YouTube religiously and "curating" an Instagram account. The fights began with a tiny conflict—the white specks on the bathroom mirror, or how Eileen never cleaned the microwave—and they finished with Claire sniveling and Eileen winning the day with cold logic. That's precisely how Eileen had expected this fight to go. What she hadn't expected was Murphy screaming at them from the back seat. In fact, she'd temporarily forgotten Murphy was there.

Now, though, Murphy was undeniable. She'd jutted her head between driver and passenger seat, red in the face, eyes wild.

"You two are the worst," Murphy proclaimed. "The apocalypse could be happening, and you would care more about your fight. It gets old. Fast."

Eileen stared at Murphy, wondering whether she should be offended or impressed. Since when had Murphy been this opinionated? Not that Eileen would ever admit as much aloud, but she had never figured out her littlest sister. She was too young, and it took too much effort, and in the end, Murphy had felt more like a house pet than a sister.

Which was a horrible thing to think, Eileen knew. Still, it was the truth.

The truth made her want a drink.

She eyed the glove compartment lustfully.

"Look," said Murphy, waving her hand in front of Claire's face. "It doesn't matter what's wrong with the van. What matters is it doesn't work. So we go into town for our food, because that's what's important. Capisce?"

Claire wrinkled her nose. "Don't say 'capisce.'"

"Why?"

"Because it's annoying, and you're Irish, not Italian."

Murphy shook her head at Claire. "And *you* are an expert at missing the point."

Eileen hadn't missed it, though. Murphy was right, *and* she was kind of a badass. Eileen hadn't known that this whole time Murphy could've done her dirty work by shooting zingers at Claire.

"Right," said Eileen. "Murph, you wearing good shoes?"

Murphy looked down at her Ugg boots, hand-me-downs from Claire.

"Define 'good,'" she said.

"They'll do." Then Eileen eyed Claire's glitter Keds, which were less than ideal for walking a mile in the rain. That was Claire's own damn fault, though, wasn't it?

Eileen got out of the van and Murphy followed suit, circling to join her on the edge of the road. There was no sidewalk here, but considering not a single car had passed them on this road, Eileen figured they could manage the walk without incident.

"Claire, c'mon," she said.

Claire hadn't moved from her seat. She was tapping at her phone.

"I'm looking up repair shops," she said. "It makes sense to hitch a ride with whoever tows us."

"I'm hungry *now*," Murphy whined.

Eileen gave her youngest sister a good looking over. How could she be badass one moment and a baby the next? Had Eileen been this obnoxious at fourteen?

Claire kept tapping her phone, visibly growing frustrated. "None of these open till six thirty or seven," she said. "Wait. There's one that's open, but it's the next town over, and . . . huh. The reviews aren't great."

"Claire," said Eileen, "I told you the van is fine. Even if you won't believe me, we'll ask at the diner about a mechanic. There's no point in staying here in the cold."

"And starving," Murphy added.

Claire didn't answer. She kept tapping.

"*Claire.*"

"Oh my *God*, I'm coming. I'm looking up the directions to the diner."

A moment later Claire was out of the van. "Okay. I think we walk that way."

She pointed down the road.

Eileen gave her a look. "Nice deduction, Sherlock."

Claire looked around, clearly taking in for the first time that the road away from the bluff was the *only* road to take. She sniffed proudly and turned up the hood of her coat, walking ahead of the others without a word. Murphy ran to join her, excitedly saying something about cheese.

This was the perfect opportunity.

"You two keep going," Eileen called. "I forgot something. I'll catch up."

Claire and Murphy didn't even look back. Good.

Quickly, Eileen crossed to the passenger side of the van and, leaning in, opened the glove compartment and removed the flask. She unscrewed the cap and took a swig. The liquid stung down her throat, filling Eileen with sweet relief. She pocketed the flask in her jacket.

It didn't take long to catch up with the others. Murphy was doing a beatbox version of a Christmas song, and Claire was saying, "Please. You're not Pentatonix."

Eileen glanced at Claire's phone screen, which showed a blue dot moving along their path, down Shoreline Road. Their destination was farther east, on a perpendicular road called Honey Street.

Honey Street. Seriously. The cuteness made Eileen queasy.

"What'd you forget?" Claire asked Eileen.

Eileen stared ahead at a pink-red dawn. "My wallet."

"The one with no money in it?"

"Yeah. That one."

The queasy feeling was growing. It wasn't that Eileen cared about lying to Claire. They weren't close, not anymore, and Claire wasn't exactly forthcoming about her own life. So, it wasn't the lying that made Eileen feel bad. It was the lying about *drinking*. Eileen knew it was gross. Gross, like the times she'd called in favors at Safeway, asking Asher to grab a bottle from Liquor Mart. Gross, like how she'd begun to think whiskey made a great pairing with her morning Pop-Tart. Gross, like the times she'd passed out in her room on the floor, tears dried on her face and vomit crusting her lips. Gross, like drinking and driving with her sisters in the van. Gross, like the letters she'd found in the linen closet. The letters that had started it all.

Documents.

What were inside those boxes at 2270 Laramie? A whole *wall* stacked with them. Maybe they contained nothing important. Or maybe they held the definitive answer Eileen had craved for two long years.

The trouble was keeping her sisters from finding out that answer. Claire seemed more interested in what the house was worth, and Murphy . . . well, who knew what the hell had brought her along. It might not be too difficult, keeping them off the scent. They couldn't know. *Couldn't.* The thought of them finding out the secret—they would never look at Eileen the same way. It was why she hadn't told them in the first place.

It was why she'd started drinking.

Eileen wanted, more than anything, to take another swig.

But doing that in front of Claire and Murphy was one gross step too far. Sure, maybe she'd drank and driven last night. Drinking *in the open*, though? For her sisters to see? Not that. Instead, Eileen dug into her other pocket, removed a piece of Dubble Bubble, and popped it in her mouth. She chewed into the hard, pink nugget, watching with sordid satisfaction as Claire occasionally wobbled and slid on the slick road, thanks to her tractionless shoes.

Maybe Eileen was imagining things, but it seemed colder than it had been before — as though, against nature, the temperature was plummeting with sunrise. She pulled her jacket tighter and tugged her beanie till it nearly covered her eyes. No cars passed them as they walked down Shoreline. The street was quiet, house windows dark. The wind was damp, sticky with salt. The sound of breaking waves was ever-present.

Only when they reached their first intersection did Eileen spy signs of human life: a brick post office and, beside it, a playground. Stop signs, storefronts, and *then* cars. A truck rumbled past them, followed by a sedan. They were in the land of the living, and Honey Street was ahead.

"There it is," said Claire, pointing, and sure enough, cattycorner to them was a squat restaurant with big windows and a light-up sign that read RAMSEY'S DINER.

The building looked as though it hadn't been renovated since 1950, and as the sisters crossed the street, the words "E. coli" and "hepatitis" came, unbidden, to Eileen's mind. There were, at least, several cars in the parking lot. This early in the morning that had to mean the place was decently popular.

"Or it's the only restaurant in town," Eileen muttered, as

Claire opened the door and a jingling bell announced their presence.

The diner was retro, with checkered tile and a glittery Formica countertop encircling the open kitchen. It was maybe a quarter full, with a few people sitting in booths, others at the counter. From the speakers, a familiar Christmas tune played, and Eileen had to laugh a little. It didn't matter where in Oregon Eileen went, Mariah Carey would find her, and all that woman wanted for Christmas was *her*.

Taking in more of the scene, Eileen noticed a figure to her right, dressed in a collared khaki button-up, a gold star affixed to the left breast pocket. Eileen inched forward to better make out the woman's features: beige-skinned and plump, with dark eyes, and a black braid emerging from beneath her wide-brimmed hat. She was reading the paper over a cup of coffee.

Claire had taken note of the woman too, and looked suddenly terrified; Eileen could practically see the tension fissuring her skin. What was there to be tense about, though? This was the town sheriff, not clairvoyant. This lady couldn't possibly know that the three of them had trespassed. All they had to do was remain chill, and Eileen had perfected that art a while back. She was chill as fuck.

"What can I do for you girls?"

A waitress appeared at the counter behind the register. She was probably in her fifties, with a pair of glasses perched on her pale, beaklike nose. She wore an electric red uniform, and the name tag pinned at her shoulder read CATHY.

"We came for breakfast," Murphy announced, pushing ahead of Eileen and Claire. "And we mean to be satisfied."

Cathy raised a brow at Murphy. "Do you, indeed?" She glanced at the clock above the register. "Pretty early to be up. If it were my Christmas break, I tell you what, I'd be sleeping in till noon."

"We come from a long line of early risers," Murphy said, conversationally.

That got an amused snort out of Cathy. She scanned the sisters before directing a question at Claire. "Just the three of you, then?"

"Yes, ma'am," Claire replied.

Eileen rolled her eyes. She knew what had happened. Cathy had been assessing them, figuring out who looked the oldest and most responsible. It didn't matter that Eileen *was* the oldest or a head taller. Of course Cathy would choose Claire. Adults always liked Claire best. She dressed right and smiled and called people "ma'am."

Cathy grabbed menus and three sets of silverware and led them to a corner booth. Eileen scooted into a seat first, and Murphy joined her. *That* was something, at least. Adults might choose Claire, but Murphy chose Eileen.

"Drinks?" Cathy asked, handing out the menus.

"Do you have mochas?" Claire asked.

Cathy studied Claire. "Beg your pardon?"

"Mocha. The coffee drink. Like, peppermint flavor, or . . ." Claire trailed off as Cathy's face went blank. "Never mind. A coffee, please. With skim milk."

Eileen watched this play out smugly before adding a coffee, black, to the order.

"Me too," said Murphy.

"Don't be silly," Claire said.

"Who's being silly?" retorted Murphy.

"No law about kids drinking caffeine," Cathy observed. "Three coffees, right up."

As Cathy swept off, Murphy leaned across the table, telling Claire, "You always act like you're way older than me."

"All I'm saying," Claire replied primly, "is Mom didn't let me have coffee when I was fourteen."

"Yeah, well, Mom doesn't care what I do."

Murphy said this blithely enough, but Eileen saw the force with which she flicked a sugar packet across the table. She recognized that force. It pressed against a small, sore spot that had existed under her skin for years. In that spot resided the knowledge that Leslie Sullivan was to her daughters what the sun was to its planets: warm, but distant; bright, but slowly burning out before their eyes.

Things had been warmer once. Eileen remembered mornings when they'd eaten Saturday breakfasts together, and Mom had asked about school and life, and they'd joked about TV shows. She remembered more distant and fuzzy days spent with Mom and Dad, her and Claire cuddled between them on the couch as they watched *Wheel of Fortune*. Dad had smelled of oranges. She remembered that clearly, even from thirteen years ago: the way the air turned citrusy when he was around.

That had been then, though, and this was now. Eileen didn't think Mom even suspected her eldest daughter drank. For one thing, Eileen was sneaky about it. She brought in the booze from Safeway in her backpack and kept it hidden beneath her bed. For another, Mom was barely around. When Eileen got drunk at home, Mom was either working a late shift at Walgreens or locked away in her room, dozing to the drone of the TV. And this holiday season? She was thousands of miles away, on the distant shores of paradise.

Eileen really needed a drink, her sisters' presence be damned. Maybe she could figure a way to slip the whiskey into her coffee. It would've been easier if she and Claire were sitting side by side. Not that she wanted Claire to—

"Three coffees," Cathy announced, back at the table. She set down the mugs and pulled out her order pad.

"You guys have cheese curds?" Murphy asked.

"Well now," said Cathy, "not a popular breakfast order. Normally, Mike doesn't start frying till eleven, or so. But I can see if he's feeling generous."

"If he is," Murphy said solemnly, "he'd make me the happiest human on earth."

"I'll have the yogurt parfait," Claire said.

Eileen ordered a short-stack of pancakes, plus a side of bacon. Once the food arrived, she intended to stare Claire dead in the eye and say, "Yum, yum, *gluten*."

Because Claire could say whatever she wanted about her "sensitivity." Eileen had grown up with her and seen Claire pack away pizza and bagels like nobody's business. Sensitivity, Eileen's ass.

"You girls from around here?"

With Cathy gone from the table, Eileen hadn't planned on any further contact with strangers. She blinked uncomprehendingly at the two old ladies sitting across from them. They were watching the sisters as though they were six o'clock news.

"Nope." Murphy answered the white-haired lady who'd asked the question. "We're from Emmet. *Ow*."

Eileen had actually *heard* Claire kick Murphy under the table, glitter shoe smacking bone.

"Emmet." The woman looked thoughtful. "Can't say I've heard of it."

"It's small," said Murphy, who'd pulled out a length of knotted rope from her coat pocket and begun messing with it.

She was such a weird kid.

"Well! We know how small towns go," laughed a man at the counter. He'd spun his barstool to join the conversation.

What is this? Eileen thought. *A town hall meeting?*

"What brings you ladies to Rockport?" asked the man. "Visiting relatives? More likely than not, I know who they are."

"That's true enough, Orson," said the inquisitive old lady. She smiled at the sisters, motioning to the man. "Orson's our mayor."

It is a town hall meeting, Eileen confirmed. Sheriff, mayor . . . who would appear next? The president of the goddamn garden club?

For a politician, Orson was underdressed. He wore a bulky suede jacket with a plaid-patterned collar and a U of O baseball cap. But as someone often dismissed for her own choice of clothes, Eileen was willing to withhold judgment. As to his question—Eileen decided it was better not to tell an outright lie. Orson probably *did* know everyone in town, and she wasn't going to risk a bogus story about made-up grandparents. She was still thinking up the best approach, when Claire beat her to it.

"We're doing research," she said, pointing to Eileen. "My friend and I, we're in the same freshman course at OSU. It's a journalism prereq, and we're supposed to report on an aspect of small-town America. So we thought it'd be a good idea to do a podcast, you know? And our angle is old homes. See, my mom used to take us on home tours of Victorians. They have *so* much history. Anyway, I got mono in October—don't worry, I'm better—but it really put me behind. So our professor was super understanding and gave us a grace period to finish the project. She said as long as we had something turned in by Christmas, she'd hold off on our final grade. Well, we've been reporting on a few local houses, but they just don't have that . . . *pizazz*, you know? Then we saw your house on Laramie written up in an article in *Victorian Times*, and we decided we had to see it for ourselves. So we've come to report on it. And this is my little sister." She pointed to Murphy. "My parents are letting her travel with us, for fun. We figure, we'll get home Christmas Day in plenty of time to open presents and everything. But when you're a journalism major, you're never off the clock."

Eileen stared, speechless, at Claire. Never in her eighteen years had she heard someone tell a lie that butter-smooth. Podcast? Mono? *Victorian Times*? She'd hadn't thought Claire had it in her: the imagination, the eloquence, the balls.

"Smooth," Murphy said under her breath.

Claire was smiling cheerily, post verbal vomit. She hadn't even broken a sweat.

"A . . . what, now?" asked the lady at the booth. "Pod-what?"

"Podcast," Claire said, patiently. "It's like a prerecorded radio show."

"Whoo," said Orson, chuckling. "I can't keep up with this technology. You millennials go too fast."

"Actually," said Claire, "we're not millennials. That's a common misconception. We're younger than that. Not that generation matters, of course. You're never too old for podcasts. Plenty of older folks enjoy them too."

Orson kept chuckling. "It's enough effort for me to maintain the Rockport website."

Cathy appeared at the counter, filling Orson's mug with coffee. "What's this I hear about Patrick's house?"

Orson pointed at Claire and Eileen. "These two, they're doing a news report. A real Woodward and Bernstein in our midst."

Cathy looked sharply at the sisters. She wore an expression Eileen couldn't read.

"Reporters, huh?" she said. "Then you know about the murders, I expect."

Claire cleared her throat. "The, uh . . . murders?"

Eileen dug her fingers into the booth.

No, she thought. *Not the secret.*

There was no stopping it, though.

"Sure," Cathy said. "The ones at 2270 Laramie."

FOURTEEN

Claire

We knew the Enrights were odd folks. But no one knew *how* odd till too late."

Cathy sat beside Claire, crow's-feet enshrining her drama-bulged eyes. She was a natural storyteller, Claire thought. In another life, she could've been a Hollywood actress. The typecast world-worn woman, wizened by time and beautiful to behold. A real star, in the vein of Meryl Streep. Claire was riveted by the performance—so riveted, she'd abandoned the parfait in front of her.

What was yogurt to murder?

And not just any murder. One that had taken place in the house she'd inherited.

Claire couldn't think of eating.

Nor, it seemed, could the other customers of Ramsey's Diner. They were listening too. When Cathy had delivered the girls their food, she'd sat right down at their booth to tell the story she'd promised earlier.

"Amelia!" she'd called into the kitchen. "Could you take over?" She'd turned to the sisters and added, "I'm using a smoke break on you, so listen up."

Since Cathy's big announcement, Murphy had gone statuesque, her jaw dropped comically low. Eileen, on the other hand, hadn't reacted a smidge. She was cutting her pancakes languidly, eyes heavy-lidded with dispassion. As though murder was no big deal. *How?* Claire wondered. Had Mr. Knutsen already told her about this? If so, how many other secrets was Eileen keeping from Claire?

Claire had lied through her teeth about it, sure, but she honest-to-God *felt* like a journalist. She wanted the scoop. Every last detail.

As Cathy spoke, her voice booming for all to hear, Claire scanned the diner. Everyone was watching Cathy, drawn in, same as Claire. The place had grown quiet. Even the Christmas music was reverent, a pensive piano version of "O Holy Night."

They must know the story, Claire thought. *I wonder how many times they've heard it, in how many ways.*

This was murder, after all, in a small town. Claire remembered when Marcie Hoffman, a senior at Emmet High, had been shot in the arm by her stepfather. Marcie had lived, and the stepfather had gone to jail. No murders, no death, and even then, that was the only thing people could talk about for weeks. It still came up five years later, in hushed cafeteria conversations.

That memory brought on an ugly thought: *Marcie got shot and still went to college. What's your excuse, Claire?*

She shook out the question and refocused on Cathy.

"The father was a bigwig in Silicon Valley back in the day.

Made bank down there. What was the company, Orson? Intel?"

"Hell if I know," said Orson.

"Well," said Cathy, "coming north was the mother's idea. Wanted to find a nice plot of land for cheap. God knows why they chose Rockport."

"Wasn't Intel," piped a bearded man sitting three booths down. "Boeing, that's what it was. In the plane business."

"That so, Wyatt?" Cathy scrunched her nose. "Boeing."

Wyatt nodded politely and sipped his orange juice.

"That'd be Seattle, then," said Orson. "Not California."

Cathy waved her hand. "One of the two. Point is, these Enrights were rich. They rolled into town around, oh, late eighties. People could tell from the first they were standoffish. City blood, you know. Doesn't mix well in Rockport. The wife was a pretty thing, though." Cathy frowned. "What was the maiden name? VanderVeer?"

"Eschenburg," supplied the talkative old lady. "German stock, I remember. Sophia Eschenburg, that was the name."

Orson chuckled from the counter and said, "Really, folks. This diner could turn into a genealogical society. Put a new sign out front!"

"It's important to get these details right, Orson," Cathy said, chidingly. She pointed at Claire. "These girls are journalists. They need the facts."

Claire smiled weakly, trying to think of something to say, like, "That's right! Just the facts, ma'am." The truth was, she wasn't sure how many of these details *were* facts. Seattle was a long drive from Silicon Valley. VanderVeer had a different ring—and origin—than Eschenburg. Claire considered the possibility that though Cathy was a good storyteller, maybe she wasn't the most trustworthy one.

Cathy carried on: "Rich as Croesus, these Enrights. Determined to buy that old house on the bluff, do it up nice. He was always away on business, but he hung around Sophia long enough to get three sons out of her. Wyatt, you grew up with 'em, didn't you?"

Wyatt shook his head. "Little after my time. John, he was three years behind me. The rest were younger, of course."

"Patrick was in my class," came a new voice, from a woman sitting at the counter.

The sheriff.

Instantly, Claire grew stiff.

If you act like there's nothing to hide, she told herself, *then she's got nothing to suspect.*

"We were on some group projects together, growing up," the sheriff continued. "He dated my friend Faith for a few weeks."

"Did he, now?" Cathy said. "Way he turned out, I couldn't picture him dating a soul."

The sheriff smiled. "Well, he was sixteen then. That was before the murders. A lot of things can change a man."

"Can they ever." Cathy pounded the table, causing Murphy to hack on one of her special-order cheese curds. "Well, we're meandering around the meat of it. Though I warn you girls, it's ugly." She stopped and peered at Murphy, who'd managed to swallow the offending curd. "How old is this one, exactly?"

"Sixteen," Murphy said, smoothly. "I look young for my age."

Claire was impressed—almost as much as she had been by her own silver tongue.

"She's fine," Claire said. "Please, Cathy, what can you tell us about the day of the murders?"

That was something a journalist would say, right?

"Oh, it wasn't *day*," said Cathy. "Middle of the night. And the murders didn't happen together. No, months apart. It started the night after high school graduation. Mark, the middle son? He'd graduated top of his class. There's one boy I *didn't* peg as odd. Out of that whole Enright clan, I'd say he was the most normal. God's truth, that's what I would've told you back then. He worked as a busboy here the summer before it happened. Mark was charming, he really was. Handsome, too. Customers raved about him. Somehow, between busing, he managed to strike up conversations left and right. Kerry, if you were in Patrick's class, that means Mark was, what, a couple years older than you?"

"I was a sophomore," said the sheriff, Kerry.

"Don't you think Mark was handsome?" Cathy shouted across the diner.

At that, Kerry smiled and said, "I don't know if I'd be the best judge of that, Ms. Hollins."

Cathy seemed to recall something, and then she smiled too. She waved off Kerry, like she'd told a big joke that Claire didn't understand. Then, sober again, she went on.

"That was Mark. Whole town loved that boy—I don't think that's too strong a way of putting it. He was class president and a real talented artist; sensitive type, but not *too* sensitive. Got a real good scholarship. PSU, was it? Or maybe Lewis and Clark."

Claire winced, and at first she was unsure why. Then she remembered.

Yale.

No college.

Her bleak, education-less future.

Of course. How could she ever forget?

"It was the night of graduation," Cathy said. "After midnight, said the police. That's when Mr. Enright was killed. Blunt force trauma to the head. There was blood all over those parlor walls. On the piano keys too, they said. Mrs. Enright's prized piano."

Claire was grateful not to have touched her parfait. She felt sick. The piano she'd seen, *admired* with her own eyes. She hadn't thought, when they'd made their tour of the house, to check it for bloodstains.

"Morning comes," said Cathy, "and Mrs. Enright discovers the body. She screams bloody murder, calls the police straight away. And what do they find when they arrive? Mark Enright has left town. Fled, in the middle of the night. Now, what innocent man would do that? Especially when he had a big homecoming dance the next day."

Claire frowned, raising a finger. "I . . . sorry to interrupt. You said it was graduation night?"

Cathy blinked. "Yes, that's right."

"But . . . then you said homecoming."

Cathy's eyes widened. "O-oh. I did, didn't I? Well . . . let's see, when was it? I thought it was spring, but . . ."

"No," called out Wyatt. "Definitely fall. I remember, it was right before Halloween. There were pumpkins on the front porch in the newspaper photos."

"Were there?" Cathy said, dubious.

"I'm with Cathy," said Orson. "I remember it being spring. It rained that night, a real April shower."

Cathy, who had begun to look distressed, shook her head dismissively. "Oh, well, it was two decades ago. You'll have to forgive our collective memory, girls. Point isn't the date; it's what happened next. And that was this: Police tracked down that boy at an Amtrak station in Portland. Brought him back, placed him under arrest, put him on trial. It was a real tragedy."

Cathy heaved a long sigh, as though she'd finished a Herculean task.

Claire was still playing the part of the journalist, though. She had to ask the question.

"Cathy," she said. "You said murders. Murders, plural."

Cathy looked weary. The silence of the diner was sticking to Claire, filling her pores like humidity. She realized, then, that Cathy hadn't meant to stop her story; she'd *had* to stop it, because it was too much of a burden to tell.

"I-I'm sorry," Claire said, gently resting her hand on Cathy's.

Cathy murmured, "That's all right, hon. It was just . . . such a horrible thing."

She kept on keeping quiet, which left Claire to reflect on how she'd found herself here, miles from home, in a tiny town she'd never heard of till two days ago, comforting a woman she hadn't met an hour ago. She glanced across the table at Murphy and Eileen and wondered if they were thinking the same thing. Who knew. They were both so different from Claire, it was hard for her to believe sometimes she had *anything* in common with her sisters, let alone thoughts.

"Sorry," Cathy repeated, but this time it was clear she meant to go through with the rest of her story. "As I was saying, they caught up with Mark and brought him back for the trial. We figured it'd be an open-and-shut case. That's sure what it seemed, in the beginning. The DA, they only had what you'd call circumstantial evidence—nothing scientific, exactly. But the youngest brother, Patrick, he testified in court that his brother told him, 'Pat, I'm going to get that old man, once and for all.' See, the father and Mark had been butting heads for years, getting involved in nasty fights. 'Course, none of us knew that. Goes to show, you don't know your own neighbors. Well, it was a real strong case before the defense brought in these so-called experts, talking about fingerprints and DNA. Then they get this girl who *claimed* to be Mark's girlfriend—an out-of-towner, some teenager with no parents to speak of—to say he was with *her* the night of the murders. And God knows why, but that jury? They believed the story. Acquitted the boy, let him go scot-free."

"*No*," Claire said, though she hadn't meant to speak. She placed a hand on her mouth, shocked as much by her reaction as the verdict.

"Hang on," said Murphy. "If Mark didn't do it, who did?"

"*That's* the real question." Cathy pointed at Murphy. "Because wouldn't you know, the night Mark Enright gets out of jail, he leaves town again. This time for good, along with the girlfriend. And in the morning? Like before. Patrick Enright finds his mother dead at the bottom of the staircase, head bashed in like a cantaloupe."

Claire felt a retch coming on. She clamped her jaw and tried her best to ride out the nauseous wave. The staircase. Those stairs she'd thought were elegant, the height of class. Now she saw splattered blood on the railing, soaking every inch of the carpet runner.

"Police ruled a suicide this time," Cathy went on. "Brought

on by grief. But others—and I'll confess myself among them—well, we think a person can get pushed as easily as they can jump. And Mark Enright had a motive. Could've even been helped by that girlfriend of his. Not that anyone's asking *me*. And I'm not blaming you, of course, Kerry," she added, nodding toward the sheriff. "Lord knows it was well before your time, and I've got nothing against the force."

Kerry gave a single, silent nod back.

"Now, Cathy," Mayor Orson called out, "we gotta let those wheels of justice turn. I'm sure the jury heard more than you and I know about the case."

"Oh, sure, Orson," Cathy called back. "Everyone's entitled to their opinion."

She turned to Claire and, very distinctly, with her back to the mayor, rolled her eyes. Claire wasn't sure if she should laugh. She was afraid that if she did, she might end up vomiting.

"Well!" bellowed Cathy, slapping her hands on the table. "I've used up my smoke break. But now you know why I say *murders*, girls. And if you intend to stay here till Christmas Day, I recommend you ask other folks about the Enrights. If you're looking for pizzazz for that pod-thing of yours, there it is."

"That's, uh . . . *pizzazz*, all right," Claire managed. "We had no idea the kind of story we'd get out of this visit. Our professor's going to be . . . impressed."

Claire was finding it increasingly difficult to lie. Her mind was fixated on an image: a woman clothed in a blue silk dressing gown, sprawled at the bottom of those stairs at 2270 Laramie. Why had Cathy said *cantaloupe*? Nothing could wash the bloody image from Claire's head.

"Whatever happened to the eldest boy?" asked Orson, as Cathy bustled around the counter, reclaiming the coffee pot. "John, wasn't that his name?"

"Off at college when it happened," said Cathy, beginning her refill round. "Other side of the country. Never came back, not even for the funerals or trial. Too much scandal, I guess, and I don't blame the boy. Of course, everyone here knows what happened to poor Patrick. Went crazy in that house, turned hermit. Eccentric as they come. It's a shame to die that young, but really, I see it as a mercy. A life like that, cooped up in that home, with those awful memories . . . you ask me, it's no life at all. God was right to take him when he did. Just a shame about that burial, insisting it be closed off. Not a soul to attend to his grave. Tragic."

"It'll be interesting to see what comes of the house," Orson remarked. "I've been curious as to what he kept in there. Who do you suppose he's given it away to?"

There was a sudden weight in Claire's stomach, pinning her to the booth. She felt as though all eyes in the diner had turned to her.

"Can tell you one thing," said Cathy, hand on hip. "It wasn't me."

She stopped at the sisters' table with the coffee pot, but Claire's cup was unrefillable. It had gone cold, full and untouched. Cathy raised a brow at it, shrugged, and headed back to the counter.

"Maybe," said the vocal old woman, "he gave it to charity."

Cathy snorted. "Hardly likely. Even if he did, that'd mean the house would have to be auctioned off, huh? And who can afford to buy it? No one I know. And no fool is going to move here from out of town. Mark my words, it'll go unsold. Some pyro delinquent will burn it down."

"Well, what about Mark?" asked Orson.

"What about him?" Cathy grunted. "Patrick *testified against him*. In a murder trial! You think he'd leave it behind to *him*?"

Claire didn't like this. Any of it.

"Cathy," she called, raising a finger. "Could we have our check, please?"

"Certainly, hon," said Cathy, before carrying on. "No, I don't think there's a mention of Mark in Patrick Enright's will. But I'll tell you my theory: We're due a visit from Mark, all the same. If anything would bring him back to this town, it'd be his brother's death. And though that house may not be his, I'm sure he'd want to claim it."

Claire formed her hands into fists beneath the table. She squeezed and relaxed them, squeezed and relaxed. She was a freshman at OSU. A journalism major. She was not Claire Sullivan, inheritor of the house in question.

Having finished her work at the register, Cathy walked to the sisters' table, setting down the check. Claire was ready with cash. She placed the bills down and told Cathy, "Keep the change."

Cathy studied the money for a moment, counting it up. Then, it seemed, she decided that Claire had been generous. And she had: 40 percent. It only felt right, given Cathy's performance.

"Didn't you like the food?" Cathy asked, eyes flitting to Claire's parfait.

"Uh." Claire looked to Murphy's empty plate and Eileen's half-finished pancakes. "Guess I got too excited by the story. You know, journalist's stomach. That's what we call it."

Her lying was getting worse. Claire scooted from the booth, and Murphy and Eileen followed suit.

"Thank you again!" she called to Cathy.

She felt she should be thanking everyone in the diner: Wyatt, Orson, Kerry, and the two old ladies. It was as though they had been in it together, this shared experience of the Enright murders.

Cathy nodded amiably at Claire. "You girls take care."

"We will. Thanks."

It was all Claire could manage. She wanted to be out of this diner, out of Rockport, out of the story unspooling around her.

They had almost reached the door when Claire felt the lightest touch on her elbow. She turned to see Kerry, the sheriff, standing there.

She knows, a frantic voice looped in Claire's mind. *She knows, she knows.*

"You girls okay?" The sheriff's words were kind, not accusatory. But maybe that was the ploy she used on people she knew to be trespassers. Made them feel comfortable, to draw out damning information.

With effort, Claire put on a smile. "Oh. Yes! We're good."

Kerry nodded, looking thoughtful. Thoughtful about what, though? Whether or not she meant to arrest them?

"I know you're college girls," Kerry said, "and I'm sure your parents have already given you the rundown. But as young women traveling alone on the holidays, out of familiar territory . . . just remember to be aware of your surroundings."

Claire stared at Kerry, and as she did, realization touched the young sheriff's face.

"Oh! Not that I'm trying to scare you." She lowered her voice, confidentially. "I don't think there's stock in these bogeyman tales about Mark Enright. I only mean, be careful in the general sense.

People can take advantage of travelers during this season."

"Sure," said Claire.

She didn't want to be rude, especially because Kerry seemed to be a nice person, and the way she spoke was gentle, like soft singing. It was hard to be polite, though, with terrible thoughts in her head. She shoved her shaking hands in her pockets and walked out the door.

What she needed was a plan.

A plan to leave Rockport as fast as she could.

FIFTEEN

Murphy

W e have to get out of here."

Claire's eyes were hard with purpose, the way they got at home when she scolded Murphy for not wiping up puddles on the bathroom sink. Only, this was more serious than puddles.

Murder. *Murders.*

Murphy was absorbing everything Cathy had said. People had *died* at 2270 Laramie. Weren't you supposed to be able to sense a thing like that? Shouldn't Murphy have gotten a bad feeling walking around that house? The way people did in horror movies, when they stepped into a room, made a face, and said, "Something *bad* happened here."

Murphy guessed her sixth sense was broken. Maybe it still was, because she didn't see why Claire was upset, or why she'd rushed them out of the diner and been rude to the sheriff. She frowned at Claire's back as her sister charged down the street.

"Hey, slow down, would you?" Murphy puffed. "We didn't ask about a mechanic."

"On purpose," Claire said sharply. "They can't know we were at that house. I don't want people asking questions, or suspecting. We shouldn't have come here."

Murphy frowned. Coming to Rockport was an adventure. Their first and probably only sister road trip. How could Claire regret that?

"Weren't you listening?" Murphy asked. "Those murders happened a long time ago."

Claire spun around so fast that Murphy pinwheeled her arms to stay upright.

"Weren't *you* listening? She said Mark Enright is coming back to town. He could be here *now*."

Eileen had been trudging behind them in silence. Now she came to a stop by Murphy's side, chewing a mouthful of bubble-gum that smacked and clicked between her words.

"She said Mark *might* come back. Dunno if you caught this, Claire, but it was a little . . . conspiracy theory in there. You pointed it out yourself: Cathy was getting tons of details wrong. Who knows how much of that was reliable?"

"Yes, okay," said Claire. "They were bound to get some things wrong. It's been twenty years. But do you think Cathy made *all* that up? Everyone in there agreed the murders happened. *And* they agreed Mark Enright was the prime suspect—who, by the way, is another uncle we didn't know existed."

"What are you saying?" Eileen scoffed. "You really think this big, bad Mark Enright is gonna come back, Michael Myers style, and kill us?"

Claire threw up her hands. "I think there are a lot of unknowns at play here. *Scary* unknowns. Why are you being so chill?"

"Dunno, Claire," said Eileen, "maybe I have less to lose."

"What does that mean?"

"It means I'm not scared I'll get arrested because I have to maintain a sterling reputation for my big, fancy, Ivy League college."

Claire set her jaw. "You don't know what you're talking about."

"Yeah, then why are you taking the word of a diner lady we just met? What, do you think this is actually true crime podcast world? Where a serial killer is on the loose in a sleepy, coastal town?"

"Oh my *God*. You're being absurd."

"Uh, no. I think that honor belongs to you."

"You're not evening *listening*—"

Murphy had heard enough. She edged around her sisters, leaving them to bicker, and kept heading down the street. She glanced back once to see that neither of them had figured out she was gone and, judging the coast to be clear, pulled out the Tupperware box from under her coat. That was the nice thing about puffer coats: You could hide turtles beneath them, and no one could tell.

"Siegfried?" Murphy whispered, tapping the container's edge. "Hey, dude, you okay?"

Siegfried didn't answer. He was dead. A tiny explosion of guilt went off in Murphy's chest, and the cheese curds she'd inhaled felt leaden in her stomach. Their remnant taste was souring on her tongue.

"I'm sorry," she whispered to the plastic coffin. "I'm gonna find you a place to do a good burial. You deserve that. You—"

"MURPHY."

She froze. At last her sisters had noticed. She shoved the coffin back into her coat and turned around.

"What?" she asked innocently.

Claire was storming up the sidewalk, Eileen unhurriedly following.

"You can't keep doing that! If I lost you, Mom would kill me."

"Nah." Murphy shrugged. "It'd take her a while to notice. You could skip town before then."

"Not funny." Claire reached Murphy, planting her feet and folding her arms. "Maybe *neither* of you are taking this seriously"— she shot a pointed look at Eileen—"but I am. Don't you get what it means, everything Cathy said? If Patrick is really our uncle, then—"

"Sure," Murphy cut in. "It means that house is where Dad grew up."

Claire blinked. "Well . . . yeah." Then she seemed to board her former train of thought: "It *also* means we're related to a murderer."

Eileen said something under her breath, brusque and derisive. Claire ignored her and added, plaintively, "I don't know why Mom wouldn't tell us any of this."

Murphy swallowed. She wasn't exactly happy with Mom for leaving the family for Christmas. All the same, Murphy didn't like to think of Mom as a liar. And something about this didn't seem fair—questioning Mom when she wasn't around to answer. She probably had a good explanation. For instance—

"Maybe she was trying to protect us."

Claire parted her lips, but Murphy pressed ahead.

"Everyone gets it, right?" she said. "Dad was the oldest brother, John. Same name. He was away at college when it happened, and the murder probably freaked him out so bad he never came home and decided to lie about it, say his whole family was dead. He wanted a fresh start. That makes sense."

Claire was glaring at the concrete, toeing a scraggly patch of grass. "Well, if that's true, it's another lie. Mom said Dad never went to college."

Murphy thought about this. "I dunno if she ever said *didn't*. She just never said *did*."

"Come on. If he had a college degree, you think he'd settle down in freaking Emmet?"

"Maybe," Murphy said, "Dad got so upset about the murders he didn't graduate."

"Whatever." Claire threw up her hands. "This doesn't matter. Mom's not here, and Dad and Uncle Patrick are dead. The only one left is this Mark person, who probably killed our grandparents, and for all we know, he's back in town."

Claire scrunched her nose, and Murphy did too. She bet the others were thinking how *weird* what Claire had said sounded. Uncles. Grandparents. Murders. Those weren't part of the Sullivan sisters' lives.

"This is the plan," said Claire. "Eileen, you're going to try starting the van again. If it works, great. If it doesn't, we call a mechanic, get the van fixed as quick as we can, and leave town. We forget this whole thing ever happened."

Murphy gaped. "Forget about our *inheritance*?"

Murphy had reached a conclusion: Sure, the house had

turned out to be a murder mansion, but it was *her* murder mansion. A third of it, anyway. There was magic in the place, and it had drawn the sisters together. It was the place to enact Operation Memory Making. She wasn't ready to leave that yet.

"Of course not," Claire told her. "But there's nothing we can do about the inheritance part right now."

While Claire had been laying out her master plan, the sisters had resumed their walk toward the bluff. This entire time, Eileen had stayed quiet. Murphy kept sneaking glances, trying to read her oldest sister's face, with no success. Eileen's eyes remained lightless, her lips drawn in a long, neutral line until, after the silence, she said, "I'm not ready to leave."

"What do you think you're going to find there?" Claire challenged. "Cathy already told us the deepest, darkest secret a family could have."

"Or," said Eileen, "she just scratched the surface. Maybe only the Enrights knew what really happened in that house. But we could know too. There could be something in there that tells us the whole story. Maybe even . . . stuff about Dad."

"You can't be serious." Claire motioned at Murphy. "What about her? Maybe you're fine being reckless with your own life, but Murphy's a kid, and I'm not going to keep her here when there could be a *killer* in town."

Red-hot indignation filled Murphy. A *kid*? That really was how Eileen and Claire thought of her: the kid, the nuisance, the *baggage*. The spare tire.

Well, this spare tire could talk.

"I'm fourteen," she growled at Claire. "We're *both* in high school. And I want to stay."

"Doesn't matter."

"Uh, yeah it does." Murphy raised her voice. "We're a democracy, and it's two against one."

Claire laughed. "You think this is a *democracy*? News flash: I'm the one with the money. I pay for gas. If you want to get home, you'll do what I say."

"You have to get home too," Murphy challenged. "You need Eileen's van. I heard you say so yourself."

Claire laughed again, like a rabid hyena. "I don't need that van. I told you, I have *money*. Enough to get a ride back to Emmet."

"Whoa," said Murphy. "For a three-hour trip? That's your college fund."

"Much good it's doing me," Claire muttered.

"What does that mean?"

Claire's eyes met Murphy's. There was a flicker there in the blue—a possibility. Claire opened her mouth to speak. Then, she seemed to reconsider, shook her head, and walked on.

They'd been ascending the bluff through a drizzle, and the rain-slicked road had leveled out, revealing the topmost gables of the house. At the sight, goose bumps formed on Murphy's arms— the weather's doing, that was all. Still, for a moment, Murphy let herself wonder if this Mark Enright dude really was a murderer. If, maybe, he'd found out who had inherited his old house and if, maybe, he was mad about that.

Murphy didn't know how a house could look scarier in the daylight than in the dark. This one did, though—its gables pointing up like teeth into a moody sky.

Blood all over those parlor walls.

Head bashed in like a cantaloupe.

What had really happened in this place?

Yes, it was an adventure. It was drama.

It was also terrifying.

But Murphy had made a point to tell Claire she wanted to stay. She couldn't act scared, like a kid. Like they expected. This was a time for being brave. For making memories. For magic.

Murphy had been to a haunted house before, on a school trip to Oregon's one and only amusement park, Enchanted Forest. It had been creepy, sure, and she'd screamed once when Derek Huggins had jumped out from behind a dark corner. But that had been for fun.

This was an actual haunted house. A place where people had been killed, *for real*.

Murphy reached into her coat pocket, grabbing hold of the rope trick she'd packed there. She didn't care about forming a knot, just needed something to hold on to. She thought of the trick's instructions: *over, under, tug through and out*. She repeated them to herself internally. A mantra. A bit of magic in the face of murder.

SIXTEEN

Eileen

I'm giving you an hour."

"Sure, Claire. Sure."

Because, seriously, with the level of absurdity emanating off her sister, the only thing Eileen could say was, *Sure, Claire. Sure*. The same way she had for months:

"I don't want pizza. Don't you know how bad gluten is for your gut?"

Sure, Claire. Sure.

"You use way too much eyeliner. If you'd watch these tutorials . . ."

Sure, Claire. Sure.

"It'd help if you could take out your own trash."

Sure, Claire. Sure.

And if Claire thought she could dictate Eileen's life now, of all times . . .

Sure, Claire.

Sure.

They'd see what came of that.

Eileen intended to spend as much time as she goddamn pleased inside this house. A couple murders weren't going to keep her away.

Especially since she'd already known about them.

When Eileen had gone snooping in the linen closet two years ago, she hadn't been looking for something that would break her life apart. Who in their right mind would do that? Who'd search for a box of letters that would tell her a dozen truths she didn't want to know? Who'd drink a quarter bottle of Jack Daniel's every night to forget what she'd read? Who'd trash her arts programs applications, because she didn't see the point? Who would, instead, work a mind-numbing, foot-killing job at Safeway forty hours a week?

No one sane.

So Eileen couldn't be sane.

But it wasn't that she *wanted* to be this way.

That's what people like Claire and her perfect Harper Everly tribe didn't get. Eileen heard what Claire called her behind her back, under her breath: *Settler.* Claire thought Eileen had a choice.

Eileen hadn't chosen to read those letters, though. She'd been looking for painter's tape and had thought maybe some could be stashed away in the shoeboxes Mom kept at the back of the closet. She figured they contained boring stuff you'd normally keep there: clothespins and spare staples and tacks—and maybe painter's tape, too.

You just don't think you're going to get bad news in a linen closet.

That's what had happened, though: In one of those boxes, she'd found the letters.

Eileen knew what hate mail was, theoretically. But nothing could prepare her for this.

The letters were addressed to "Leslie." Her mother.

Well. Some of them read "Leslie," while others opened with "You bitch," or "Sinful whore."

There were nine letters total, composed in various handwritten scrawls and on different kinds of stationery. Nine letters from several strangers, and Eileen knew the shortest of them by heart:

Bitch,

We know it was him. You defended a murderer, and one

day you will pay for your great sin.

No one had signed the letters. Eileen guessed if she were to draw a Venn diagram, "People Who Write Hate Mail" would be a perfect overlap with "Goddamn Cowards." No outside space.

Did that mean it wasn't a Venn diagram?

The point was, the letters were bad, and they made Eileen realize, sharply, how bad *people* could be.

Here was what she'd pieced together, after she'd read the letters many times over:

These people were accusing her mom, Leslie, of defending a man they called Mark. And this Mark was a murderer. Each letter-writer knew this for a fact. Mark Enright was a cold-blooded killer, and Leslie had taken his side, and she was going to pay one day for these sins. The element that varied from letter to letter was the hypothesis for *why* Eileen's mom had done these things. Some wrote she'd been deceived, or misled. Some said she'd been beguiled by "sexual sin." (One of them actually said that, like a televangelist: "sexual sin.") However, the majority of letter-writers were of the opinion that Leslie Sullivan was as guilty as the murderer named Mark. They wrote she was probably in on the killing of Mr. Enright, too. Those were the writers who included the most vivid prophecies of Leslie's fate—how she'd burn in hell or die of cancer or, best of the lot, be murdered herself.

"Whoso sheddeth man's blood," read one, "by man shall his blood be shed."

Straight from the Bible.

Eileen wasn't religious, but she recognized that much. Quoting the Bible, telling a woman she deserved to die. And these people could sleep at night.

Eileen hadn't slept, though. Not for days. Those letters had given her an answer to a question she'd never asked.

Eileen looked different from her sisters. That had been obvious since she was a kid. It was hard to mistake their blue eyes, or to miss Murphy's fiery curls and Claire's blond bun. And then there was Eileen, with her black coffee eyes and hair. The family's recessive genes had blatantly passed her over, and Eileen had been okay with that for a while. It made her unique, and she'd liked that.

Until she'd found the letters.

Until she'd put together the pieces, and everything made perfect, horrible sense:

Eileen didn't look like pictures of her dad, because he wasn't her dad.

She didn't look like her sisters, because they were only half related.

She'd noted the dates on those letters: 2002, the year of her birth. She could put two and two together. For months Eileen had believed she wasn't John Sullivan's kid. She was the daughter of a murderer.

She didn't know where this Mark had run off to, but she'd guessed why her mom had married John Sullivan so soon. She'd figured out, too, where the murders took place. One of those letter-writers had been brave enough to label their letter with a return address. They'd written from a town called Rockport, Oregon.

All it took was a Google search of the town, plus "murder," plus "Mark," and Eileen had found out a whole lot. About Mr. and Mrs. Enright and their deaths, the trial, Mark's acquittal, and how a woman named Leslie Clark had defended him on the stand. Eileen had even found Mark Enright's artwork.

Eileen knew everything. She hadn't needed Cathy's version of things.

Mr. Knutsen, by contrast, had told Eileen something new: John Sullivan was really John *Enright*—not a random dude her mom had married, but Eileen's uncle. As for Mom . . . she'd had a thing for Enright boys, hadn't she?

Eileen still didn't know what to make of *that* development. She was processing, and she needed this house and its contents to do that. Maybe Patrick or one of his brothers had left behind a clue, a confession, *anything* that would give Eileen a definitive answer.

Because if she hadn't known about John Enright, what else

had she missed? Or gotten wrong? What if the horrible truth she believed *wasn't* true?

Eileen was sick of the secret. She wanted solid proof. Either she was Mark Enright's kid, or she wasn't. Her heart beat with possibility. The chance of a *no*.

Ch-change, ch-change, ch-change.

Sure, she hadn't wanted her sisters to know about the murders, but they still hadn't learned Eileen's possible connection to the story. She could keep that under wraps while searching for the truth.

If it took longer than an hour to find that, then Claire could wait.

Eileen stood in the parlor, studying the picture she'd found. Here were the three Enright sons: two fair-haired, one dark. A perfect male mirror to her and her sisters. The news articles she'd read online hadn't included photos of Mark—something about his age and a judge's court order. But Eileen didn't need anyone to point out which of these brothers he was. She knew: He was the one who looked like her. The one with the dark hair and eyes, and the mole beneath his lip. She had a mole too, under her left eye.

Was that the sign of a killer? Proof she had Mark Enright's blood in her veins?

If so, Eileen hadn't been able keep all that blood inside herself. It had leaked out in an unlikely way, through brushes onto canvas, infusing the very paint with its wickedness, earning the reactions "bizarre" and "unstable." Eileen had thought of her art as a way to find herself, to explore who she was, deep inside. Then, when she'd learned the secret, she hadn't wanted to explore any further.

Because what the hell might she find?

Here he was, the killer himself, dressed in green plaid, dappled sun on his face. He was very real to Eileen, standing alongside Patrick and John. She looked into his photographed eyes. She almost *hoped* Mark Enright was coming back to town. She wanted to ask him a question, or two, or three thousand.

She guessed that made her a bad sister. She'd known more than Claire and Murphy had when she'd started this trip, and maybe she should have warned them about the risks: that there was a possibility the murderous Mark would show up at his old house to claim what he thought was rightfully his. That seemed to be the theory of everyone in Rockport, anyway.

What a theory it was, too. Probably bullshit.

Still.

Eileen needed someone to ask, because it couldn't be Mom. Way before Eileen had found those letters, Mom had pulled away, spending longer shifts at work, claiming the family needed the money to cover their growing debt and the landlord's hike in rent. Maybe that was true, but when Eileen had started working at Safeway and offered to give Mom half the money, Mom had cried and straight-out refused, telling Eileen that money was hers alone. At the time Eileen had thought Mom had simply been ashamed, insisting the job of breadwinner was hers, not her children's. Now she wondered if Mom had felt guilty about taking the money for other reasons.

After she'd found the letters, Eileen had suspected this: Mom didn't *want* to spend time with Eileen. She'd stopped hanging out with her, stopped asking questions other than a perfunctory, "Doing okay?" And it could have been Eileen was imagining it, but she sometimes found Mom looking at her in a way that could be described as . . . frightened.

Was it because the older Eileen had gotten, the more she looked like *him*? Did that make Mom afraid of her? Then again, Claire and Murphy weren't murderer spawn, and Mom had pulled away from them, too. Had they been collateral damage?

Those weren't questions Eileen dared to ask. But *these*, about her real dad and what had happened in this house—she might have luck there. Eileen set down the photograph and, returning to the real world, found Murphy sitting at the piano, pressing a single key again and again.

The kid could be a real freak.

Claire was hanging outside, an asshole, refusing to enter the home on principle.

"For all you know," she'd told Eileen, "Mark could be waiting for us in there."

Claire didn't really believe that, though. She was using fear to prove her point, a politician's move.

Fear didn't work on Eileen. Not anymore.

Once she was out of Claire's sight and Murphy was in the foyer, poking around, Eileen seized the moment—the one she'd been waiting for. She pulled from her flask, welcoming the electrifying sting. The promise of good things to come: no fear, just resolve.

Over the past two years Eileen had become an expert in measuring, gauging, knowing her limit—the line between buzzed and drunk. It was a fine art, drinking, though it hadn't started out that way. It had begun with Asher from Safeway offering her a beer after their shift and Eileen drinking it down, thinking it tasted like liquid Wonder Bread mixed with piss. Then, when the bad taste was over, she'd felt a bubbliness on the surface of her mind, a lightweight feeling, not of her body, but of her brain. And she'd liked that, because since she'd found the letters a month earlier, her brain had been heavy as lead.

She'd lightened her mind, and she'd kept on doing so, day by day, testing her limits, making a survey of what her over-twenty-one coworkers were willing to offer, from wine to beer to vodka to gin to—her favorite poison—Jack Daniel's. She'd vomited, she'd rambled incoherently, she'd raced Asher around the parking lot in a shopping cart, once. She'd figured out what worked, and what accomplished the job of brain-lightening most efficiently.

She'd stopped drinking with coworkers and started bringing the booze straight home. She'd figured out how much to swig before driving, and how much before bed. Some nights, like the night she'd opened Mr. Knutsen's letter, she overdid it. For fun. She only lived once.

But somehow along the way, despite Eileen's gained knowledge and expertise, the alcohol began to be less of something she measured out and more of something that measured *her* out.

She'd considered the word. The one that began with an "a."

That wasn't her, though. That wasn't what this was.

Eileen's need to drink didn't make her an alcoholic. Plenty of teens her age got shit-faced, and no one was dragging their asses to rehab. She was fine. And she could drink from this flask. Hell, she could drink it all down, if she wanted, in one go.

160

Eileen headed for the parlor wall stacked with filing boxes. She took down the first of them, tugging off the lid and inspecting its contents. There were folders filled with papers and labeled with the words "Utilities," "Bills," and "Receipts." Eileen didn't trust labels, though. The prosaic had fooled her before.

She opened the first of the folders, and as she did, a sound reached her ears. It was forceful and even and everywhere at once, pinging against the windows and juddering on the roof, two floors up.

Rain. Not everyday Oregon drizzle; hard, driving *rain*.

Funny, Eileen thought. She hadn't been looking skyward earlier. Had a storm been building?

She glanced from the box to the parlor's threshold, where Murphy stood.

"Whoa," said Murphy.

"Yeah," Eileen replied.

She listened longer, and as she did, she noted the jagged way the rain hit the house. She looked to the window and found the world outside was a mess of bouncing bits of white. Sleet.

There was rain in Oregon—a usual occurrence, abundant as dirt. Then there were storms—occasional, warranting your best parka. And there was this—not a storm, but a *storm*. A coastal tempest, sent straight from hell.

"Claire!" cried Murphy.

Eileen turned, and there indeed was Claire, at the French doors, ghost-faced and shivering like a junkie.

"Well, this is perfect," Claire announced.

Inside, Eileen thought, *Sure, Claire. Sure.*

This time, though, she meant it. She agreed.

The van had been one thing, but now there with this: a heavy-duty storm, *sleet*, forcing them inside. Allowing Eileen the time she needed to find her document. To discover the truth of her secret, once and for all.

That was as perfect as perfect could be.

SEVENTEEN

Claire

W e're leaving."

Claire spoke with authority. She had allowed Eileen and Murphy their fun. She'd told herself it was a fair compromise, since the Caravan was, technically, Eileen's. She'd stood outside, tapping out of open apps to save her phone battery, which was at a threadbare 11 percent. She'd tried *not* to think of the gruesome things Cathy had told them at the diner. Before, walking the halls of this house had felt akin to discovering Atlantis. It had been her golden moment. Now, Claire felt she'd been conned—though by who? Patrick Enright? William J. Knutsen, attorney-at-law? Harper Everly? The house itself?

Whoever was to blame, it wasn't fair, falling in love with a home only to be told it was the setting for heinous crimes. The gables no longer looked elegant, but severe. The wraparound porch was hardly romantic. The turret, jutting proudly from the house, struck her as malevolent.

It wasn't as though Claire would ever live at 2270 Laramie. Doing that would require living in Oregon, and Claire still planned to get out of the purgatorial Pacific Northwest. She guessed what was bothering her, deep down, was that she'd wanted to believe her world was righting its wrongs. She'd thought, *Okay, Claire, you've been summarily rejected by your dream college, but there must be good waiting for you in Rockport.* She'd thought, mere hours ago, that she could sell this place for a profit in four years' time. And maybe—a wild thought—that she'd learn about a father she'd barely known, which would, most likely, be good for her personal growth.

She'd been attempting to think like an Exceller.

But as the sleet had begun to rain down on her head, Claire realized she was only being delusional again.

There was nothing for her, for any of them, here. And if the sleet was a portent of what was to come, Claire wanted to be nowhere near this place. Eileen could call her paranoid, and Murphy could call her mean. She was used to no respect at home; wasn't that always a middle child's plight? She was the Exceller of the family though, and, it seemed, the only sister with a plan. If that required her to give orders, so be it.

"Did you hear me? We're leaving, before it gets any worse." Claire held up her phone, at 8 percent, close to death. "They're calling for sleet and freezing rain. The roads are going to be brutal. We have to go."

"But Eileen said the car has to *reeest.*" Murphy whined.

And she wondered why Claire treated her like a baby.

Claire and Murphy had never been close. Three years was a weird age gap. It seemed whenever Claire was leaving a stage of life, Murphy was getting into it, and maybe that wasn't Murphy's fault, but she could be so *annoying*—a babbling toddler when Claire was a bookish seven-year-old; a gangly, too-loud middle schooler when Claire was starting high school; an awkward freshman when Claire was a seasoned senior. The timing was never right.

When she'd been younger, Murphy had constantly asked if Claire would play with her, help her with homework, watch a magic trick. Claire had kept saying no, no, *no*. Murphy was always a little too little, and the magic obsession and silly jokes didn't help. Eileen, weirdly enough, had been closer to Murphy. Years ago, on those nights when Eileen had babysat, she'd almost always taken Murphy's side in a Claire versus Murphy fight. That had driven Claire crazy, back when she and Eileen had been close, and Claire had actually cared about Eileen's opinion. Lately, though, neither of them had been spending time with Murphy, and Murphy had stopped asking the annoying questions.

Claire had wondered if, maybe, over that time, Murphy had grown up.

But no. Not a chance. Murphy had stowed away in the Caravan, clamored endlessly for cheese curds, run off despite Claire's instructions, and broken into this house. And *now* she was sitting at the grand piano, plunking out a clumsy version of "Heart and Soul."

Claire watched, stomach turning. Murphy had heard Cathy's story as clearly as Claire had. How could she possibly choose to sit there, knowing what she did? Claire thought of bloodstained keys, of a broken skull. She retched.

"Whoa," said Eileen. "Take it easy."

165

Claire swallowed the nausea and said, "I'll take it easy once we're on the road."

"It's bad out there?" Eileen squinted at the ceiling, as though that was a better indicator of the weather than an up-to-date app.

"It's *bad*," Claire insisted, "and it's only going to get worse."

"Then why would we go out in it?"

Claire gaped. Eileen loved being a smart aleck, but this was not the time.

"Seriously," Eileen kept on, "you know what a piece of shit the Caravan is. Even if it starts up, there's no way I'm going out in that. We could get stranded on the road."

"We're already stranded here," protested Claire.

"Exactly," said Eileen. "Here. In a home. With electricity and a roof over our heads. You want us to go on the road for hours, when we could skid off the highway? Or the Caravan could break down again and we freeze to death on I-5? I'm not risking that."

Claire was realizing something against her will. Eileen wasn't just being stubborn; she was being the older sister—the way she had once upon a time. In those days Claire had come home from middle school crying and Eileen had poured her a soda and told her it'd be okay. Back then talking to Eileen had felt like consulting someone wise and fierce, who would back Claire up and fight her enemies, no matter what. Eileen had been the babysitter in charge, the one to come up with solutions if there was a leaking dishwasher while Mom was at work. She'd been the *eldest*.

But she'd officially given up that title two years ago. She'd slunk into the garage and stopped caring about anyone else. And she didn't get to reclaim a position she'd willingly relinquished. Not now.

Still, Claire was beginning to see Eileen's point: The Caravan wasn't reliable, the weather was bad, the journey home was long. Going out could be dangerous, even deadly. What Claire wasn't sure about was the conclusion Eileen had reached, that staying here was their best option. If they were at a Days Inn, Claire could understand. This wasn't a motel, though. This was, essentially, a haunted house.

"We could walk into town," Claire offered. "Ask at the diner about lodging."

"I thought you wanted to keep a low profile," Eileen challenged at the same time Murphy shouted, "I'm not going out in *that!*"

Murphy pointed upward, toward the sound of *thunk, thunk, thunk*s on the roof. Claire had been out in that sleet. She'd run while ice chunks the size of peas pelted her body. She didn't want to walk through this weather any more than Murphy did. But she didn't want to stay the night inside a murder house, either.

Why had she come on this trip in the first place? Trusting impulse had utterly failed her, put her in the worst position. Where was her golden moment? *Where?*

Exhaustion waxed so large inside Claire, she started to cry.

No, not now, she scolded herself. *Excellers don't cry about things like this. They take action.* She brushed her knuckles along her eyes, wiping up traces of weakness. She couldn't fall apart.

"Fine," she said to Eileen. "It might not be safe out there, but it might not be safe in *here*, either. If we're going to stay, we need to secure the house."

"*Secure the house*," Murphy parroted. "Black-ops style, okay."

"This isn't a joke," Claire told her.

167

"Everything's a joke." Murphy spoke slowly, like she was reminding Claire that two plus two equaled four.

Claire focused on the sister who could at least see reason. "If we broke in here," she told Eileen, "anyone could. I say we go over the house again, and this time we make sure to check every closet and crawl space. Every corner. One of us stays here and watches the entrance." She motioned to the French doors. "Then, when we're sure we're alone, we barricade. We hang tight for however long it takes this storm to let up, and when it clears, we leave. Can we agree to that?"

"I volunteer for patrol!" Murphy shouted.

Eileen shrugged, because clearly it would kill her to acknowledge that Claire had good ideas. She said, "Fine, Murph and I will check the house."

"Thoroughly," Claire emphasized.

Claire was pretty positive Eileen said "bitch" under her breath. She rose up above it, focusing instead on finding a power outlet for her phone charger. By the time she had, the others were gone, up the stairs.

It wasn't that Claire was paranoid, as Eileen had accused. There wasn't a huge part of her that thought Mark Enright could be in town. It was more that she needed a plan—even a plan of house inspection—to feel in control. If the house was secure, then she could be secure too.

And yes, there was a *small* fear that Cathy's horrible theory might be true.

As Claire plugged her phone into the outlet by the sideboard, she noticed the copy of *The Three Musketeers* that Murphy had brought down from the library. Claire flipped open the cover, checking the print year: an 1894 edition. Claire was no expert, but she guessed 1894 could catch a good price on eBay—maybe a hundred dollars? And this was only one book of hundreds. Who knew how much that library was worth? With the proceeds, Claire could get out of Emmet for good. She could comfortably support a move to New England, pay for months of rent, buy furniture. . . .

Stop it, Claire instructed herself. *The book isn't yours yet. You're trespassing.*

She sat herself on the hardwood floor, cradling the phone in her lap, watching as the red battery icon inched from 8 to 9 percent. There was an itch in her fingers to open the Internet, log in to the Yale admissions portal, and verify for the fifty-first time that the news was not, in fact, a mistake.

Don't be obsessive, she ordered herself. *Don't dwell. It's over. Focus forward.*

Focus forward—a Harper Everly original. It was such an iconic phrase of hers, she sold totes and jersey-knit tees featuring the advice. Claire didn't own one of those, but she'd bought other merch, including a tumbler with NO EXCUSES scrawled in loopy, rose-colored script.

Those phrases were painful to her now, each one a dart sticking her skin:

LONG-TERM DREAMS > SHORT-TERM PROBLEMS

ELECTRIC SUCCESS IS ONLY GENERATED BY POSITIVITY

A BABY STEP IS BETTER THAN NO STEP AT ALL

DREAMS DON'T WORK UNLESS YOU DO

DON'T PLAN FOR FAILURE

The itch in Claire's fingers grew stronger. Maybe a lowly intern had made a data-entry mistake, and they'd only caught it a week later. Maybe it was worth checking the portal one. More. Time.

Claire was too weak to resist temptation. Her fingers tapped the phone screen in what had become habit. Moments later she was on the webpage, staring down a fate that remained unchanged: not accepted. Rejected. Spat out.

Early admission application hadn't changed a thing. Neither had chairing five student council committees, nor working long hours at the Emmet soup kitchen, nor hounding three AP teachers to write additional letters of rec.

Claire wanted to face a flesh-and-blood human at Yale, not a URL. She would be polite, and she'd only ask one question: "Where did I go wrong?"

She needed to know. The lack of an answer was driving her mad.

Claire opened her texts, tapping on the abandoned thread between her and Ainsley St. John.

Ainsley's last text glared at her, a blue-bubbled accusation:

Hey, you alive?

"Yeah," Claire whispered, "but my dreams are dead, thanks."

She knew she was being melodramatic. Maybe that's all it had ever been, this weird Harperette connection between her and Ainsley: *melodrama*. Claire had concocted such an elaborate story, for so long. She and Ainsley would both go to Yale, would be roommates there, and Ainsley would *get* Claire, and then she'd realize Claire was irresistible, and they would fall in love, and Claire would get her first kiss, and everything would be fine, would be *right*.

Never mind the photos of Ainsley and her new girlfriend.

Never mind that she and Claire lived thousands of miles apart. Was Claire really that desperate? Just because no other girls were out at high school, and because Ainsley was the first person Claire had felt remotely connected to in a long time?

Delusional.

The word rang in Claire's ears.

She'd thought that she was excelling. She'd thought that if she reached for the moon, at least she'd fall among the stars. Yale wasn't *impossible* to get into. And even if Ainsley had a girlfriend, she'd have to leave her behind for college. Everything was going to work itself out.

That had been Exceller mindset.

Or, it had been a pipe dream.

As Claire stared at the phone, a notification banner slid into view. It was an e-mail informing her that Harper Everly had uploaded a new video. Claire tapped the banner, following the heading to the full e-mail. That's where she saw the title of Harper's newest vlog:

STAYING POSITIVE THROUGH LIFE'S STORMS.

"*Wow*," said Claire.

She couldn't.

She simply couldn't.

Claire wrenched the phone from its charging cord and hurled it across the room. It smashed against the opposite wall.

Then Claire was on her feet, preparing herself for what she would find. She wanted to look away, pretending this temper tantrum had never happened.

It had, though. And the screen was shattered, splintered into a dozen spider web strands.

When Claire attempted to turn on the phone, nothing happened. No light flooded the screen. No life.

She'd paid $800 for this phone.

She'd saved for two years.

The supply trips to Michaels, the hours spent forming delicate bracelets beneath her desk lamp, the hundreds of trips to the post office.

In one second, she'd smashed—literally *smashed*—all that.

The worst part was this: She was laughing.

At plans.

At golden moments.

At Harper Everly.

She laughed so hard that her arms began to shake.

She tried turning on the phone again, and again. The screen remained dark.

She thought to herself, *I'm alone. I am cut off from the world.*

And all she could do in the face of that truth was laugh.

EIGHTEEN

Murphy

D o you hear that?" Murphy asked.

"What?" said Eileen.

"Someone's laughing."

"Not funny."

Her sisters sure loved saying stuff like that: *Not funny, it's not a joke, stop being dramatic.* Which was *great* for a performer's morale.

This time, though, Murphy wasn't trying to be funny.

"Leenie, I'm serious—"

"We're not on Scooby-Doo, Murph. Shut up."

Murphy liked Eileen better than Claire. She always had. That didn't mean she actually *liked* Eileen, though. When she chose to, Eileen could be a stone-cold bitch, and she'd only gotten stonier over the years. Sometimes, Murphy wanted to jump to Eileen's way-high eye level and shout—for Eileen to notice her, to be nicer, to give Murphy some good memories to hold on to.

That was the big goal, wasn't it? Operation Memory Making. But how did you make memories with people who barely acknowledged your presence?

Murphy gave up talking about the laughter, only because it was possibly Claire's. Murphy couldn't be sure, because she hadn't heard Claire laugh—really laugh—in years. Who the heck knew what Claire found funny. Probably old nineties shows about rich people, like *Frasier*.

Maybe she was watching *Frasier* on her phone.

Murphy settled on that explanation because she was creeped out already, and she didn't need to add "mysterious ghost laughter" to her list of "Signs the House Is Haunted."

Regardless of what Eileen said, this could be a funny story one day. How Murphy and her sisters got winter-squalled into an old house and were almost ax-murdered by their long-lost uncle.

Ha . . . ha?

No. Diner Cathy had to be wrong. Murphy bet that once Mark Enright had left town, he'd gone off to live in Argentina, or Switzerland, or wherever else morally dubious creeps went. No way he'd care about a house in Nowheresville, Oregon.

If he was around, though, they were armed. Eileen was brandishing a large kitchen knife she'd found downstairs. She'd given Murphy her open switchblade.

"Aren't these illegal?" Murphy had asked.

"So are intruders," Eileen had countered. "Anyway, blades are best. If someone tries to take your weapon, they'll end up cutting themselves. Just keep a good grip."

"And I'll yell if I see something suspicious?"

"You won't, Murph. No one's here. We're doing this to make

Claire happy, because she's a freaking princess, and I don't want to deal with her bitching the rest of the night."

Eileen had seemed confident, and that made Murphy feel better about their mission. For . . . a minute. Upstairs, though, things felt scarier.

Maybe there wasn't an intruder. What about ghosts, though?

"Murph, stop breathing down my neck."

Murphy shot back to reality, where she was *kind of* breathing on Eileen. She hadn't realized how close beside her she'd been walking. It wasn't because she was scared, though.

It wasn't.

"Check that one," Eileen ordered, swatting Murphy toward the bedroom across the hall.

Murphy was about to say, *Why me?* but stopped herself. She didn't care if Eileen thought she was a whiner, but a *coward*? That was different. So Murphy shrugged like it was no big deal and went to the other room.

This place hadn't been touched since the 1970s, at least. The wallpaper was striped mustard yellow and mud brown. Murphy squinted till the lines went runny, blending together in one putrid glob. She wondered, was this what it was like to be high on weed, or LSD? Is *that* why everything was barf-colored back then?

First, Murphy checked under the bed. She had to psych herself up, telling herself that no one had gotten their brains bashed in here, and there was definitely *not* a rotting corpse awaiting her on the other side of the bed skirt, à la "A Rose for Emily" (thanks, Ms. Hutchinson's seventh-grade English class).

"You're cool," she told herself, gripping the switchblade. "You're totally cool."

She flung up the crocheted lace. There was nothing there. No storage boxes, not even dust. Was Uncle Patrick a neat freak till his dying day?

Murphy told herself to focus on the positive: no corpse. She felt a lot more confident when she got to her feet and checked the closet. No corpses there, either, or ax murderers. No dust bunnies, no anything.

She let herself wonder, what if this had been her dad's room? It was a weird thought, and the weirder thing was, these rooms were old, but none of them contained a ton of old stuff. Murphy hadn't found clothes in the dressers, papers in the desks, or picture frames on the walls. The only photo she'd seen had been the one Eileen had found. As for personal stuff, maybe Uncle Patrick had gotten rid of it. Or maybe it was stored away in those boxes downstairs.

"Clear!" Murphy yelled, but when she turned for the door, her eyes locked with another pair. Blue. Unblinking. Dead.

"HOLY—" Murphy started and didn't finish.

It was a doll. The creepiest, ugliest porcelain doll she'd ever seen. Its hair was a mountain of ratty blond curls, and its lips were painted blood-red, slightly parted to reveal rabbitlike teeth. It was wearing a pink dress and pinafore, and Murphy wasn't sure which was more disturbing: that the doll's nails were painted, or that Murphy knew what the word "pinafore" meant.

Her heart revved to three hundred beats per minute. She clutched at it like an old woman and tried to breathe.

Everything was fine. It was only a doll.

She glared at the offending hunk of porcelain.

"Not cool, Winifred," she said.

Because the doll was Victorian, and that seemed a safe bet, as far as names went.

Winifred stared back at her with those utterly dead eyes, and Murphy's heart slammed the accelerator again. She booked it out to the hallway and slammed the door shut. Eileen was standing a few feet away, a single brow raised.

"There was . . . a doll," Murphy tried to explain, which made her sound like the greatest coward who ever lived.

Eileen shrugged and said, "Yeah, dolls suck."

She could be a stone-cold bitch, but she could also be decent.

Murphy smiled a little. "You think so too?"

"Sure. I had this Raggedy Ann once named Deidre. Creeped me the hell out."

"What'd you do with her?"

"Gave her to Claire."

Murphy giggled, and Eileen actually smiled. Then she pointed to the spiral staircase at the end of the hall. "Turret's the only place left, huh?"

Murphy was glad to be almost through with their reconnaissance mission. Eileen was right: Claire was paranoid. There was no one in this house aside from them. No hoboes, no ghosts, and *no* Mark Enright.

Murphy's heart had turned law-abiding motorist once more as she and Eileen headed up the stairs. Midway up the spirals, there was an arched window. Rain slammed against the glass, torrential. Beyond, hard wind was on the Pacific, whipping out angry waves. They'd been right to stay. If they'd gone out in this weather, they wouldn't have made it home. They'd have been swept away in a flash flood, or smashed by a fallen tree. Dead.

Dead as Siegfried.

Murphy winced. She'd gone a few minutes without feeling totally guilty about that. At least she was treating Siegfried properly in death. His Tupperware coffin was safely deposited in the grand piano downstairs, resting inside its frame on the bottommost strings. That had seemed the classiest alternative to a turtle funeral home. Murphy had noted a slight odor emitting from the coffin, like trash gone bad. Nothing noticeable outside the piano, though. She'd find Siegfried a proper burial site before the stench got worse.

"Murph. Move."

Eileen jabbed Murphy's shoulder, and the sisters headed up the remaining stairs. When they reached the top, Eileen flipped on the light, revealing the round room with its hundreds of books. Murphy's imagination ran wild. What had gone on in this place? Tea parties? Secret meetings? Torrid love affairs?

Or maybe this was where Mark Enright had first fought with his father. Maybe he'd whacked him over the head in this very spot. Maybe they'd painted over the bloodstains. Maybe—

"AAAAAH!" Murphy shrieked.

Something was headed straight for her face—small, black, and fast. Panicked, she threw out her hands. Then she got really scared because *Eileen* was screaming.

It was pandemonium. Murphy waved her arms, tripping backward, falling, butt slamming onto the floor. The switchblade flew from her hand, skidding across the room. Eileen, too, had dropped her knife, and her screams transformed into words: "FUCK" and "VAT," and then Murphy realized she wasn't saying "VAT" but "BAT."

When Murphy was brave enough to open her eyes, she saw the truth for herself: the mystery object that had come for her face was indeed a bat, flapping haphazardly around the room.

"*Fuck!*" Eileen shrieked again, grabbing Murphy by the shoulders and trying to haul her to her feet. Murphy had only stood partway up before they were tumbling down the stairs. She hit her shin against the railing. Pain meant nothing, though; Murphy was focused on her hair. What if the bat got *in her hair*? She stumbled to her feet, and then she and Eileen were neck and neck, racing down the hallway and the next flight of stairs. She didn't know where the bat was anymore. She could only hope she was getting farther away from its claws and beady eyes and *fangs*.

There was only the grand staircase left. Murphy took the steps three at a time, advancing like a track star, flinging herself over invisible hurdles. She collapsed on the parlor floor, gasping for breath. Digging her fingers into her curls, feeling all over, she shouted, "It's gone, right? Where is it? Is it gone?"

When she looked up for an answer, she found Claire standing over her, big-eyed, brandishing a soup pot above her head.

"What?" Claire looked wildly between Murphy and Eileen. "What's going on?"

Eileen was puffing as loudly as Murphy, hands on her knees. Neither of them could speak.

Claire shook the pot, menacing. "What's *going on*? Is someone here?" Then she called out, "We're armed down here, you hear that? WE ARE ARMED."

"Fuck," said Eileen, but there was no longer urgency in the word. She shook her head at Claire, breath regained. "Hey, it's fine. It's *fine*. There was . . . a bat."

Claire was staring blankly at Eileen, like she'd spoken in Russian.

"A bat?" she repeated.

Murphy sat up and cleared her throat, ready to give the performance this moment deserved: "It was a *big* bat. In the turret. It was attacking us!"

Claire looked at Murphy. Murphy looked at Eileen.

"Good to know we're armed, though." Eileen pointed at the pot. "If that was Mark Enright, you could have souped him to death."

Claire looked at Eileen. Looked at Murphy. She dropped the pot to the ground. It rolled across the floor, hit the wall, and clattered to a stop.

Claire was going to yell, telling them how impossible they were. She was going to say they should've listened to her and left this place when they'd had a chance. Murphy was ready for that.

Only, Claire didn't yell.

She laughed.

And when she did, Murphy knew for sure that the ghost laughter from before *had* been hers.

Claire's giggles were shallow. She was pressing a hand to her forehead, and tears leaked from her eyes. She laughed and laughed, and Murphy was starting to freak out about it, but then something weirder happened: *Eileen* began laughing too. She stayed stooped, hands on her knees, producing a big, brassy howl.

Murphy stared at them like they'd both gone mad. Then she noticed her heart, back at Indy 500 speed. There was energy building inside her—so much it could snap her bones, or bust through her arteries. Then it was rushing out her mouth, and *she* was laughing. It happened involuntarily, like a sneeze.

The three of them laughed, and then Murphy was laughing *because* they were laughing, and she thought they might keep going for hours, maybe until the end of the world. It was happening, just as Murphy had hoped it would: They were making a memory.

That's when the lights went out.

TWO YEARS

BEFORE

CAYENNE CASTLE

In its fifth year the castle had neither towers nor parapets. In fact, it had lost most of its walls.

"You aren't putting your backs into it," Murphy complained. She was struggling to hoist a bedsheet above her head and secure one of its ends on a floor lamp. This would've been easier if someone tall was helping. Like Eileen.

But Murphy's oldest sister sat in the corner of the room, crossarmed, in the La-Z-Boy.

"It's good enough, Murph," she muttered. "Leave it alone."

Eileen had been doing a lot of muttering lately, as well as sullen staring. Murphy thought the new bedroom was to blame. Why had Eileen needed to clear out the garage? She and Claire had always lived together happily. Murphy knew the story of how, when Murphy was born, Eileen had begged Mom to let her and Claire keep sharing their room, rather than moving Murphy in with Claire.

"I don't *want* oldest kid privileges!" she'd shouted when Mom had tried to change her mind.

Murphy had thought the story was cute, and she'd definitely liked the result: a room to herself. But she'd seen why sharing worked for Eileen and Claire. They were basically best friends.

That's what she'd thought, anyway. Then, two months ago, out of the blue, Eileen had moved out.

Why the heck resort to a cold, drafty garage? The only explanation, Murphy decided, was that Claire had to be a really bad snorer. It made more sense than the idea that Eileen and Claire weren't getting along. That was impossible.

But on this twenty-first of December, all Eileen and Claire had done was fight.

"If she wants to make the castle, or whatever, let her," said Claire, who was stretched on the couch, eyes glued to her phone. Claire was *always* on her phone.

"What's the point?" Eileen shot back. "She's gonna break that lamp, and *we'll* get the heat from Mom."

Another something that had been happening lately: Murphy's sisters talking about her like she wasn't in the room. *She* this, and *she* that, and none of it nice stuff, either. About how Murphy was too young and naive, while they were older and infinitely wise. Like, what was the point of Murphy being around?

Well, she was going to impress them today. She'd been working on this act for weeks, with Cayenne Castle in mind.

Murphy had long known she was destined for the stage, but until recently she'd been half-hearted in her magical pursuit— trying to learn new tricks and abandoning them after a few days. Now, she'd become a scholar. She was getting good at the illusions in her library book entitled *Stage Magic: A Beginner's Guide*. With committed practice, she was going to get better.

Maybe good enough to get Claire and Eileen and even *Mom* to stop with their busy lives long enough to pay attention.

That could happen.

With magic, anything was possible.

"Seriously?" Claire sniffed at Eileen. "Like Mom's going to notice a lamp."

Claire had a point: Mom didn't notice dirty dishes in the sink, or the certificate Murphy had stuck to the fridge—an award for Best Solo Act in drama club's Winter Holiday Revue. Why would Mom notice a broken lamp?

"Anyway," Claire went on, "you've broken more stuff in this house than any of us." She held up a hand, enumerating: "Mom's ashtray, the bird soap dish, the outlet cover in my room—"

"*Our* room."

"Uh, not yours anymore."

"Whatever. And sorry, I didn't realize you were keeping a freaking *list* of my mistakes."

"I'm not, it's just obvious who the real breaker is here."

"*Breaker?* Wow. Nice vocab."

"Better than yours, Ms. F-Bomb."

"I haven't—"

"GUYS." Murphy threw down the sheet.

Begrudgingly, the sisters looked to her.

"No one's helping," Murphy said, hands on hips. "It's like you guys don't even want to do Cayenne Castle anymore."

Eileen and Claire exchanged a look across the room.

Shrugging, Eileen said, "Sorry, Murph. We don't."

187

"We're too old for it," Claire added, gaze drifting to her phone. "We have been for a while."

"It's . . . blankets," Murphy said, nonplussed. "Who gets too old for blankets?"

"You know what we mean," said Claire. "The made-up names and tea parties. It's kiddie stuff."

Murphy pursed her lips. Her eyes were getting scratchy.

No. She wasn't going to cry. Especially not when Claire was calling her "kiddie." Like Claire and Eileen were *way* older. The two of them sure hadn't acted too old for the castle last year.

Something had changed. It had been changing for months. Eileen and Claire had been closing their bedroom doors. They no longer whispered, sharing secrets; they shouted, trading insults. Like they'd forgotten how close they'd been before. Forgotten their royal titles of Princess Paprika and Sir Sage.

Then, a few weeks ago, Eileen had said, "Let's not do the present thing, huh?"

Murphy had stared, uncomprehending. "But . . . that's our tradition. We've been doing it for years."

"Yeah, well, it's old now."

Claire had shrugged at Eileen's pronouncement—the only thing she'd agreed with her about lately. And they'd left Murphy in the kitchen, staring at her lukewarm mac and cheese. She hadn't told them she'd already bought their gifts: a black-handled, iridescent paintbrush for Eileen and a pink flower statement necklace for Claire.

She'd been scared since then, suspecting it: that Eileen and Claire were *over* the castle. Still, she'd kept her chin up. She'd prepared her show. She was determined to raise these walls and make them remember.

But now . . .

"You're ruining it," she whispered, focusing on the ground so she could swallow the tears. "I was going to put on a show, and you've messed up everything."

"Don't be dramatic," Claire said, scrolling on her phone.

Eileen threw her combat boots over the side of the La-Z-Boy. "What show, Murph?"

It felt silly to say now: *I've been preparing magic.* It was the *worst* thing to say when she was being accused of immaturity. The deck of cards in Murphy's back jeans pocket felt hot, burning into her leg.

"Never mind," she mumbled. "It's already ruined."

Something flickered in Eileen's eyes—a place where, recently, Murphy hadn't seen light.

"Hey," she said, softer than before. "Sorry for what I said. I know you're not gonna break anything."

The tears Murphy had suppressed came back with a vengeance, pouring down her cheeks.

"It's . . . not that," she croaked out. "It's *everything*."

She couldn't say more. She could only cry, like the little kid Claire and Eileen thought she was.

Well, if that's what they thought, then fine. She'd prove their point. Murphy yanked down the nearest blanket she'd clothespinned. She ripped out a sheet she'd tucked into the couch's back cushions.

Then she ran, escaping to her room, slamming the door behind her and locking it shut.

Come back, Murph, she waited for them to call. Or, *Don't be like that,* as they pounded on her door.

No one even knocked.

The longer Murphy cried in her room, the better she understood: Her sisters weren't coming after her. They didn't care enough.

The castle had crumbled, never to be rebuilt.

DECEMBER
TWENTY-THIRD

NINETEEN

Eileen

"Claire, for the love of God, let me," said Eileen.

Because, as it turned out, her seventeen-year-old sister couldn't light a match.

"I know how to do it," Claire insisted.

"You keep freaking out. You have to make sure it's lit before throwing it in. The box is worn down, it'll take a few strikes. You're not stopping to make sure."

"I *know* what I'm *doing*."

Eileen's best guess, in the wake of the lights going out, was that the electricity company had finally caught on to the fact that their customer at 2270 Laramie was deceased. That, or the storm was to blame. Either way they were screwed. Eileen could already feel the winter cold seeping through the old windows, overtaking the artificial heat that had formerly filled the house. They were in for a frigid, dark night. The sisters had decided, though, that it was better to stay inside, with blankets and a fireplace, then risk going out in the deluge. They'd stick it out one night, said Claire, and tomorrow they'd get out of town. Storms had to stop eventually.

"Stop dicking around and let me do it," Eileen said, making a grab for the box of matches Claire had scavenged from a kitchen drawer.

Claire avoided Eileen's grasp, twisting her arm to shield the box behind her back. "I can light a fire."

"Then stop being a wuss and do it already. Put your back into it."

"Put your back up your ass."

"Excuse me?"

Eileen wasn't offended, just impressed Claire had cussed. It had only taken half a day for her prim and proper ways to break down. What would her lord and savior Harper Everly have to say about that?

Then something more unexpected happened. Claire struck a match and this time waited for the flame to spark. Without flinching, she crouched toward the firewood and the crumpled newspaper the girls had placed in the hearth, and threw the match the short distance left between her and the kindling. The flame caught the paper alight, and the fire started to grow.

Claire stood, tossed the matches to Eileen, and said, "I'm *not* a wuss."

The box hit Eileen soundly in the chest. She'd forgotten this side of Claire: the stubbornness and resolve. When they'd been little, how many times had Eileen shamed Claire into being brave? Like the time she'd convinced her to get on the Area 51 spinning ride at the county fair, or how she'd given Claire endless grief about being too scared to shave her legs until she'd finally done it, knee cuts and all. In retrospect, maybe Eileen could have been gentler in her methods, but Claire was better for them. Of course, the way Claire behaved, you'd think Harper Everly had taught her to walk and talk.

Murphy joined Eileen and Claire in a trip upstairs to gather blankets and pillows from the bedrooms. She refused, though, to go into the bedroom with the porcelain doll, and no one approached the bat-infested turret. Eventually they returned to the parlor with enough bedding to make a decent campfire arrangement.

It would've been a cute setup in an alternate universe. Not in this dimension, though. Claire griped about the littlest things, like getting stuck with the scratchy blanket and the lumpy pillow. The only good thing she'd had to say all afternoon was when she'd emerged from the downstairs bathroom and announced that the plumbing, at least, was working.

Now that the three of them were gathered around the fire, Eileen looked to the windows, trying to figure out the time of day. There was no trace of sun in the storm, but the rain-ridden outside had turned from a sickly white to a deepening gray. It was nearing sunset—four o'clock, Eileen guessed.

"Hey," she said to Claire. "What time is it?"

Claire gave her a bizarre look, like Eileen had asked her to offer forth her firstborn.

"What?" Eileen said.

Claire pointed to the curtainless windows. "It's getting dark. What more do you need to know?"

This wasn't the first time Eileen had wanted to call her sister a bitch. She had before, but saying it again would be a waste of breath. Instead, she headed to the kitchen to check the oven clock, only to remember that, of course, the electricity was out. There were no analog clocks that Eileen could see, either. For such an outdated house, Patrick Enright sure had kept his clocks in step with the digital age. As Eileen soon discovered, upon further kitchen inspection, he'd also kept his pantry stocked. She gave its contents a once-over and grabbed what looked best: an unopened box of Pop-Tarts. When she returned to the parlor, Murphy was at the piano and Claire was sitting on a stack of pillows by the fire, that bizarre look still smeared across her face.

"I broke my phone," she said, once Eileen was close.

"What? How?"

"I threw it across the room."

Eileen processed this fact. Then she said, "Good for you."

Because honestly, whatever the reason Claire had for throwing a phone, that was a sign she was partly human and not entirely a YouTube influencer–bot.

Over at the piano Murphy was playing the bass chords of "Heart and Soul" on loop.

"Mozart caliber," Eileen told her dryly.

"Thanks," Murphy replied, without looking up.

Weird kid, as always, but there was something in the simple song that gave Eileen's heart a twist. Something so very *Murphy* about it—bouncy, and in a major key. Eileen hadn't noticed that about Murphy until now: how, even when she was whining, she always *sounded* positive.

Eileen took a seat by the fire, tearing open the box of frosted strawberry Pop-Tarts. Wordlessly, she offered one to Claire.

Wordlessly, Claire pushed the pastry away. Right. *Gluten.* Jesus. If Claire wanted to voluntarily starve, so be it. Eileen ate in silence as Murphy ran over the same chords, again and again. As she did, Eileen noticed Claire's hands, folded across her knees. Polish had chipped off her right thumb, forming a jagged triangle of bare nail.

The Pop-Tart was good. Sweet and carby, and not the least bit stale.

"Remember when Mom took us to the coast?" Claire suddenly said.

Murphy looked up from the piano. "I remember."

Eileen did too. She hadn't thought about that day since . . . the day it had *happened*, she guessed. It had to have been at least three years ago. Leslie Sullivan had pulled her daughters out of school that day, piled them in the Subaru, and told them she was taking them to a surprise. That long drive northward, Eileen and Claire had sat in the back seat, laughing over a copy of *Star* magazine. That was back when the two of them would walk to Fred Meyer and spend change on sour gummy worms and tabloids.

The nostalgia hit Eileen punishingly. It ricocheted in her ribcage, and she felt for a moment that she might spit out her food. They'd been close, she and Claire. What the hell had happened? *How* had it happened? It had been like a breakup, only afterward they kept sharing the same house, same blood.

Murphy kicked Eileen out of her thoughts by saying, "What was Mom *on* that day?"

"No clue," said Claire, staring into the fire. "I kept trying to figure it out."

Eileen had too. From the moment her mom had ordered

them into the car, to the moment they'd arrived on the shore and walked along the sand under the late summer sun, to the moment they'd stopped at Arby's on the way home and Mom had said they could order whatever they wanted—shakes and extra curly fries, *anything*. Mom had never given an explanation, and she'd never done anything else like that again. The next day she'd gone back to working twelve-hour Walgreens shifts. As though their coastal trip had never happened, but rather been a mass-hallucination, shared only by the Sullivan sisters.

It hadn't been make-believe though, Eileen knew. She remembered the colors vividly: stark blue sky meeting gray sea in a perfect line. Jagged rocks had stood up from the water, cloaked in algae. The sand had reflected the sun, precious and bright.

"I want you to take it in," Mom had told them, smiling. "Sink your toes into the sand, enjoy it."

And they had. Claire had turned cartwheels, perfectly balanced rotations. Murphy had dug their names in the sand— "LEENIE + CLAIRE + MURPH"—and drawn a massive heart around the words. Eileen had walked close to the water, allowing the chilly waves to lap over her toes. She couldn't remember the name of the beach, or the route they'd taken. She hadn't known the *why* of the trip at all.

It was clear to Eileen tonight, though, in a way it hadn't been at fifteen: Maybe Mom had been saying sorry the only way she knew how. Maybe she'd been trying to make up for being a mom who never attended PTA meetings, who hadn't counseled them on the best mascara to buy, or warned them about menstrual cramps.

Yes, Mom provided accommodation, utilities, basic needs.

She'd never been cruel to them. She hadn't shouted or fought. She wasn't bad, she simply wasn't around.

That day on the coast, though, Leslie Sullivan had been a normal mom. She'd spent time with her kids. She'd *been* there. It was the normalcy that had made it strange.

Eileen had been to the coast plenty of times since then—for school trips, and back when she'd actually hung out with a friend group in her first two years of high school. The coast was simply a place to *go*, only an hour's drive west. Why not see the Pacific? And why not eat some good seafood, while you were at it? There was nothing noteworthy about a trip out there. Only *this* trip stood out.

Murphy dropped an elbow on the piano keys, producing a dissonant jumble of notes.

"Maybe that was the start of Mom's menopause," she said. "Or, like, she was having a midlife crisis."

Eileen didn't know where to begin with that.

Claire said, softly, "Who knows what it was about."

Murphy hopped up from the piano and joined her sisters by the fireside. She grabbed a new packet of Pop-Tarts from the box, ripped it open, and bit into both pastries, double-layer style.

Through a full mouth she said, "Uncle Pat had bad taste. Didn't he know strawberry is the lowest of Pop-Tart flavors?"

Uncle Pat. The familiarity made Eileen's skin prickle. Had he known about her mom's affair? Had she been sleeping with *him*, too? Was it a brother fetish? God only knew.

But maybe Eileen would know too, if she finally got the chance to go through the boxes. Her gaze drifted to the wall, stacked high with them. Eileen couldn't have dreamed this shit up. And for this to fall in her lap, right when she was feeling her shittiest, most directionless—it was almost enough to make her believe things happened for a reason.

Almost.

Not entirely.

Of course not. That idea was bullshit.

Claire lay out on the ground, stretching her arms above her head. The firelight danced on her face in patches of orange, and her eyes were intensely blue. So opposite of Eileen's.

"Remember what we did with the shakes?" Claire said.

"Oh my God," said Murphy. "FLAVORNADO."

Claire nodded, repeating the word as a reverent prayer: "Fla-vornado."

The memory hit Eileen in a sensory-packed punch. The three of them had conspired in the back seat of the Subaru while in the drive-through line at Arby's. They'd each ordered a different flavor milkshake and asked for an extra-large soda cup. They'd pooled their shakes into the cup and mixed the flavors with a plastic spoon. Then, with the finesse of a practiced mixologist, Eileen had poured the concoction into their individual cups. So flavornado had been born. A perfect combination of vanilla, mocha, and mint. They'd only had flavornado that once, but clearly it had been enough to make a memory.

That queasy feeling was inside Eileen again. She was thinking of three years ago, of the way things had been. Some of those things had stayed the same: Mom's absence, the clogged bathroom sink, rainy winters and springs. Other things had changed, though, and for the worse: what they'd had as sisters, how they'd goofed off, joked, confided, kept their doors open. Eileen had shared a room with Claire, then. She'd given Murphy regular piggyback rides. She'd believed she was one of them—a Sullivan sister.

Then, after the letters, she'd begun to think differently. She'd pulled away, barricading herself into the garage. Because Eileen knew a secret they didn't, and that secret would change everything. Telling them, or confronting Mom . . . that made it too real. Saying the truth aloud was impossible, and if Eileen had mustered the guts to do it, she knew what would've happened: Claire and Murphy would've looked at her differently, treated her differently, *known* she was the daughter of a murderer.

That's what Eileen had decided.

Only now? She watched the firelight dance on Murphy's freckles and in the blue-gray flecks of Claire's eyes. And she wondered if, maybe, she'd misjudged her sisters. Even if the worst was true, and she was Mark Enright's kid, would Claire and Murphy turn their backs on her?

Claire, who—for better or worse—had given Eileen gas money and not allowed her to drive drunk? Murphy, who'd had the guts to stow herself away and to call Eileen and Claire out on their bullshit?

Maybe Claire was less of a bitch than Eileen had painted her to be. And maybe Murphy wasn't so little or weak. Maybe they were kind and strong enough to hear the secret and be okay. They *were* her own goddamn sisters.

But . . . what if sisterhood wasn't enough?

Eileen was growing numb, the way she had the first time, when she'd discovered the letters. She wondered if she would remain this way, frozen, no matter how close she scooted to the fire.

She really needed a drink.

She'd needed one hours ago, and the lingering taste of flour and sugar on her tongue made the craving worse. Digging into her jacket pocket, she found one precious Dubble Bubble left. She made quick work of unwrapping the gum and popped it into her mouth—her powdery pink salvation, for the time being. As she chewed, Murphy and Claire talked on, not fighting for once. *None* of them were fighting, so why did Eileen need a drink more than ever?

The conversation had turned into a game of Remember When.

Murphy started with, "Remember the tire swing?"

Eileen did. She'd swung on it before Murphy was even born. Dad had pushed her. Then the tree branch had broken off one night in a summer windstorm.

Claire said, "Remember the marionberry contest?"

The three of them had gone to the county fair and stood in a gray-sky drizzle, gawking as contestants pursued the most stereotypical Oregonian feat: shoving their mouths full of as many marionberries as they could, in front of a screaming crowd. When the sisters had returned home, Murphy had reenacted the event by standing on the kitchen counter and cramming twenty stacked pieces of Kraft singles into her mouth. She'd puked in the backyard a minute later, but they'd all found it hilarious. Eileen thought maybe that was the last time the three of them had laughed together.

The last time until today.

Claire and Murphy continued to reminisce, jumping on each other's words like eager crickets. Eileen didn't join in. She couldn't anymore. She could only viciously chew her gum down to its stringy, sugarless core. It took the others minutes, maybe an hour, to notice. Murphy nudged Eileen's foot and said, "Why're you quiet?"

Eileen had been staring at the wall of boxes. Waiting for her chance to look inside, without the fear of either sister looking over her shoulder.

She shrugged and said, "Worn out, I guess."

"Leenie." Murphy ducked her head, looking oddly shy. "What's your favorite memory with Dad?"

Eileen blinked, her throat growing rigid. The question should have been an easy one to answer—logistically, at least. Eileen had multiple memories of Dad. She should have been able to pick one she liked best.

It wasn't as simple as that, though.

Back when they'd been close, Eileen and Claire had swapped memories of their father, and Eileen had found out that Claire had barely any; she didn't even remember the funeral. Eileen had thought that was strange, that they could be a year apart, and yet Eileen got the lion's share of memories. Was it something about the human brain, how its memory-making magically clicked on when you were four, but not three years old?

For whatever reason, Eileen had been given the responsibility: She was the designated memory keeper of John Sullivan. How twisted was that? He was *their* biological dad, not hers, and she got the memories.

The memories had been good, though, and John Sullivan had *acted* like her dad. She could tell Claire and Murphy that. She could recall the time they'd finger painted together in the kitchen, or how high he'd pushed her on the swing in the front yard, before its demise. She could recall his swishy bangs and solid presence and citrusy scent.

But doing that wouldn't be fully honest, would it? Talking about *their* father when she knew she had *another* father too. A killer, with no good memories attached to his name.

Eileen couldn't.

"Murph, I'm tired, okay?" It came out more irritably than Eileen intended.

An injured look cracked across Murphy's face as she said quietly, "Okay."

"Mom used to take us to his grave," Claire said.

Murphy frowned. "I don't remember that."

"It was a long time ago when she stopped. You were little."

"Oh," Murphy said, looking deflated. Moments passed before she murmured, "I'd like to see it sometime."

No one replied, and to Eileen's relief, the conversation broke apart after that. It was as though her talk of tiredness cued Claire to yawn, and then Murphy caught it. Claire stayed where she was, sprawled out, eyes closed. Murphy burrowed into a pile of quilts, wrapping her body around a needlepoint pillow and, minutes later, producing delicate snores. Eileen watched her sisters sleep and the fire crackle, as shadows waxed and waned on the parlor walls.

Wind and rain pushed against the house, sending low creaks through the room. It was peaceful. In a state like this Eileen couldn't imagine Mark Enright throwing his mother down the stairs or bashing in his father's brains.

That had happened, though.

And it was time, at last, to seek out the full truth.

Eileen rose from the couch and, with care, tugged an object from her left pocket—not the gum pocket, the alcohol one. The flask was half empty, and she decided she could spare a whole half of that tonight. Sure, it was more than usual, but this was a special occasion. Eileen needed the liquid courage to see herself through her clerical task.

She crossed the parlor, surveying the stacked boxes, and took a pull of the liquor, allowing it to burn down her throat. Then she pocketed the flask and got to work, taking down one box, removing its lid, and sitting with the contents.

At the moment it was only electric bills and tons of old issues of *The New Yorker*. Eileen wasn't deterred, though, and she wasn't thrown off the scent. What she was looking for might be wedged between an insurance bill and an old Christmas card. There was no knowing.

As she sat, meticulously sifting, a memory came to her. One of her very own "remember whens." She'd been thirteen, and Claire had been twelve, and they'd decided to walk the forty-five minutes from their house to the Emmet Walmart in an unusually sweltering August heat. Claire had needed shoes for the start of school; she'd worn her only pair of sneakers down to peeling rubber.

"I don't know what I want," she'd told Eileen. "It has to be good, though. It's seventh grade; I need to make an impression."

Eileen had told her impressions didn't matter, and she should just be herself. Claire had told Eileen she sounded like Mr. Rogers. Eileen had said thank you for the compliment. It hadn't been a fight. They'd bantered, goaded, teased—but they hadn't fought back then.

"I don't know what I want," Claire had repeated as they entered the store, stepping into the cool bliss of air-conditioning. "I'll know what it is when I see it, though."

Those words echoed in Eileen's brain, relevant five years later, as she sat in darkness, with only firelight to illuminate her search.

She needed an answer to this question: Am I the daughter of a cold-blooded killer?

She didn't know in what form she'd get the answer.

She only knew she'd know what it was when she saw it.

DECEMBER
TWENTY-FOURTH

TWENTY

Claire

C laire. Yoo-hoo!"

It was a rude awakening. Claire's joints were stiff as marble, skin ice-cold, and here was Murphy hanging over her, red curls tickling Claire's nose. This close, Claire could smell her sister's stale morning breath.

"Murph, *stop*." Claire swatted her away.

"Whoa, sorry!" Murphy threw up her hands. "I tried nudging first. You're a hard sleeper."

That wasn't true, though. The past month Claire hadn't slept well at all. Before the early admission decision came in, she'd been kept awake by jumpy anticipation. Then the rejection had come. Claire hadn't been sleeping hard for a while.

Who knew that what she'd needed to do for a good night's sleep was drive through the middle of the night, be sleeted upon, and break into a dead man's house?

A life of crime, she thought wryly. *The new Ambien.*

"What time is it?" Claire asked, pushing out of her quilted cocoon.

Murphy shrugged. "You were the one with the phone. It's light outside, though."

She pointed to the parlor's row of windows, through which gray light illuminated rain hitting as hard against the house as it had the night before. Claire grimaced.

"Yeah, still storming," said Murphy. "I bet the whole town's going to flood."

"Comforting." Claire rubbed her temples.

At this rate the Caravan had most likely been swept off the side of the road and cast into the ocean.

You're being pessimistic, warned the internal voice of Harper Everly. *Excellers don't think negatively. They're not sarcastic, either. You must—*

Claire punched the voice in the face. For the first time in over two years, she wasn't listening. She'd made her decision yesterday, when she'd smashed up her phone. Today, she would do and be whatever she pleased.

"Where's Eileen?" she asked, glancing around the parlor. Her eyes landed on a figure slumped against the opposite wall.

There was an open box in Eileen's lap. Her head was lolled to one side, mouth hanging open. Though Claire couldn't see the drool from this distance, she could imagine it well enough. She rolled her eyes. What did Eileen hope to find in this house? A tall stack of hundred-dollar bills?

"Leenie," she called across the room.

Eileen didn't stir.

Murphy *tsk*ed and said, "She's a harder sleeper than you."

Claire's stomach let out a gritty howl. She clutched it, wincing at the gnaw of hunger coming on fast.

"Right?" said Murphy. "I'm starving."

Claire glanced at the box of Pop-Tarts on the coffee table. There had to be more where that had come from.

"Come on," she said, getting to her feet. "Let's look in the kitchen."

"Okay, cool," said Murphy, sounding inexplicably relieved.

When they set foot in the kitchen, Claire understood why: This room was creepy. There was only one window, small and frosted, over the sink, which cast the surroundings in an ominous gloom. The checkered tile floor was old, thirties style, as were the wooden counters. The appliances weren't new either; Claire's guess was that the fridge had been around since Reagan's presidency. Murphy approached it so quickly, Claire didn't have the chance to warn her.

"*Bleugh,*" Murphy said, upon flinging open the door. She threw an arm over her nose, covering a gag.

"I wouldn't trust anything in there," Claire said.

"No kidding," Murphy said, but she remained standing in front of the darkened fridge, taking in its contents: a carton of milk, myriad jars of pickles, dressings, and condiments. There were Styrofoam takeout boxes crammed onto the bottom shelf, and Claire shuddered to think how long they'd been there.

She frowned, thinking it through. Whose job was that? A postmortem fridge clean-out. Who dumped out the food of a recluse once he'd died? Who had even found Patrick Enright's body? And why had his burial been closed off from the public? She'd had endless questions when she'd first read the letter from

William J. Knutsen—too many to ask, or have answered, so she'd temporarily stuffed them inside. Now, though, Claire's mind was wandering. *Why* had Patrick left this home to nieces he'd never met? Maybe, if Claire had directly asked Cathy at Ramsey's Diner, she would have had an answer even to that.

Thinking of the diner caused Claire's stomach to growl again. She wished she'd eaten that yogurt parfait. But yesterday morning she'd thought they were going to get out of this town. That had been before the skies had opened up and belched out a freak storm, and before she'd lost all faith and dashed her phone against the wall. A lot had changed in twenty-four hours' time.

The scent of rot was tickling Claire's nose. She shook herself from her thoughts.

"Murphy, close it already," she ordered, crossing to a wooden door that was very helpfully marked PANTRY.

When she opened it, she gaped in wonder. Here was the Holy Grail. How had Eileen kept this a secret? More importantly, how had she seen its contents and only taken away a box of Pop-Tarts? On the shelves before Claire were bags of potato chips, hazelnuts, chocolate chips; there were boxes of crackers and cereal, and additional Pop-Tarts. It was a sight so heavenly, it almost made Claire forget the legion of articles she'd read on why gluten was bad for you.

"Yeah!" Murphy cried from behind her. "The mother lode!"

She pushed Claire aside and grabbed the chocolate chips, flinging off the clothespin that had been sealing the half-full bag. Murphy dug in and shoved a handful of morsels into her mouth.

"Mmmm," she groaned. "Claire, *try.*"

Claire looked at the bag, wavering. Semisweet chocolate was junk food, but it wasn't glutenous.

Murphy seemed to become aware of Claire's inner battle. "Do it," she whispered salaciously. "C'mon, just a few."

She held out the bag, and the chocolate scent wafted into Claire's face. She could no longer resist. She took a handful of chips and popped them into her mouth, then embraced the earth-shattering sensation that followed: sweet, chocolatey goodness exploding on her tongue. The chips weren't even stale. She surveyed the rest of the pantry, on a hunt for treasure.

"What's up?"

Claire turned to find Eileen standing behind them. Her eyeliner had smeared, turning her face raccoonlike. The messiness made her appear younger. Gentler. Claire almost smiled at the sight.

"Breakfast," she said, nodding to Murphy's chocolate chips.

Murphy obligingly offered the bag.

"Eh," Eileen said. "I'm feeling savory."

Reaching over Murphy's head, she pulled down a can of Pringles.

"More for me," Murphy said, shoving in another handful of chocolate.

This time, a strange expression followed. Murphy's nose lifted, her eyebrows lowered, and her mouth flattened. She made a choking sound.

"Murph?" Claire said, cautiously.

Murphy opened her mouth wide, and a torrent of chocolate chips burst forth, scattering onto the floor.

"Holy *shit*," Eileen yelped, jumping back. "Murphy, what the hell?"

"Oh God," Murphy wailed, pushing past them. "Oh God, oh God."

Claire watched, bewildered, as Murphy yanked on the kitchen tap and splashed water into her mouth with clumsy abandon.

What was wrong?

What was wrong . . . with the chocolate?

She looked to the bag Murphy had dropped, then to the spit-out pile of chocolate. It was difficult to see in the dim light, but not impossible. There was movement in the chocolate. Small, white movement. Crawling. Squirming.

Maggots.

Then Claire *felt* them—slight little shiftings in her mouth.

She spewed out the chocolate onto Eileen's boots.

"FUCK," Eileen shrieked, running from the room and then yelling from the parlor, "I DON'T WANT TO KNOW."

"Move, *move!*" Claire shoved Murphy from the sink, angling her mouth beneath the faucet, filling it with water and spitting out. Filling, then spitting. Stumbling back, she raked her fingers across her tongue.

She was almost sure the maggots were gone, but the shifting sensation remained, a memory that made Claire heave out clear, sticky liquid into the sink.

Murphy was sitting on the floor crying, snot flowing from her nose.

"Ewww," she wailed. "*Ewww.* It serves us right, eating a dead guy's stuff!"

Claire couldn't be sure if Murphy was joking, but laughing felt better than retching, so she laughed. She wiped her stinging eyes and slumped down to the floor beside Murphy.

"W-we're okay," she told her. "Murph, it's fine."

"Speak for yourself," Murphy cried, wearing a strange, hysterical smile.

How absurd was this? Sitting in their dead uncle's kitchen, spitting out maggots on Christmas Eve. Claire cried a little and laughed a little and dragged her molars across her tongue, while Murphy made snuffling, spitting sounds.

Moments later, Eileen appeared at the door.

"Much good *you* are!" Murphy shouted, pointing an accusing finger.

Eileen shrugged. "What could I do about it?"

"I dunno," Murphy conceded. Then she said, softer, "If Uncle Patrick's a ghost, I tell you what: He's mad at us."

"Sure you don't want one?"

"Leenie, for the *last time*."

"What? You gotta be hungry."

Claire stared at Eileen in disbelief. After several additional rounds of mouth-washing and retches, she'd managed to leave the kitchen with some dignity intact. Now she and Murphy sat with Eileen in front of a rekindled fire as Eileen chomped merrily on salt and vinegar Pringles. It didn't matter that Eileen claimed the can was well sealed, or that there was no trace of infestation on those chips. Claire's appetite had been ruined. She didn't know if she'd ever eat chocolate again. One thing was for sure: She wasn't touching another item that came out of the pantry.

Murphy, it seemed, was of the same opinion. She lay on the couch, hands clenched over her gut, a martyr's expression drawn over her face. She was dramatic, that one, but she was also paler than usual beneath the freckles. Claire didn't blame her. For once, for maybe the *first time*, she completely understood Murphy's position. Like Claire, she refused Eileen's offerings.

"Your loss," Eileen concluded, chomping into four layered chips. "Hope it doesn't bother you."

Claire didn't know what to say to that. At the moment, food in general bothered her, as did the fact that they were stuck in this house, held captive by a winter storm. Ravenous wind drove into the walls, and vertical rivers ran down the windows.

"This is one messed up Christmas," Claire said, looking into the fire.

She was going to indulge in as much pessimism as her heart desired, Exceller status be damned.

"That's what *I* was saying the other day," Murphy offered from the couch.

"Aren't all our Christmases kind of messed up?" Eileen said, crunching into a chip.

Claire reflected on this. If a *good* Christmas meant snuggling with your family and opening nice gifts and drinking eggnog by the fire, then yes, comparatively, every Sullivan Christmas had been messed up. Mom tried to make things nice, but half the time she burned dinner or forgot about the stockings, and when she remembered, she filled them with junk from the Dollar Tree: off-brand antibacterial gel and cheap boxed candies. Christmas in the Sullivan home was a parody.

Then again . . . there had been those few years when the sisters had exchanged gifts inside the castle. Their own private ritual, on the twenty-first. Claire couldn't forget Eileen's gift that one year: the secondhand iPhone, an answer to Claire's prayers.

That had been the second-to-last Christmas they'd been okay, the two of them. And then Eileen had moved from their room, and a month before Christmas announced they wouldn't be exchanging gifts. Claire had hidden away the set of paints she'd bought for Eileen—a hard-to-find brand she'd only been able to track down at a craft store in Eugene.

Yes, Claire reflected. Most Christmases of theirs had been messed up.

"You gotta admit, though," said Murphy, "this one's, like, extra screwy."

"A memorable last Christmas," muttered Eileen.

Claire looked up from the throw pillow she'd hugged to her chest. "What's that supposed to mean?"

"Well, c'mon." Eileen snorted.

"Come on, what?"

"You'll be in Connecticut next year," Eileen elaborated, "as you've made us aware *countless* times. So here's a Christmas for the books, huh? Before you leave."

Claire tried to swallow the barb-edged tickling in her throat.

"Maybe we could visit though?" Murphy said from the couch. Her voice was tentative, as though she was expecting a no.

Wasn't that reasonable? Why would Claire invite Murphy to Yale? Claire never spent time with her younger sister as it was. She'd had an online shop to run, high school to conquer, extra-curriculars to add to her résumé. What she hadn't had was the energy to put up with Murphy's bad jokes and attempted "magic shows"—card tricks resulting in wrong guesses, mystical quarters that ended up falling out of turtleneck sleeves. Murphy had been a *kid*, and she still acted like one. Was that the way it was with babies of the family? Claire wasn't sure. She just knew that she'd been too busy to deal.

Why would Yale have changed any of that?

The shifting sensation was back, only this time it wasn't on Claire's tongue. The tiny creatures were writhing *inside* her, in the ventricles of her heart. Restless. Relentless. An itch she couldn't dig deep enough to scratch.

It was terrible, the feeling of regret.

Because what if she'd been doing it wrong, all this time?

She looked to where Murphy lay on the couch, red hair tangled, limbs akimbo, then to where Eileen sat, propped up on her elbows, black smudges lining her cheekbones. How had Claire lived with these two humans, so close inside one house, but so far away? How had she been seeing them for years, but not *seeing* them? Somehow, in the midst of Claire's goal charting and vision boarding, Murphy and Eileen had transformed. They'd stopped being her sisters, and they'd become part of Emmet, Oregon, instead. They'd turned to mere landscape, part of the life she had to leave behind.

Maybe it was the regret, or the aftershock of eating maggot-filled chocolate. Maybe it was that this was the most messed up Christmas anyway. Whatever the reason, Claire said the words.

"I didn't get in."

Speaking them out loud was a dagger stab to the throat. The blade pierced through skin, and the blood ran down, hot on Claire's neck.

"Wait, what?" Murphy sat up on the couch.

"I didn't get in," Claire said, louder, feeling strangely euphoric. At last she was announcing it for everyone to hear: She wasn't the Exceller she'd tried to be. "They rejected me. Yale. They said no."

Eileen was staring at Claire, face slack. "What the hell?"

"Yeah." Claire shrugged. "What the hell."

"What about other colleges?" asked Eileen. "U of O, or OSU? You applied to those too, right?"

Claire didn't speak.

"Shit," said Eileen.

Claire dipped her chin into the throw pillow. "Go ahead and tell me what an asshole I've been, and how Harper Everly is a joke, and that's what I get for trying so hard."

Eileen remained quiet. Claire felt pressure on her arm—the lightest graze of three fingers. It was Murphy, leaning off the couch.

"Sorry, Claire," she said, and nothing else.

Eileen's jaw had tightened and her eyes shone, rabid, in the firelight.

"Fuck them," she said. "Elitist pricks. You're the goddamn smartest, put-together asshole I know. If they can't see that, they're idiots. So, fuck 'em."

Claire blinked. Her blood was pouring out slower, euphoria gone. Despite her night of hard sleeping, she felt exhausted. And maybe she was delirious, because she was almost certain Eileen was being nice to her.

Like the Eileen from five years ago, who'd listened when Claire had told her she was gay. Not in so many words, because Claire was thirteen then and figuring things out, but Eileen had understood what she was trying to express.

She'd said, "That's cool, Claire. It's more than cool." And she'd added, "Don't take shit from anyone."

Claire had forgotten that. Not that Eileen knew her secret—you couldn't ever forget who you'd told—but that she'd accepted it easily, and well. She'd been . . . a good sister.

The way she was being now.

Claire wasn't ready for that. For any of this.

"I need to be alone," she said, realizing as she stood how true the words were. "I . . . just . . . need to be alone."

She stumbled out of the tangle of blankets, heading for the grand staircase.

"But Claire!" Murphy called after her. "It's dark and cold up there!"

Claire ignored Murphy. That was easy to do; she'd formed the habit.

She'd formed all the wrong habits, hadn't she?

She took the stairs quickly, wiping tears as she went, and reeled into the hallway at the top of the landing, throwing herself into the first room she saw. She slammed the door and sank to the ground, and then, for the very first time, Claire cried about the bad news.

The rejection.

The shattered future.

The forever loss of Ainsley and Excelling and what could have been.

TWENTY-ONE

Murphy

O peration Memory Making was at a standstill.

And things had been going so well.

Last night amid all the "remember whens," Murphy's heart had filled with hope. She, Claire, and Eileen had shared a moment. They'd talked, really *talked* to each other, reminiscing on the past by firelight. It had practically been a scene from *Little Women*. Yes, Eileen had been sort of distant, but this was progress. A step in the right direction.

And now?

After Claire had run upstairs, Eileen and Murphy stayed quiet. What was there to say after that announcement?

Claire hadn't gotten into college.

Bam. The big, awful truth had gone off like an explosion. Murphy wasn't sure how to make a memory out of *that*.

So she lay on the couch, absorbing her sister's news, while Eileen finished off the rest of the Pringles. When she was through,

Eileen stood, crossed the parlor to the wall of boxes, took the open one she'd fallen asleep with, and began to go through its contents.

What was she searching for? Murphy wondered. The only thing those boxes were good for, from what Murphy could see, were proving that Uncle Patrick had been a big-time hoarder.

Murphy army-crawled to the side of the couch, peering over its edge.

"Looking for buried treasure?" she asked Eileen.

"Something like that," Eileen replied.

"What makes you think it's in those boxes?"

"A hunch." Eileen sifted through papers, looking them over and setting them aside, one by one.

"They're just bills and stuff."

"No one's asking you to look through them."

"But *why* are you looking?"

Eileen huffed, throwing down a stack of newspapers. "Because all it takes is a letter, okay?"

"Uh, yeah. Okay."

Clearly, Eileen didn't want to talk to her. What else was new? Murphy couldn't help wondering, though—all *what* took was a letter? A letter about *what*?

From her pocket, Murphy pulled out the rope trick. *Over, under, tug through and out.*

As her fingers fell into the practiced routine, she raised her eyes to the windows. Rain beat against them, sluicing down the glass, forming a stormy curtain between the house and the world outside.

You wouldn't even know a world was out there, Murphy thought. And then, *Maybe it's not. We could be in a vacuum. A void. A nowhere place.*

The thought sent a chill through Murphy. She wondered, if you were cooped inside a house long enough, could it drive you insane? To *murder*? Is that what had happened to Uncle Mark? Was that why Uncle Patrick had turned hermit?

Maybe this house possessed magic.

Not the good kind, though.

Not the kind meant for a stage.

Tragic magic.

The kind that snuck up on you, from behind, and slithered a noose around your neck before whispering, *Ta-da*.

The rope went limp in Murphy's hands. She felt a little like hurling. Maybe that was because of the maggots.

And maggots made her think of death.

Murphy's gaze flicked to the piano, Siegfried's temporary funeral home. It wasn't right, keeping him trapped in there. She looked again to the rain-sheeted windows, imagining what she couldn't see: the ocean, bluffs, and sand. She bet it was pretty here, on a summer's day. A turtle's paradise.

Siegfried hadn't deserved a smelly cage or a broken heating lamp. He'd deserved Rockport on the Fourth of July.

Sometimes you didn't get what you deserved, though. Take Claire, for example, and college. If *she* couldn't get into college, who the heck could?

Murphy was gladder than ever that her entertainment career wouldn't require a diploma. When she turned eighteen, she'd be off to Vegas, and that was that. No applications for her, no tests, and no AP classes. She would attend the school of hard knocks, the way all performers did.

"Uh, Leenie?" Murphy craned her neck over the couch.

Eileen sifted through papers. She didn't reply.

"*Leenie.*"

"For the love of God, Murph."

"Should we check on Claire?"

"No. She wants to be alone."

"Because it's got to be cold upstairs. And she was crying really hard."

"She'll get over it. Leave her alone."

Murphy huffed. *She* was over it. Over being overlooked.

She pocketed the rope and got to her feet, shuffling toward the door that led from the parlor to the front rooms.

She waited for Eileen to say, "Where do you think you're going?"

She didn't even glance up.

"Whatever," Murphy muttered. "Find your mystery letter."

The foyer was big and high-ceilinged, same as the parlor. The front door was red. Blood red, Murphy thought. Out of nowhere, the voice of Cathy at the diner reminded her, *Bashed in like a cantaloupe.*

Murphy's mouth felt maggoty again. She fled into a sitting room.

Even though there was no fireplace here, the room felt cozier than the parlor. Maybe it was the pink floral wallpaper, or the fact that there were three couches, all comfy looking.

"Why didn't we sleep on *these* last night?" she wondered aloud.

They clearly hadn't been thinking. In fact, everything they'd done since arriving at the house had been haphazard. Like the sisters had been knocked off a trajectory in Emmet and were careening into deep, dark space.

Murphy ran her tongue along her teeth. Maggots. In the chocolate. She'd been *eating* baby flies.

"Ugh." She sank onto the nearest couch, resting her head in one hand.

For a long moment she remained that way.

Then something caught her eye, glimmering from beneath the opposite couch. Murphy got up, approaching the shiny object for closer inspection. It wasn't beneath the couch, exactly, but attached to its velvet upholstery, under the centermost cushion. Murphy crouched, tugging at the pull. *That's* what it was: a metal pull. Nothing happened when she yanked forward, so instead she yanked up. The couch groaned, and Murphy froze, startled. Then she understood. Releasing the pull, she threw off the couch cushions, revealing a hinged plank of wood. This couch was, in fact, a *chest*.

Murphy's hands trembled with excitement as she took hold of the pull again and lifted. Inside she found . . .

Blankets. Quilts. Sheet sets. They were folded neatly, stacked upon each other. She'd found a linen chest.

Murphy felt a prick of disappointment. Then a memory hit her. A memory, and then *an idea*.

"Holy crap," she breathed. "Merry Christmas."

She raised up the first of the quilts, crocheted in deep magenta and gold. She held it to her face, breathing in the scent of Decembers past.

This house and its murders and maggots weren't getting her down tonight.

Operation Memory Making was back on.

TWENTY-TWO

Eileen

There was nothing in the boxes.

Eileen had reached the last of them and come up empty.

Nothing.

No life-altering document.

No answer to her question.

Nothing earth-shattering disguised as innocuous junk. This really *was* innocuous junk.

And what was she looking for, anyway? A letter from Mark Enright, laying it on the line, confessing everything in explicit detail?

I *am* guilty of parricide.

I *did* have an affair with Leslie Clark, who later married my brother in a severely twisted way.

I *am* the father of Eileen.

I *am* a psychopath, and she's got all my traits—ask anyone who's seen her art.

Nothing like that, though.

Bills, newspaper clippings, expired coupons, tax forms, and partially filled-out Nielsen rating surveys.

No answers.

"Goddamn you, Mark," Eileen growled, pushing away the final box and sprawling on the ground, sapped of will.

What the hell was she doing? Following a vague hunch that there was a reason Uncle Patrick had left her this house, and a reason why William J. Knutsen had told her there were "documents"?

She'd grown so reckless, she hadn't even cared about sifting through contents in front of Murphy, telling her sister precisely what she was looking for. She'd felt she was *so close,* and she had to make up for the time she'd lost when she'd fallen asleep last night. The storm had been a gift. This was her chance. She had to seize it.

Only there was nothing to be seized.

Her heart beat slower, each thump a sad defeat—*ch-change, ch-change,* until the word had faded altogether.

Nothing had changed.

Now Eileen was stuck in this house on Christmas Eve with no electricity, rained and sleeted into captivity. All along, the storm hadn't been a blessing, but a curse.

God, she needed a drink.

She didn't have one, though. She didn't even have Dubble Bubble left.

She'd drained the last of her Jack Daniel's the night before, during her search, and for a few hours she'd been numb. Removed.

A headache was forming, angrily pulsing under her temples

in erratic red bursts. Eileen knew the cycle. She'd been in it for a long time.

Sometimes, Eileen tried to remember what it had been like to *enjoy* life. She had once, and then one day she hadn't. There wasn't a definable breaking point—not even the night of her junior art exhibit, or the day she'd found the infamous letters. The loss of liking life had happened gradually. A fade from Technicolor to gray scale, pixel by pixel, over months, until the color was gone completely.

She'd looked around and found no friends. She'd checked her calendar, and the arts program deadlines had passed—which was just as well, because she hadn't drawn or painted anything worth a damn since the exhibit.

She still had the drinks, though, and those could be easily bribed out of Asher. For a while she'd lived her life in black and white, no feeling. A drink. A shift at Safeway. A drink. A shift. A drink. The drinking replaced art, friends, even TV.

She'd made money in the meantime. She'd used it to buy a van, and she'd equipped that van's glove compartment with additional drinks. It had been a nice routine, until it wasn't anymore. Until it got harder to wake up, pointless to draw on eyeliner, draining to work another shift of scanning and bagging and taking coupons. Until the drinking itself got dull.

Then one night, filled with more whiskey than she'd ever contained, Eileen had gotten real with herself: She was no artist, as she'd thought at fourteen. She was an illegitimate kid, with a murderer for a dad, two sisters who'd become strangers, and a mom as distant as the moon.

And it all seemed suddenly, suffocatingly heavy.

The heaviness pushed down hard—so hard that Eileen didn't have the energy to feel sad. In that blank space she'd been free from feeling anything. And feeling nothing, she'd almost felt fine.

Why didn't she feel fine anymore?

Patrick Enright, and the law offices of Knutsen and Crowley, and Murphy with her freckles, and Claire with her god-awful heartfelt confession—they'd upset the order of things, and the stabbing sensation beneath Eileen's ribs wasn't going away, no matter how hard she dug her teeth into sugary gum.

She really, *really* needed a drink.

There was none to be found in this house though, Eileen knew. She'd already surveyed every inch of it on what Murphy had called their reconnaissance mission, making careful note of hiding places for life-changing documents and whiskey bottles alike. No drop of liquor in the pantry, no worthy documents in any of these forty-seven boxes. She'd exhausted her options, on both counts.

From her shut-eyed sprawl, Eileen listened to the sounds of the winter storm. The squall had been going on for so long, it had become white noise—slatting rain, pressing wind, occasional bursts of sleet.

Eileen didn't believe in omens, but she did believe in ebbs and flows. The tide of life drew back, surged forward. Time was as cyclical as her drinking routine. Once, three siblings had lived in this house. Three brothers, each with their own unique tale of woe. And here, three siblings lived again. Three Sullivan sisters, alone in their separate corners. Just as they'd been in Emmet.

A new sound reached Eileen's pricked ears: creaking wood.

She opened her eyes to see Claire on the grand staircase. Her makeup was, for once, imperfect, exposing a reddened nose and dark-circled eyes. She'd been crying, of course. Moping around in one of those upstairs rooms.

A few days back, Eileen might have said something cutting: *Feeling sorry for yourself, huh?* Today, she didn't have the energy. Or maybe she didn't have the heart.

"Hey," Claire said, soft and flat.

She descended the remaining stairs, stopping feet from Eileen and, after seemingly thinking it through, sitting crisscross on the floor.

"Didn't find what you were looking for in those boxes?" she asked Eileen.

"Nope."

If only Claire knew the half of it. Eileen wondered, if she'd found the letters five, not two years ago—would she have shared them with Claire? Or had the letters been part of the problem, a reason why she'd pulled away?

"You, uh . . . cool?" Eileen asked.

What kind of question was that? No, Claire clearly wasn't cool.

"I guess I'm in shock," Claire said, idly tapping the soles of her glitter Keds. "I was *sure*, you know? I'd never been so sure of something in my life."

"I mean," said Eileen, "if we were placing bets on college admission, I'd put my money on you."

Their eyes caught—blue on brown. Claire parted her lips, widened her eyes, looking almost . . . grateful? A way she hadn't looked in a long time. Maybe not since the day Eileen had given her that old iPhone.

The knifing sensation sharpened at Eileen's ribs.

"My counselor told me not to get my hopes up," Claire said. "That it was a long shot. A ton of people get good test scores and GPAs, and I needed something that made me stand out. If I'm honest? I wrote about being gay in my admissions essays because of that. Like, you know, take pity on a gay girl growing up in a tiny town."

Eileen's eyes widened. "Jesus, Claire."

"I feel gross about it now. Not about being honest, just—I opened myself up, you know? To strangers. I *undressed* for those admissions officers. Like I was, I don't know, pimping myself out. And it wasn't even worth it. Like, of course not. It's Yale. As if they don't have enough small-town gay kids."

Claire produced a self-deprecating smile.

"Why the hell didn't you apply to Oregon schools?" Eileen asked. "U of O is queer friendly as hell. You're acting like it's goddamn Westboro Baptist Church."

Claire shook her head severely. "That's not why I didn't apply there. I wanted to go to . . . a *prestigious* school. One that's hard to get into. One where it rains less and is close to an actually glamorous city, where life happens all the time. I don't know, I got Yale lodged in my head. Like it was the perfect solution. Yale, or bust."

"Don't plan for failure," Eileen muttered.

Claire looked to her sharply. "How do you know that?"

"It's on one of your fucking coffee mugs, Claire."

"Oh. Right."

"You think I escaped that Harper Everly bullshit? I practically got half her pep talks through osmosis."

Eileen wasn't being kind, she knew, but Claire wasn't being

defensive, either. They were almost having an actual conversation.

"Claire?" she said.

"Hm."

"I'm sorry. That seriously blows. Like I said, they're idiots."

"Yeah, *Yale*. A bunch of idiots."

Eileen pushed up from her sprawl, fixing Claire with an unflinching stare. "Fuck national rankings, Claire. You know who makes those? Elitist assholes. People who didn't grow up like us, in a shit town, in a shit house, working shit jobs. Fuck rankings, period. Only rich, pretty people make those. And you're better than that. Better than *them*. The Harper Everlys. Don't waste good tears on them."

The knifing—the *feeling*—was excruciating. Eileen was mad at Claire for making her care, but she was madder at every vapid YouTuber who'd ever made her sister feel less than.

"You're not a loser," she said, forcefully. "You're not a Settler, or whatever dumb-ass term you use. You're just a person, Claire. Someone who does good stuff and bad stuff too. Someone who's complicated. Who's really goddamn smart and started her own business and didn't let life's shittiness drain the hope out. So apply to U of O next year. Or don't. Keep making your jewelry and move away on your own. You're not doomed. It's college. It's an overrated, overpriced school."

Claire was looking at Eileen intently, a critic taking in a piece of art—absorbing the lines and colors before forming her opinion.

Then she said, "I'm the one who needs to say sorry."

Eileen made a nasty face on instinct. What was this, a trick?

"For what?" she asked, dubiously.

Claire looked askance, to the burned-out fire.

Without meeting Eileen's eyes, she said, "I didn't get into my program, but . . . you did."

TWENTY-THREE

Claire

News flash, Claire: I haven't applied to any programs."

Claire was expecting this. She'd braced herself for caustic dismissal, because that was classic Eileen. And why would Eileen suspect Claire of doing what she'd done? It made no sense.

It *had* made sense months ago, when Claire had been in Harper Everly's thrall. Life itself had made sense. Not to Eileen, though. She was a mocker of inspirational quotes, a scoffer at all things related to the lifestyle vlog. If Claire was going to make this confession, she'd have to do so slantwise. It might ruffle Eileen's feathers, but at least it'd be an approach she would understand.

"Leenie," she said, "why did you stop painting?"

Eileen balked. "What?"

Claire didn't repeat the question. She waited. She'd wanted to know the answer for a long time, and in this moment she actually hoped Eileen would give it. Because in this moment Eileen had light in her eyes, and Claire hadn't seen that light in what felt like ages. These past two years Eileen's eyes had been dull, words monosyllabic. Claire had told herself that sometimes that's how sisters turned out: You were close for a time, and then you grew into the people you were meant to be. Plenty of adults didn't get along, sisters included.

Sisters *especially*.

Claire had thought Eileen was turning into a Settler. She'd thought it was for the best—the fights, at first, and then the complete lack of talking—because Harper Everly said you had to hang with the people you wanted to be.

That was the funny part: Once upon a time, Eileen *had* been someone Claire wanted to be. When Claire had been fourteen and Eileen fifteen, Claire had thought her sister was the most beautiful person on earth. More gorgeous than any Instagram model she followed. Claire's theory was that Eileen simply didn't try. She didn't contour or pluck her brows. She went to school barefaced, showing her prominent nose, sharp cheeks, and piercing eyes—all features Claire herself didn't have. Eileen's hair had been long back then, past her waist, and she'd only worn jeans and tees, but she'd made them look effortlessly elegant.

And then there was her artwork. Paper brushed with bold watercolors—aquamarine and sage, gold and violet. Eileen had drawn portraits of girls with wistful gazes and purple hair. She'd drawn sunsets over apocalyptic worlds and done still lifes of trivial subjects, from crumpled-up candy wrappers to ripped tea bags. She'd been *good*. Her teachers had said so. In high school she'd begun to submit to contests and exhibits. A painting called *The Unholy Trinity* had even been featured in Eugene's *Register-Guard*.

Then Eileen had stopped.

She'd cut her hair and begun to line her eyes, and she'd told Claire one night in late October, two years ago, that she didn't want to share a room anymore. And Mom, distracted as always, had granted Eileen permission to clear out the garage and make it her drafty, concrete home.

That had been the beginning of the fights. The beginning of the end.

Claire knew the timeline very well. She just didn't know why Eileen had quit painting, or why she'd lost the light in her eyes. So when she'd seen that light tonight, she'd decided to confess. Only, first, she was asking for a confession from Eileen.

"I just stopped," Eileen said.

"No," said Claire. "That isn't it. What *made* you stop?"

"Nothing."

"It can't be nothing."

"It *can*. I used to like art, and then I stopped. Simple as that."

"You didn't *like* art, Leenie; you breathed it. You were brilliant."

"Stop fucking saying that. I hate when you're fake nice."

"I'M NOT BEING FAKE NICE. I HAVEN'T BEEN NICE AT ALL."

Claire hadn't meant to shout, or for this to go wrong. Maybe, on reflection, there wasn't a good approach. Maybe that was an excuse for her to avoid saying the skeletal truth. She clenched her jaw, a part of her desperate to keep it in. As she did, she could see the light fading, bit by bit, from Eileen's eyes.

"Harper Everly," said Claire, and when Eileen derisively snorted, Claire talked louder, to shut her up. "She has this thing she calls the 'Selfless Act Challenge.' What you're supposed to do is, you choose someone you know who has potential but isn't living up to it. You encourage them somehow. You write them a note or tell them how proud you are, or you do something for them that they don't have enough faith to do for themselves."

Eileen said, "What the hell are you talking about?"

"I took your paintings. A few of them. I made copies and put them in a portfolio. It wasn't hard. I filled out an application, and I sent it to this arts program in Eugene. It's called the Myrtle Waugh Fellowship—this chance to work with local artists, program expenses paid for the full year. I sent your application the same time I sent mine to Yale. And you got past the first round of applicants. They want to interview you in person next. I've known for a week, but I didn't tell you because . . ."

Claire didn't voice the because. That was still too difficult to say. She hadn't told Eileen because it was too cosmically unfair that Claire would do a good turn for her Settler sister, and Eileen would be the one to succeed. Eileen over *Claire*, the most intentional Exceller. It wasn't right, how Eileen's golden moment had come the same day as Claire's rejection. And as the days had passed, reality had only seemed more unjust, and Claire had kept on not telling Eileen.

Until now.

"I did that behind your back," Claire said, "and then I didn't let you know. I think . . . I didn't want you to be happy. Not if I couldn't be too."

There wasn't a real expression on Eileen's face. She breathed and blinked and offered nothing else.

Claire wasn't waiting for a thank-you. What she'd done was

messed up—invading Eileen's privacy, sending art without her consent. And Claire wasn't pretending she'd done all that out of the goodness of her heart. She'd done it because Harper Everly had said selfless acts were good for one's self-esteem. Really, Claire had been selfish to be selfless.

So she wasn't expecting a thank-you. In fact, she was ready for Eileen to yell at her that this was none of her business and how dare she interfere.

Time passed, but Eileen didn't speak.

"I'm sorry," Claire said, at a loss for anything else. "I'm . . . sorry."

The light in Eileen's eyes suddenly burst, intensifying tenfold. A supernova, set in sockets.

She said, "Do you remember my junior art exhibit?"

Claire did. Even though she and Eileen had fallen out by then, Claire had attended the show, blending into the crowd of adults and students gathered in the high school gym. Every May, on the Saturday before graduation, upperclassmen at Emmet High were invited to display their works of art. It was typical fare: angsty poem board pastiches and decent self-portraits and the occasional out-of-the-box venture, like modeling clay–based "interactive art." Claire hadn't come for the other students, though. She'd wanted to see what Eileen had on display, and she hadn't been disappointed.

There had been five pieces, propped on rusted school easels. The most prominent was an oil-based painting on canvas—a portrait of three figures, their limbs disproportionate and their faces elongated, grotesque. They put Claire in mind of vampires, or ghosts, or a hybrid of the two. They were upsetting to see, but they were beautiful, crafted with deft precision.

Eileen had labeled the painting THE UNHOLY TRINITY.

And Claire had been proud of her, even then.

"I remember," Claire said.

Eileen nodded. "Yeah, so. Afterward, there were comment cards. This great idea Ms. Medina had, for people who stopped by to leave anonymous notes about how our artwork 'spoke' to them. I think her head was in the right place, but, like, shitty idea, huh?"

Claire hadn't known about the cards.

"I read my comments. And a lot of them? They were saying how disturbed I was. Not the paintings, *me*. They said, 'This girl is super unstable.' Or, 'Way too bizarre for me.' One of them? They called me a psychopath. 'Eileen paints like a total psychopath.'"

"Leenie," said Claire. "It was high school. People are horrible. You know they were wrong."

"Do I?"

There was a strange look on Eileen's face. Claire had to look away as she said, "I don't see what the issue is."

"No," said Eileen. "You wouldn't."

There was a pause, and Claire panicked, afraid this was over and Eileen was shutting down.

Then Eileen spoke again. "Did you know Mark Enright was a painter?"

Claire was thrown by the question. "I . . . remember Cathy saying something like that. What has that got to do with anything?"

"YOU. GUYS."

The parlor echoed with sudden sneaker squeaks. Murphy was barreling into the room, beaming.

Thoughts had been circling densely in Claire's head. Now they scattered.

"I have something to show you," Murphy said breathlessly. "Come on. Come *on*. Stop fighting, or whatever. Come and see."

Annoyance plucked Claire's chest. If Murphy could read a room, she'd see that Claire and Eileen were the furthest away from a fight as they had been in two long years. She had shattered the moment, oblivious as she squawked on.

"Please? Come with me; I made us a surprise."

Claire looked to Eileen, and her heart sank to find that she was already on her feet.

"Okay, Murph," Eileen said. "If we see, will you lower the volume?"

"No promises." Murphy smirked and fled from the room.

Irritably, Claire followed her out into the foyer. Murphy landed on the threshold of a sitting room, bouncing on the balls of her feet. Then Claire saw what her sister had to shout and bounce about:

The room was a fortress of blankets and sheets, tied to curtain rods, swung over couches, fastened to floor lamps.

Memory hit Claire, a brass-knuckled punch, as Murphy announced, "Welcome to the castle."

TWENTY-FOUR

Murphy

"Cayenne Castle." Eileen breathed the words out like a curse.

"You remember it, right?" Murphy looked earnestly between Claire and Eileen with the unspoken plea, *Be amazed. Notice. See.*

She'd known nothing good was happening when she'd peeked into the parlor and seen them there, sitting close, talking low. She was tired of them fighting, and it was Christmas Eve. Here was her trick: She'd pull back the curtain, reminding them of the past, and they *would* be amazed. They'd remember Cayenne Castle and the way they used to spend time, lazy stretches of hanging out together. No fights, no silences, and no closed doors. Murphy was going to remind them of everything the Sullivan sisters had been. It would be her greatest feat, worthy of a standing ovation.

So far, the act was going according to plan. The best way

to describe her sisters' expressions was . . . *wonderstruck.*

"Whoa," Claire said, stepping into the room and reaching for the hanging quilt that doubled as both wall and castle entrance. "I haven't thought about this in ages."

"Two years," Murphy supplied.

"Princess Paprika," Claire said, under her breath. She turned heel, pointing at Murphy. "And Prince Pepper."

Murphy beamed. It was working. Operation Memory Making was a go.

She pulled back the door-quilt and said, "Go in."

Eileen and Claire didn't protest; they ducked their heads and walked through the castle gates. Murphy followed them, seating herself on the circle of couch cushions she'd arranged inside.

"The throne room," she explained. "I mean, the whole castle's kind of the throne room. It's a big downsize from last time, but there weren't a lot of blankets."

Eileen was wearing a crooked smile. "You're weird, Murph."

"Thanks," Murphy replied.

"Do you remember?" said Claire, eyes unfocused. "Remember the year I was trying to bake? Like, all the time?"

"Because of the British show," Murphy said, encouragingly. She meant to coax out every memory she could.

"I made those holiday Bakewell tarts," Claire said, before laughing a goosey honk, "and I forgot about them, because we were playing Apples to Apples."

"Oh my God," groaned Eileen, swiping a hand down her face. "And you still made us eat them. Damn, they were bad."

"Yeah, whatever, Leenie. You ate, like, a bite."

"And you spit it out," Murphy added.

"Yeah!" Claire said. "And Murphy was a trouper and ate the whole thing."

Murphy felt luminescent. Claire remembered *that*, too: Murphy had consumed her entire slice of charred peach-mint tart, so Claire wouldn't feel like a failure.

"The icing was . . . good?" Murphy offered.

Claire turned up her nose and smacked Eileen's knee. "Hear that? It *was* good. I had a perfect feathering technique."

"Remember when Mom tripped?" asked Eileen.

"Oh man," said Murphy, giggling. "Oh *man*."

That had been one for the books. Leslie Sullivan had made a rare and unexpected appearance early in the evening of December twenty-first. She'd opened the front door and run straight into the west wall of the castle—a fitted sheet tied taut between two curtain rods. The girls had seen it from outside the castle, where they were drinking ginger ale on the west veranda. The sheet had smacked into Mom's forehead, sending her reeling out the open front door, tumbling backward onto the rain-slick porch, and from there, careening into the yard. The sight had been so cartoonish, and the sisters so shocked, they'd broken into stifled laughter.

Then, of course, they'd run out to be sure Mom was okay, watching as she pulled herself out of the wet mulch. She'd laughed a little too and vaguely patted the girls on the shoulders, telling them she was fine. Then she'd slunk down the hallway, shut herself in the master bedroom for a rest, and that had been that.

Mom, the originator of the closed bedroom door.

But before that door had closed, a memory had been made,

and it had the sisters laughing louder than they'd dared to then.

"It was *ridiculous*," Claire said. "Like something from Looney Tunes."

"Exactly!" cried Murphy.

Eileen had turned quiet, looking around the castle's fabric walls. "Can you imagine Dad living here?" she said. "As a kid. Growing up in this huge house. I wonder how rich the Enrights were, how he and Mom ended up the way they did."

"You mean *not* rich," Claire clarified.

"Cathy said he never came back from college," Murphy said. "Not even for the funerals. Maybe he wasn't on good terms with the family. Maybe they'd disinherited him."

"Well, obviously something like that happened," said Eileen, "or Uncle Patrick wouldn't have a whole house and its contents to give away."

"Maybe that's why he left it to us," said Claire. "Guilty conscience about inheriting everything?"

"Maybe," said Eileen, looking thoughtful. "Though if that's the case, why didn't he leave it to Mom?"

Murphy considered what she knew of her mother, which admittedly wasn't much. The long work hours, her frazzled trips to the grocery, the glaze Murphy had seen in her eyes when she passed by the bedroom and found Mom propped on the bed, watching late-night TV.

"Yeah," she said. "I guess Mom could use an inheritance too."

"What?" Eileen snorted. "Look, Murph, we're not telling Mom about any of this."

"When did we agree to that?" asked Claire.

"You were the one who suggested it," Eileen challenged.

"When we first got here, remember? Don't get on your Harper Everly high horse now."

"I didn't say we'd *never* tell her. Keeping it a secret wouldn't be . . . emotionally healthy."

"Oh, man." Eileen slapped her forehead. "That's right, I forgot, we've got an emotional health expert in our midst."

No. *No.* The trick didn't go this way. These were supposed to be warm, bonding memories, not fight fodder. Murphy had to act, to save the show.

"Who do you think Winifred belonged to?" she asked.

"Winifred?" asked Claire, frowning.

"The doll upstairs. I mean, if it wasn't *theirs* . . ."

"What're you saying, Murph?" Claire asked irritably. "Boys can't have dolls?"

"Of course they can," said Murphy. "I only mean—"

"Who knows about the doll," Eileen cut in. "About any of it? We don't because Mom never told us anything."

Murphy studied her fingertips, calloused from the rope work. True magician's hands. She wanted to say, *When do* you *tell* me *anything?* She wanted to say that a house wasn't their only family inheritance.

That wasn't the point of Cayenne Castle, though. The point was to get along.

"Hey," said Claire. "Do you hear that?"

Murphy looked up, at attention. She listened hard for a sound and then concluded, "I don't hear anything."

"Exactly," Claire said, in a low, rapturous voice.

She scrambled over the cushions, ripping back one of Murphy's carefully hung sheets. Murphy blinked, adjusting her eyes to the light Claire had let in. It was bright, no longer shrouded by rain.

Murphy stared, openmouthed, out the sitting room window.

The storm had stopped.

A grand finale befitting her magic act.

TWENTY-FIVE

Eileen

F inally," Claire murmured, one hand pressed to the window. *"Finally."*

She looked, quite frankly, unhinged.

"Calm down," Eileen said. "It just stopped. Even if it doesn't start up again, they'll need time to clear the roads. Probably black ice out there."

Claire turned back from the glass, eyes infused with zeal. "You said the Caravan needed a few hours to rest. Well, it's had plenty of those. If not, we walk to the diner and ask Cathy to call a mechanic."

"On Christmas Eve?" Eileen snorted. "I guarantee you, no one's gonna be open until the twenty-sixth, at least."

"Well, what if they aren't?" Claire was growing fervent. "We'll get an appointment first thing on the twenty-sixth. Mom isn't back from the cruise until late that night. We'll have the van fixed and get home before she does."

Annoyance crackled inside Eileen, electric and volatile. She wasn't sure why she felt irritable. Claire had a point, didn't she? They had to get home, and what was left for them here, at the house? Eileen had searched those boxes and found nothing. What was the point of staying? Claire was right. So why did that piss off Eileen?

You wanted things to change. The realization sliced through her mind. *You wanted to find something, or someone. You still do. You'd be happy if Mark Enright showed up right here, right now.*

It was messed up, Eileen knew, to want a murderer to appear, especially with two sisters around. Claire and Murphy had nothing to do with him. They'd just come along with Eileen as annoying stowaways. That was why they didn't understand. They didn't know why this trip had been important to her.

Admitting that Claire was right would be the same as admitting defeat. William J. Knutsen's letter hadn't meant anything in the end, and all that was waiting for Eileen in Emmet were day shifts at Safeway and nights spent spiking her bloodstream.

Or at least, that was all that *had* been waiting.

Eileen was still trying to process what had gone down between her and Claire in the parlor. She'd told Claire something big—half of a big thing, anyway. About what had happened that night at the junior art exhibit, only a month out from the day Eileen had found the letters.

People are horrible, Claire had told her. *You know they were wrong.*

Claire didn't understand, though, because she hadn't read the articles Eileen had, about how wildly talented high school artist Mark Enright had slaughtered his father in their family home.

His blood. Eileen's veins.

It had been clear that night, when Eileen had read the word on the notecard: "psychopath."

Was she really? The artistic finesse and the twisted soul — were those both traits she'd inherited from dear old dad? Eileen had told herself not to be ridiculous. She cried when dogs died in movies, and sick kids, too. She wasn't devoid of empathy.

Still, the next time she'd sat at her desk to paint a still life, her paintbrush had hovered over the canvas, faltered, and failed.

It was crazy to say out loud, but she'd *felt* him. He'd been breathing down her neck, and it had been his hand, not hers, holding the brush. Mark Enright had seized her until painting — this sacred, lifelong passion of Eileen's — wasn't hers anymore. It was *his*. Part of the sordid past contained in those letters.

She'd tried again and again to draw in charcoal, pencil, pastel. No medium had been left to her. Every last one was contaminated, because *she* was their poisoned root.

So Eileen had stopped trying. She hadn't drawn anymore. She'd closed her portfolio, set it aside for good. She'd let the art school deadlines pass over her like distant planes, bound for destinations she'd never see.

If she tried to explain that to Claire, it would involve telling the secret. And Eileen had been close to doing just that when Murphy had shown up.

Would she really have told Claire about Mark Enright?

Would it have made a difference?

Then there was the other secret — the one Claire had confessed. Eileen couldn't understand why the hell her sister would apply to an arts fellowship on her behalf. And Eileen had made it. They wanted to *interview* her.

Did that matter anymore?

Could it matter, if she let it?

Could she go home and face the question?

No.

That was it: She wasn't ready to go home.

That's why she wanted to wipe that hopeful smile off Claire's face. Why she wished the skies would open back up and let out freezing rain for the next ten days.

She didn't want to go home.

"Let's go to the diner!" shouted Murphy, who'd unfortunately caught Claire's enthusiasm. "It's still sort of light outside. We can walk there—it's not too far—and get some real food."

"There's real food in the pantry," Eileen countered.

Murphy gagged. "*Maggot* food."

"Because that bag was opened, and you don't know for how long. The Pringles and Pop-Tarts were totally fine. Anything in a closed container will be."

Murphy waved Eileen off. "Easy for you to say. You didn't get a mouthful of bugs."

"You just want cheese curds."

Murphy gave Eileen a look that said *duh*, before asking, "How is this a bad plan? We get food, we get someone to fix the van, if it needs it. Then we go home."

"It's still icy out there." Eileen motioned to the window. "And it won't be light for long."

It was true. The deep orange sun was already slipping behind the horizon of the bluff.

"I've got a better idea," she added. "Let's get a good night's sleep. Then we'll leave first thing in the morning."

"We don't know if the diner will be open Christmas Day," said Claire.

"We don't know if it's open Christmas Eve *night*," argued Eileen, grateful that her desperate points made sense. "I mean, we could have checked the hours, but *someone* smashed their phone."

Claire narrowed her eyes. "Someone else doesn't believe in phones."

"Another someone can't afford one," groused Murphy.

"Whatever," said Eileen. "Point is, it's not a good idea to go out. We don't know if the storm's let up for good, and we've walked this hill before—it's steep. Covered in ice? We could break our goddamn backs."

Claire peered at Eileen. "I don't get it. Why don't you want to get out of this place?"

"I *do*. I just want us to be safe."

"Bullshit," said Claire, shocking Eileen with both the curse and the insight. "What's up with you?"

The electric crackles intensified, popping inside Eileen. "Nothing's *up*. We just don't need diner food when there's plenty of stuff in the pantry. And we don't even need a goddamn mechanic, okay? The van was never broken."

She'd said the words in anger, in a rush. She hadn't considered. Now it was too late, and they were out, circling the thin, linen walls of Cayenne Castle.

Claire blanched, staring at Eileen. "Excuse me?"

Eileen licked her lips. "I meant, it's the Caravan. It's always a little broken, so it never really is."

"No," Claire said slowly." That's not what you meant."

Eileen had hoped Claire would let it go. She always saw the big picture, though, in the end.

"You told us the van was dead," Claire continued. "You said it needed rest."

She'd been found out. So why not drive the nail through this coffin fully? Eileen set her jaw. "Okay, fine. I lied about the van. Is that what you want to hear? I lied because, if I hadn't, you would have forced us to go home. Just like you forced your way on the trip and forced yourself behind the wheel. Because you have to be in control of fucking *everything*. It has to fit into Claire's perfect master plan. Only *I'm* not in your plan, and this trip wasn't about you. It was for *me*. But you couldn't possibly understand that, could you?"

"Oh my God." The full truth had come to Claire, contorting every muscle of her face. She got to her feet, and when her head collided with a blanket, she ripped it down, ignoring Murphy's squeak as she tossed it aside.

"Wow, Eileen. I'm the control freak, huh? I'm not the one who basically held her sisters *hostage* when we had a perfectly working van down the road. So maybe look in the mirror."

Eileen snorted. "Yeah, whatever."

"That's your best comeback? Well, here's mine: You get your wish. Clearly, you never wanted me or Murphy on this trip. It's for *you*, right? So have it. Enjoy Christmas in this godforsaken house, all alone. Murphy and I are leaving."

"W-w-what?" sputtered Murphy.

Claire didn't wait around. She was out of the castle, out of the room. Then locks were turning, and she was out of the house. By the time Eileen had fought her way free of blankets, Claire was halfway down the front steps.

"What the hell are you doing?" she shouted after her, clomping onto the porch.

Claire wheeled around. "What do you *think*? I'm going to the diner, and I'm calling a cab. Because I'd rather blow my money on a freaking cab ride home than stay in this house."

"It's *my van*. I'm allowed to lie about it however much I want!"

Eileen knew she was acting batshit, but there was no way back from this place. She and Claire had dug their trenches. It was battle time.

"Yeah, *keep* your van." Claire threw out her arms. "You stick around here, Leenie, as long as you want. Whatever you're waiting for, *searching* for, it's creepy. I'm not here for it, and neither is Murphy."

Murphy was hanging at Eileen's side, eyes wide. "I . . . I . . . ," she stammered, patting inexplicably at her purple puffer coat.

"I don't know what's wrong with you, Eileen," Claire said, "but figure it out, okay? I paid the expenses for *your* trip, and all you've done is look through those boxes for . . . what? *What?*"

Sparks showered in Eileen's chest, igniting, exploding.

"Don't you dare," she said, through gritted teeth. Salt-gorged wind was biting her face and tears stinging her eyes. She stomped down the porch steps until she was a foot from Claire. "You paid expenses because that's the only way you could come on this trip. You wanted to know what you'd inherited and how many Chanel purses you could buy with the proceeds. Which, spoiler alert, you won't get till Murphy's eighteen and we can sell the house."

Claire tried to speak over her, but Eileen talked the loudest. "So *stop* being a self-righteous pain in my ass. No one asked you to

253

come here. Or to apply to a fellowship on my behalf. Or to lecture me, when you've got enough goddamn problems of your own."

"What problems?" Claire near-shrieked. "What problems do *I* have? Obviously it's something big and bad, for you to move out of our room and pretend I don't exist."

Eileen scoffed. "*You* stopped talking to *me*. Because you thought you were better. With your makeup. And your designer necklaces. And your fucking Harper Everly videos. With your whole perfect life, all planned out. You wanna know your problem, Claire? You're a self-righteous bitch."

"It's. . ." Claire seemed to be searching for words, but nothing came out. How could she fight what she knew to be true?

Then the uncertainty in her face disappeared.

"Fine," she spat, and Eileen felt the heat of her breath. "If that's what you think of me, fine. Better to be a bitch than a burned-out drunk like you."

"You guys!" Murphy cried, at their backs. "Guys, *stop*."

"Murphy, *shut up!*" Claire shrieked. "You don't know anything about this!"

"But you—"

"MURPH, FOR THE LOVE OF GOD, NOT NOW!" Eileen shouted, whirling around.

Immediately, she regretted it. Murphy shrank toward the house, looking small and terrified, like a hunted rabbit.

"Come on," Claire called to her. "We're leaving."

But Murphy was shaking her head. "I'm not going anywhere. Not with either of you."

She turned and ran into the house.

"Great," Claire threw a hand at Eileen. "Great job."

"Seriously?" Eileen laughed darkly. "That's my fault?"

They locked eyes, and in one moment Eileen saw everything: pillow fights and late-night talks, confessions and reveals, sing-alongs and inside jokes, poolside chats in summertime, cafeteria lunches, and Cayenne Castle, and every moment they'd shared. She saw all that in Claire's cold, blue stare.

The visions vanished. Claire had turned away, walking fast across wet gravel, headed for the road that led down the bluff to Rockport and, beyond it, a place far away from Eileen. Her messy bun bobbed in the fading light as she tugged her peacoat around her waist. She slipped once, nearly wiping out, but caught her balance and walked on vehemently until she'd descended so far down the road the horizon had eaten her up, and there was no remaining trace of Claire Sullivan.

TWENTY-SIX

Claire

The damp air stuck to Claire's cheeks, drawing out a shiver. She hadn't thought to go back in the house for her scarf, hat, or gloves. She hadn't thought to drag Murphy out, insisting she come along. She hadn't thought, period. She'd been too angry for thinking.

Eileen had lied. She'd deliberately put them in danger, stranding them in a strange town. This entire time, the Caravan had been fine. They could have escaped before the storm hit and been safely in Emmet for Christmas. Instead, Eileen had kept them holed up in that house . . . for what? What could she have possibly hoped to find in those boxes?

Claire had come on this trip on impulse, a desperate whim that a golden moment awaited her. She'd assumed, wrongly, that Eileen had come for an equally rudderless purpose. Only now it was clear that in this new, inverted reality, Claire had been planless and Eileen had been the intentional one.

Claire had caught Eileen asleep, with a box in her lap. She'd seen the wistful way Eileen had glanced, midconversation, to the stacked parlor wall. She'd heard her say, "*We could find some answers here, if we stick around.*"

Eileen was a confirmed liar; she'd probably lied about the boxes, too. For all Claire knew, William J. Knutsen had given Eileen a detailed map and instructions for uncovering rare jewels. A selfish secret Eileen had kept to herself.

And Eileen had called *Claire* a self-righteous bitch.

What a small stone to throw, when Eileen lived in a glass palace. She was the garage-dwelling Settler who hadn't bothered pursuing her art and instead continued a dead-end job at Safeway, living at home. She was the teenage alcoholic.

Did Eileen really think Claire hadn't noticed?

She had seen the bottle-shaped paper bags Eileen brought home, had passed her in the hall enough times to catch the sharp stench of whiskey. She'd witnessed Eileen staggering to the bathroom late at night, watched as she'd trudged, bedraggled, into the kitchen in the morning with obvious hangovers.

It's bad, Claire had thought to herself. *But it's a phase. She's being an angsty teen, hanging out with a Settler crowd.*

Claire hadn't spoken up, because what would be the point? Eileen would only yell, telling Claire to mind her own goddamn business. So Claire had, preemptively, done just that. She'd zipped her lips when she could've talked. She'd turned a blind eye when she could've stared. Until tonight, when so much rage had collected inside her that the words had shot out like bullets, aimed to kill: *Better to be a bitch than a burned-out drunk like you.*

Claire walked the slick path down the bluff, warding off guilt.

Why should she feel bad for what she'd said? For all Eileen's lying, maybe she deserved a good slap of truth to the face.

Claire had nearly reached the base of the long, sloped hill when she lost her footing, rubber soles skidding across a patch of ice, and this time she couldn't right herself. Her legs gave out beneath her, and she was airborne for one alarming second. Then her back hit the asphalt in a *whump*. Pain screamed through Claire as she pulled in her limbs and, wincing, sat up.

Her backside hurt, and tears sprang instantly to her eyes. The chilled Pacific wind drove into her, harder than before, and Claire allowed herself the indulgence of crying. She let the tears fall fast, soaking the collar of her peacoat. Still crying, she managed to find a foothold on the frost-bitten ground that bordered the road. She got to her feet, limping onward toward Ramsey's Diner, or whatever public place she found first that was open and had a phone.

If Murphy wanted to be a whining child, then fine. If Eileen chose to be a liar, okay. Claire had been the responsible one in this family for far too long. Her sisters could fend for themselves, spending another night in that house. Claire was going home.

The sun was setting fast, turning the world the color of a bruise. Streetlights kicked on along the road as Claire limped forward, careful to look for the telltale glimmer of ice near her feet. This was the street where they'd abandoned the Caravan. She scanned the road, sure that at any moment she'd catch sight of the van's wood paneling.

But the Caravan didn't appear.

Maybe, Claire reflected, she'd gone crazy. Or maybe the more likely explanation was that someone had reported the abandoned van, and it had been towed away.

Serves Eileen right, she thought viciously. *I hope they impound it.*

She walked on for minutes, listening to the distant crash of waves and watching her breath plume in powdery bursts. Lights glowed from inside the houses she passed—cheery windowpanes dressed with garlands, mailboxes sashed with red bows. No cars had passed Claire on the street. Who would be out tonight, on Christmas Eve, in the aftermath of a violent storm? Especially when they had warm, welcoming bungalows to retreat to.

You'll be home tonight too, Claire told herself. A phone was all she needed. A phone, and she'd be out of this living nightmare.

A new sound reached her, coming up from behind. A running engine. Claire turned in time to see a massive SUV headed her way. A bar of sirens stretched across its roof, and in the fading light Claire could just make out the words painted on its side: ROCKPORT POLICE.

"Hey!"

Claire froze, hands clenching at her sides.

Peering out the open driver's side window was a face Claire recognized: Kerry, from Ramsey's Diner. The Rockport sheriff.

"U-uh," said Claire, as the SUV braked to a stop across from her.

Take me, Claire thought, resigned. *Lock me up for trespassing, As long as it's not with my sisters, I don't care.*

"Podcast girl!" Kerry called.

She was smiling pleasantly, which Claire assumed was a trick.

"Uh, that's me. I mean, my name's Claire."

Any other day Claire would have been on her game. She'd

play the role of adult perfectly, saying the right things to cast off suspicion. But today she was utterly spent.

Kerry asked, "What're you doing out here? Research?"

"N-no. I was walking to the diner, for some food."

"Where's your sister and friend?"

"Oh, um. Back at the . . . hotel. My sister wanted cheese curds, and when the storm broke, I volunteered as tribute. But, you know, we thought the roads could be bad, so I walked."

Kerry frowned. "The hotel? You mean Barbara's B and B?"

"That's the one."

Claire was tired of playing games. If Kerry was setting a trap, Claire would go right ahead and step in it.

Kerry merely nodded again. "It's been nasty weather. You know, some folks come to the coast *for* this? Storm watching. They love to see a good wave crash on the shore. I don't get it. Locals clearly don't care for it either; haven't seen anyone out on these roads. Been a good couple days for desk work, though. You wouldn't believe how it piles up around the holidays."

"I can imagine," said Claire.

Inside she screamed, *What is this? Small talk? What do you want?*

"You been able to get any research done?" Kerry inquired. "Any interviews?"

"A few."

Kerry looked thoughtful as ever. "You kids care way more about a class project these days than I ever did. Missing Christmas at home for a *podcast*."

Claire laughed—a nervous, gulpy sound. "Yeah, overachievers, what can I say?"

She knows, Claire thought. *She's the sheriff, she has to know about the van, if they towed it away.*

"You're heading to Ramsey's?" said Kerry. "Hate to be the one to tell you, but they're closed. Fact is, no one's going to be open tonight."

Claire's heart caught on her ribs, slicing in half. "O-oh."

"I tell you what, though," Kerry went on. "I can drive you back to Barbara's. Doesn't she have a dinner menu tonight?"

"Uh." Claire blinked. "She . . . does, and it looks great. Murphy just really loves cheese curds."

"Then you're a good sister."

Claire's eviscerated heart gave a pitiful lurch. *If only you knew, Kerry.*

"I feel guilty, you know," Claire said. "She thought it'd be an adventure, coming with us, but now that it's Christmas Eve, she's starting to feel homesick."

Claire paused, reflecting. Was that a lie or something near the truth? Murphy hadn't signed up for the yelling, or for Claire's college confession. She hadn't asked for Eileen's deception any more than Claire had. She probably *was* feeling homesick, and what had Claire done? Yelled at her to shut up, and then left her behind.

She and Murphy had never been close—that was a fact of life, and Claire had blamed that on Murphy being too young and annoying. For the first time, Claire considered the possibility that she had always just *found* Murphy annoying. Murphy had only asked questions. Claire had been the one to answer every one of them with a no.

"Claire?"

She was suddenly conscious of tears edging her eyes. "Hmm?"

Kerry looked concerned. "Would you like me to drive you to Barbara's? It's a long walk there, and you don't look that bundled up."

Claire clenched her hands in her coat pockets. She'd been trying for minutes to squeeze feeling into her numbed fingers. She looked down the darkened road she'd walked this far. Ramsey's wasn't open, and this Barbara person probably had a phone Claire could use at the front desk. Worst-case scenario, she could pay for one night's stay at the bed and breakfast. Maybe she'd even go back to the house early in the morning to apologize to Murphy and take her away.

One way or another, Claire could plan her way out of this.

"Yeah," she told Kerry. "Actually, that'd be nice."

Kerry nodded toward the SUV's passenger seat.

It could be a trick, still, Claire reminded herself. Kerry could know about the lies, trespassing, and abandoned van. Claire could be headed straight to jail.

"Why not," she mumbled, opening the door and sliding in.

"Seat belt," Kerry instructed.

Claire obeyed, clicking the belt in place, and Kerry began to drive.

"Sorry for the trouble," Claire said.

"No trouble," Kerry replied. "It's on my way home, and anyway, I'd hate the thought of you walking all that way back, especially if the storm picks up again."

Claire's skin prickled. "Is it supposed to?"

"Not according to the latest report. Weather on the coast this time of year can be finicky, though. I'm glad to be off duty. These roads are hazardous after freezing rain. Plenty of accidents in the making. Luckily, most folks here use their common sense and stay put."

"How many accidents do you see in Rockport?" asked Claire.

"Not many. When they happen, it's mostly summer tourists. People distracted, looking at the view. All told, they're few and far between. Portland, though? That was a different matter."

"You were a cop there?" Claire asked, surprised.

"Eight years. Born and raised in Rockport, though. Eventually, I figured it was time to come back. My wife likes the coast, so that was a plus."

Claire's brows shot sky-high. "Your . . . wife?"

"Five years," Kerry said cheerily, lifting her left hand from the wheel and waving a bejeweled finger toward Claire.

"*Oh*. I mean, uh . . . nice."

Kerry looked askance at Claire. "You *can* be a gay cop in a tiny town, turns out."

"N-n-no, that's good to know." Claire coughed. "I mean, I'm the same way. Queer, I mean. Not a cop."

Kerry laughed loud. "And you can be *not* white in Oregon. A real shocker, I know. My parents were the first Vietnamese family in Rockport."

"Was that hard?"

"Yes. It was."

Kerry didn't offer anything else on that topic. She flipped a turn signal and headed up a road marked BEACHFRONT. Claire made a mental note.

"Whoo," Kerry exhaled. "Tell you what, this whole holiday season's been off. Patrick dying, and now the freak weather. You sure picked a time to come visit, Claire. I hope you're not too hard on Rockport when you do your reporting. You should come back in June, July."

Claire nodded vaguely. She was absorbing what Kerry had said. First, about having a wife. Second, about Patrick's death. She said, "At Ramsey's, you said you knew the Enrights."

Though Kerry's eyes were trained on the road, she arched a brow. "Are we in reporting mode?"

Claire laughed nervously. "No. Off the record. I swear."

"Well, in that case, yes, I knew them. Mark, especially. It's a shame, what happened to him. To all of them, but especially Mark."

Claire swallowed. "You . . . don't think he did it?"

"No," Kerry said, with conviction. "This town likes its gossip, wants its little world to be as dramatic as possible. For them, that meant pinning the blame on Mark. This golden-boy-gone-wrong was a better story than the boring truth that Mrs. Enright wasn't a good person."

"What do you mean?" Claire asked, in a hushed voice. "You think . . . she killed her husband? And then herself?"

Kerry drove in silence.

"It really is off the record," Claire said meekly.

Kerry cleared her throat. When she spoke again, she did so slowly.

"From what the brothers told me, Sophia Enright had so many rules in that house. Not rules you'd expect, either. Neurotic ones, about cleanliness and locked doors and tucked shirts. When the smallest thing went wrong, she went into these . . . *rages*. She'd had some kind of incident in California, before. That's why the family moved up here. I think Mr. Enright thought the change

264

would do her good, but the raging started up again. She'd scream for hours, threaten the boys, throw things in the house if one of her rules was slightly disobeyed. Mr. Enright was gone on work trips often. When he came home, she turned on him as well. To hear Mark talk about it, it seemed every day in that house was a nightmare. John was the oldest, so he was able to get out first, for college. Patrick and Mark didn't tell anyone how bad it got after that. They were afraid. We were practically kids then. We didn't know what to do. And then the worst happened, and . . ."

Kerry left the sentence unfinished. She slowed the SUV and shifted into park. That's when Claire saw the sign in the headlights' beam:

THE VIOLET INN

SEASIDE BED & BREAKFAST

"I'll say this," said Kerry, turning to her. "Mark was a good friend of mine. What happened to him was wrong. He was ruled innocent, but this town would never look at him the same way. Those things Cathy said, they were more vicious twenty years back. Most people here still think Mark got away with murder." Kerry shook her head. "Rumors last forever. They change everything."

"You thought Mark was a good person," Claire said, tentatively.

"He was," Kerry said. "I know you might think I'm biased, but my going into law enforcement? What happened here played a big part in that. I've looked over the evidence since, read every document from that trial. You might call it a pet project of mine. I can tell you, there's no doubt in my mind he was innocent."

"But Cathy said Patrick testified against him. Wouldn't Patrick know best what happened in that house? And John . . . if he believed Mark was innocent, why wouldn't he come back to town to defend him?"

"You have a sister, Claire," Kerry said, her expression flat. "Tell me, is it always black and white at home?"

Claire stared at Kerry, her torn heart juddering.

"Family's complicated," Kerry added, "wouldn't you say?"

Claire coughed the answer: "Y-yes."

"If you were to ask me, I'd tell you his girlfriend knew him best. Leslie stuck to that boy through thick and thin. She's the reason he got acquitted, everyone knows. Only eighteen, and they ran without a cent to their names." Kerry let out an unexpected laugh. "Nothing but that damned turtle of his. Won him at the county fair and named him Tortue. Know what that means in French? *Turtle*. Mark could be bizarrely simple like that."

Claire's throat had gone dry, though she wasn't sure why. Heat poured from the dashboard vents, flushing her face.

"I wish they'd kept in touch," Kerry murmured. "Lots of nights, I wonder what happened to them."

Discomfort fitted over Claire like a second coat. She shrugged under its weight, feeling this moment was private, and she was an intruder on Kerry's thoughts.

"I'm sorry," she managed. Then, looking toward the inn, "Thanks for the ride. I'll get out of your hair."

She opened the door, setting one foot out.

"Claire."

Her muscles tensed. This was it: the moment Kerry cried "Gotcha!" and took her in to the station for her sins.

"You and your friend, and your sister—you take care, okay?"

"I . . . of course," Claire said, stepping out the rest of the way, eager to be gone.

Kerry was studying her, a stitch worked into one brow.

"Is something wrong?" Claire dared to ask.

Kerry shook her head, eyes clearing as though she'd been nudged from a dream. "No. I'm thinking too hard of them, I think. Sometimes I see their faces in total strangers."

Claire edged away from the car.

"Well, thanks again!" she shouted, forcing a smile and shutting the door. She hurried down the drive, up the stairs of the inn. She turned the handle of the front door, and to her overwhelming relief, it gave way.

The room inside was cozy, papered in cheery yellow wallpaper. A fire burned in one corner, and a sign on the counter ahead read RING BELL FOR SERVICE. There was no need to ring, though. A commotion sounded from upstairs, and moments later a woman dressed in an oversize sweater came bounding down.

"Oh, heavens!" she cried. "Was that door unlocked? I'm sorry, dear, but we're not open. Not for Christmas. No rooms tonight."

Claire still felt overheated from the SUV.

"I-I-I . . . ," she stammered. "That's okay, I don't need a room. I just wondered if I could use your phone?"

The woman puffed at the base of the stairs, looking over Claire quizzically. "A phone?"

"My car broke down," Claire explained, racking her brain for one last good lie. "I was on my way home, and the battery died. I wondered if I could call my parents? They only live one town over, in . . . in . . ."

"Seaside?" the woman supplied.

"*Yes.*" Claire gave an embarrassed smile. "Sorry, I ran all this way, my mind's —"

"Well, of course, of course." The woman cut her off, bustling to the counter, grabbing the landline phone from its cradle and handing it over. "You call them dear, that's fine. How far away did you break down?"

"Um." Claire motioned vaguely out the window, supplying no details. "Do you have the number for a taxi company, maybe? Some way I can get a ride? I figure it'll be easier to get home tonight and worry about towing on the twenty-sixth."

The woman slowly nodded. "Oh, yes, I see. Well, I don't know how much luck you'll have. A place as tucked away as Rockport. . . . You could try getting someone to come out west from Salem, but that's a good two hours' drive. Or — ma'am, are you all right?"

Claire stared at the phone, wordless.

A revelation had broken in. A truth she'd been too uncomfortable and anxious to see in Kerry's SUV.

Leslie.

Kerry had said that Mark's girlfriend was named Leslie.

That there was a turtle named Tortue.

She'd said, *I see their faces in total strangers.*

"Oh my God," she breathed out.

"Ma'am?" The woman in the horrible Christmas sweater pressed. "Do you need to sit down?"

"No," Claire whispered. "I need to go."

She set the phone on the counter, dazed, and headed for the door.

"Ma'am!" the woman called. "Young lady, I don't think you

should go out. Why don't you let me—your parents—"

Claire didn't listen. She stumbled down the front steps.

Kerry's SUV was gone. Good. Claire didn't want the sheriff following her. Not when she had to get back to Laramie Court.

"Ma'am, please come back!" called the innkeeper—Barbara, was it?

Claire paid no mind. She started to walk, then kicked up to a run, following the road Kerry had driven to bring them here. Down Beachfront, then a left on Shoreline, then back, *back* to Laramie. Claire pumped her legs as streetlights blurred, vignetting her periphery. Cold air filled her lungs, wind stung her face. Her ponytail holder must have come loose, because her hair was no longer bunched atop her head in its proper bun, but flying wildly about.

Mark.

Leslie.

Tortue.

The three words rang in her mind.

Then, as Claire turned sharply on Shoreline, her heel gave way, skidding across ice, and Claire hurtled forward, toward the ground. She was going to wipe out again, and she braced for impact.

Then something slammed against her head—a pole, perhaps, a branch—and the world went black.

TWENTY-SEVEN

Murphy

Murphy sat on the parlor sofa, hands formed into fists, and counted her protruding knuckles one by one.

One, two, three.

These were real.

Four, five, six.

Flesh and blood.

Seven, eight, nine.

Smaller, maybe, than other knuckles, but visible to her.

Ten.

Yes, these were real, she'd confirmed.

So why was Murphy a ghost to her sisters?

Was she such a good magician-in-training that she'd managed to pull off an invisibility trick, without even trying?

Murphy, shut up.

Murph, for the love of God, not now.

Their words looped inside her ears, the final in a long line of dismissals. In Emmet no one asked how the day had gone, or how school had been. No one asked Murphy's favorites, or dislikes, or whether life was easy or hard. It hadn't always been that way, though.

She treasured the old days of Cayenne Castle, the make-shift blanket fort, and her role as Prince Pepper. There were gut laughs then, and singing, and made-up stories. She'd been part of a shimmering kingdom.

Then the Dark Ages had come—slammed doors, eye rolls at her jokes. Murphy hadn't understood why. Is that what it meant to grow up? One moment her sisters hadn't been that different from her. Then they got to high school, and Claire started say-ing, "You're too little to get it," and Eileen stopped saying things, period.

They no longer shared a castle.

They no longer shared anything.

The others had simply forgotten Murphy existed. They'd left her to fade, fade, and one day disappear.

The way she'd left Siegfried to starve, starve, and die.

That was the trouble: Murphy was guilty too. She was more restless than ever, and, picking up the Tupperware coffin resting on her knees, she rose and crossed to the parlor sideboard. There she found *The Three Musketeers*. Sniffling, she opened the cover, flipping through its pages, wondering why it couldn't be like *this* with her sisters: One for all, and all for one.

As she flipped, a scrap of paper loosened and fell out, flutter-ing to her feet. Frowning, Murphy set the book aside and picked up the scrap. It was an ad for carpet cleaning, shorn in half.

"Huh?" Murphy said.

Then, turning the scrap over, she found the true clipping: an obituary.

For John Enright.

Dad.

Murphy stared through bleary eyes at the text, frowning.

"*What*," she said, because what she was reading didn't make sense.

Was she delirious? Maybe. From the crying and lack of sleep. Or maybe this house was messing with her head. She set down the paper, rubbing away tears and lifting her eyes to the window.

Wind had kicked up over the ocean, leaning into the house, making slow work of warping its floorboards and loosening its nails. This murderous place was decaying with Murphy inside. *Decay*— she could smell it, there was no doubt. A horrendous stench was leaking from Siegfried's coffin, akin to a pizza gone rancid.

"I'm sorry, Siegfried," she said through tears. "I'm going to make it right."

Because, at last, Murphy knew what to do.

The sun had gone down hours ago, and neither of her sisters had checked on her. From her place on the couch, huddled in blankets, pretending to be asleep, Murphy had watched Eileen slam open the front door and tear through the parlor, heading up the grand staircase.

She hadn't seen Claire at all.

There was a part of Murphy—a wormy, wriggling part— that wanted to be smug. If her sisters chose to shout her down and exclude her, they deserved to be miserably mad at each other, too. Another part of Murphy—the better, bigger part— was only sad.

Because she remembered Cayenne Castle.

Even though those royal days were distant, she'd seen sparks of the sisters they'd been before, when they'd huddled by the fire, remembering the beach trip. Now that the storm was over, her sisters had instantly scattered, and they'd left her behind. Murphy, the spare tire. The baggage. The invisible one.

The way it had been in Emmet. Same story, different house.

The house on Laramie was silent. The parlor fire offered fewer crackles, clinging to the remaining splinters of wood, dying out. Murphy made work of counting her knuckles again, reminding herself she *was* real, no matter how easily her sisters passed her by.

Operation Memory Making had failed. But in the growing darkness Murphy made a new plan.

She'd known what to do since the moment she'd seen the sea from the Caravan's back seat. She'd allowed herself to be distracted by a beachside mansion and whispers of murder. She'd failed Siegfried this long, but the failing ended tonight.

Murphy rose from the couch, crossing to the parlor's double doors. She tucked Siegfried's coffin into her puffer coat and, with one steeling breath, stepped outside into the wind. Her coat hood was pushed back almost instantly, forcing Murphy to tighten the toggles. After the false start she set out again across the wraparound porch, clomping down its steps into the front yard and then making her way down the steep, slick road, toward sea level. Down she went, and down farther still. With care, she stepped over a gaping pothole, reaching the base of the road. She followed the street to the beach, walking past a worn wooden fence until her feet were sinking into loose, damp sand.

The sky was pockmarked by clouds, which occasionally parted to reveal a half moon. The ocean spread before Murphy—an eternal vastness, hemmed in by a pushing and pulling tide. The wind pressed into her, dowsing her face in salty cold. In the distance, a dog barked in vicious tenor snips.

"Welp," Murphy said. "Ominous as heck."

She didn't know who she was talking to—Siegfried, maybe, or herself. She only knew she needed to talk, to keep her heart beating and her feet moving. If she could make this funny, she'd be all right.

Murphy forged through sand, sinking ankle-deep with each step. Uggs definitely weren't meant to be worn on the beach, but Murphy was through with excuses for why it wasn't time to pay Siegfried his due.

At last she came to the water's edge. The tide reached for her, hungry, and water stained the tips of her sheepskin boots. She removed Siegfried's coffin from her coat, holding it reverently in both hands. She didn't peek into the Tupperware for one last good-bye. The smell would be too bad and, anyway, that wasn't Siegfried in there, just shell and decomposing goop.

Her breath plumed out, and she eulogized: "This is it, my dude. The final resting place. You were a good turtle and never hurt anyone. Rest easy in the knowledge that you were the perfect pet. It's not your fault you had a sucky owner."

Murphy let guilt pour over her, like frigid water. She let herself feel it, deep down in her pores. She felt it for a full minute—breathing in, breathing out.

Then, it was time.

"Don't mess it up, Murph," she whispered, and with all her

strength, she swung the plastic coffin back, then released it in a powerful arc, hurling Siegfried A. Roy into the sea.

Maybe he would wash up on the shore; Murphy wasn't clear, exactly, on how the physics worked. And sure, she knew Siegfried was a freshwater pet, not a sea turtle. In this moment, though, she felt she was doing him justice, returning him to the water, a place he belonged. For once, in his death, she was doing something right, and the weight of his shell and decaying body, wrapped in a candy cane napkin, was no longer suffocating her.

Murphy's feet were cold and her bare hands colder as she surveyed Siegfried's watery grave.

She wondered what time it was. If it was past midnight.

A Christmas burial. What a nice and terrible thing.

"I'm sorry I didn't see you," she whispered. "I'm sorry you were invisible, and I forgot."

There was nothing else to say.

The world was quiet and dark, and Murphy's thoughts were loud—so loud, she felt her head might explode. Her legs felt too weak to stand. She sat right there on the sand, legs crisscrossed, breathing in deep, the cold stinging her lungs. Shutting her eyes, she laid back in the sand and listened to the drudging crash of waves.

She pressed her fingers into the sand, one at a time:

One, two, three.

Four, five, six.

Seven, eight, nine . . .

FOUR DAYS
BEFORE

CAYENNE CASTLE

It was December twenty-first, and the days of Cayenne Castle had been forgotten.

The town of Emmet was swathed in gloom, mist spitting down on the spruces and cracked concrete, and the Sullivan sisters sat around a fake Christmas tree. Mom had made instant hot cocoa for everyone, and she wore a Santa-red toboggan upon her head. The TV was on, volume low, playing *Frosty the Snowman*, and discarded wrapping paper lay on the ground.

They'd had another early gift exchange — though not one the sisters had planned. Mom had been the one to insist they celebrate early, since she wouldn't be here on Christmas Day. She didn't know what today's date had once meant to Murphy, Claire, and Eileen. She didn't know they were sitting in the ruins of a razed castle.

Her smile faltered when, from the couch, she said, "You can go through your stockings, if you want."

Eileen's arms were crossed. She studied the present in her lap—a biography of Dante Gabriel Rossetti, with colored pictures. Mom wasn't aware, clearly, that Eileen hated the Pre-Raphaelites. That was no surprise, though. When would Eileen and her mother have had the time to chat about art?

And Eileen knew what was waiting in her stocking: hand sanitizer, hard candies, tiny tissue packets. She was missing her morning shift at Safeway for *this*.

Eileen studied Mom, whose eyes were darting from daughter to daughter. Her face was filled with weary hopefulness, asking them to tell her they were okay with this, that an early Christmas was as good as a real one.

She *was* making an effort, with the cocoa she'd heated and the tinsel she'd put on the tree. It just wasn't enough—hadn't been for a while. Mom was a shell of a person these days, eyes watery, posture stooped. She claimed she *needed* this trip, the chance to relax. And hell, maybe that was true.

Eileen didn't care what Leslie Sullivan did with her life. That wasn't her being petulant, either; she simply didn't care about anything, save when she could get to Safeway, talk to Asher, and get a bottle of Jack Daniel's for tonight.

Murphy took down her stocking and poured out its contents, which included two boxes of Hot Tamales. Murphy couldn't stand cinnamon, but she'd never told Mom that. Mom hadn't asked.

All she said was, "Thank you."

"Of course, sweetie." Mom smiled warmly, and for a moment, Murphy's heart leaped. Mom was looking at her. Did she see? Could it be like old times, when Murphy would sing an original song, and Mom would applaud? Would *hear*, and more than hear, *listen*?

That's when Mom's phone went off, a text alert. She jumped from the couch, checking the screen.

"Oh, God," she said, touching her forehead, where a deep crease had formed. "Melodie says the traffic report is bad. I need to get going."

She rose from the couch, and as she did, Murphy's hopes dissolved.

". . . should be enough meals in the freezer," Mom was saying, bustling from the den to the kitchen. "I left twenty bucks on the fridge for one pizza night. I want you girls to treat yourself. And . . . am I forgetting anything?"

When she returned to the threshold, her face was pinched, like she'd been told the exact time of her death. Murphy was used to this expression. When Mom was home—and that wasn't a lot—she wore it constantly. Perpetually worried. Looking, not seeing. Hearing, not listening.

Tears wobbled under Murphy's eyes. She wiped the right but kept the left one wet. Maybe she wanted Mom to see she was sad. Maybe she wanted *anyone* to see her, period.

Claire watched her mother, resentful of everything: the sweepstakes, the Lean Cuisines in the freezer, the predictable rain pattering on the roof. In New Haven, she was sure there were no rainy Christmases, but pristine, snowy ones. She'd thought she could escape dreary Decembers for good. She'd been wrong.

Claire felt chilled to the marrow. Mom was leaving them for Christmas—such a Settler thing to do. Claire could picture Mom sunning herself on white shores next to waters that needed

#nofilter. Not that she'd know how to take a good Instagram shot.

Mom hadn't even earned this vacation. She'd won it in the Local Market sweepstakes: a five-day, all-inclusive Bahamian cruise for two. When she'd gotten the call, Mom had jumped and screamed like an animal, and since she couldn't choose just one daughter to go along, she hadn't chosen any of them. She'd asked her work friend, Melodie. *Melodie* from Walgreens. It was unjust.

"How many of the meals contain wheat?"

Claire had followed Mom into the kitchen from the den. She watched, arms folded, as Mom rolled a suitcase toward the carport door.

"What?" Mom looked up. Then realization flooded her pinched-up face. "Oh no. Claire. I'm sorry, I forgot your new . . . thing."

"It's not a *thing*. I have a sensitivity. That's why I've been having those stomachaches, I told you."

Mom was riffling through her purse on the kitchen counter. "Well, we don't know for sure," she said, distractedly. "You haven't seen a doctor. This is from your Internet videos."

Claire dug her nails into her palms. Eileen and Murphy had joined her in the kitchen, Eileen loudly chewing a piece of gum.

"I haven't seen one," Claire said, "because you won't *take* me."

"Sweetie, I told you, with the insurance—we can book an appointment starting next year, but the out of pocket for tests—"

"And they're not just Internet videos. There are plenty of books, too. Everyone knows about gluten."

Mom stopped riffling. It seemed as though she were steadying herself, possibly counting to ten.

"I get that, Claire," she said, slowly. "And I'm sorry I forgot.

The pizza place has gluten-free crust, though, don't they?"

Claire felt the need to scream. Mom was being kind, but she wasn't getting it. That's the way it had been for years: Though Mom was here, she wasn't *here*. She'd given them presents and cocoa and tried to make things nice, but in the end, she was leaving them, *at Christmas*, for a cruise. And the most unjust part was this: Mom, a Settler, was getting her dream come true. And Claire's dream? It had been dashed to pieces. That was something to scream about.

Screaming wasn't Exceller behavior. Harper Everly had taught Claire that, long ago. But this once, Claire broke down.

"Okay, go, then," she said. "You obviously don't want to be with us for the holidays, so leave. Sunbathe and drink your piña coladas with Melodie. Be the Settler you are. Just *go*!"

Claire had detonated a bomb, and she wasn't going to stay for the aftermath. She stormed away to her bedroom and slammed herself inside.

"Oh, God," Mom said hoarsely, shutting her eyes. "I don't want to leave her this way."

Her shoulders slumped, toboggan gone askance. She looked drained of life.

Don't leave this way, Murphy thought. *Don't leave at all.*

Mom's phone went off, blasting a polka-style tune. Murphy saw that the screen read MELODIE.

"I . . . really need to go," Mom rasped, ignoring the call. "There's no telling, with the traffic in Portland, and . . . girls." She looked pleadingly to Murphy and Eileen. "It's just gluten, right?"

Then it happened again. Mom noticed Murphy.

"Sweetie," she said, "why are you crying?"

Murphy wiped at the tears and shrugged. "I dunno. I'm . . . fine."

The exhaustion in Mom's face intensified. "I asked you girls about this. We went over everything."

That was true. When Mom had gotten the phone call informing her that she was the lucky winner of the Bahamian Cruise Sweepstakes, she'd called Murphy and her sisters into the den and explained.

"It's a once-in-a-lifetime chance," she told them, "but I don't have to go."

How were you supposed to say "don't go" to *that*?

So Murphy hadn't. None of them had.

She wiped more tears and said, "I'm totally fine."

Mom nodded hesitantly. Murphy could see she needed to believe.

"You have the emergency numbers," Mom said, as though that made it better. Then she opened her arms to Murphy.

Hugging Mom felt like hugging a ghost—embracing a presence not fully there.

Eileen raised a hand when Mom turned to her, and said, "Not my thing."

A flash of hurt crossed Mom's face, and she glanced toward the hallway where Claire had run off, barricading herself in the bedroom. There was conflict in her light eyes—a decision unmade. Then, sighing, Mom turned to her purse and pulled out a printed plane ticket.

The time for deciding was, it seemed, over.

Mom rolled the suitcase out the carport door, down the driveway, and toward the family's old-as-rocks Subaru.

"This is bullshit," said Eileen, not loud enough for Mom to hear.

Eileen didn't care, maybe, but it *was* bullshit. She took a final look at Leslie Sullivan opening the driver's side door. When the car started, a song blasted from the speakers: Mariah Carey crooning about what she wanted for Christmas.

"Bullshit," Eileen said again—softly, to herself.

She turned from the scene and walked away.

"Wait!" Murphy called. "Aren't you going to say good-bye?"

But Eileen already had.

Murphy stayed where she was, hugging her jean jacket against the cold. Mom rolled down the window and waved one gloved hand out.

"Bye, sweetie!" she called. "I'll see you in five days!"

The day after Christmas.

Murphy waved as the car backed out of the driveway and clunked off the curb. She squinted against the rising sun, watching the Subaru fade into the horizon. Then she kept standing there, watching, waiting . . . for what? A twist ending? A real-life magic act?

It didn't come.

"It's fine," the last standing Sullivan sister told herself. "It'll be fine."

She was wrong, though.

At that moment Eileen was going outside to check the mail.

Claire, curled up with her phone, was looking at the Yale admissions portal.

And there was a dead body in Murphy's room.

DECEMBER
TWENTY-FIFTH

TWENTY-EIGHT

Eileen

I n the dream Eileen was younger. Twelve, maybe thirteen. Claire was there too, only she'd remained the same—seventeen, with a perfectly painted face and messy bun. Murphy was only a baby, dressed in a pink cotton onesie. She was strapped into a car seat, which was odd, because they weren't in a car; they were standing on the shore. Eileen turned to see her mother by her side, wearing an uncommonly calm expression.

"I want you to take it in," Leslie Sullivan told Eileen. "Sink your toes into the sand, enjoy it."

Eileen did. She walked along the water's edge. Houses dotted the shore with prominent gables colored like the sea: teal and white and deep blue.

And then, red.

The sun shone upon the nearest house, cutting through wind and rain, illuminating the redness of its walls, which only grew redder. Because the red wasn't dried paint, but liquid, pouring out between the wooden slats, leaking from the windows, pooling beneath the doors.

"Oh no," said Eileen, though it wasn't a shock to her.

Somehow, she'd expected the blood. She'd known this was coming, because she knew this place. She'd been here before.

Eileen woke.

The air was frigid, and her rapid breaths emerged as clouds in the pale light of dawn. She felt around her body, grasping at soft sheets.

Then the memory returned. She'd stalked away from her fight with Claire, furious, and made her way upstairs to the bedroom at the end of the hall. She hadn't been in the mood to suffer Murphy's whining or to face her own guilt for yelling at the kid. Not in the mood to do anything without the aid of alcohol. The ache for it had been crawling up her throat, weakening her joints.

Claire had been savage. She'd cut into Eileen's deepest, most hidden artery with surgical precision. Then she'd walked away.

Of course Claire had known.

Eileen had thought she'd been careful, sneaking the bottles into the house, imbibing only in the garage. Until Claire had called her out on the trip up I-5, Eileen had assumed that Claire was the same as Mom: unaware.

Even then, Eileen had thought the drunk driving—*okay*, that's what it had been—was her first slip. A single misstep. She'd clung to the belief that Claire didn't suspect the extent of the problem.

Was Eileen that far gone?

Claire had known, and she'd kept quiet. She'd been sharpening her blade, waiting for the moment to plunge it in deep, and twist.

A *burned-out drunk like you.*

With so much blood lost, Eileen hadn't had the willpower to do anything but sleep. She'd taken herself to this bedroom and shut herself inside, and for the first time in three days, she'd slept in a bed. She hadn't minded the cold last night, or the dark. Now, though, fresh from a malevolent dream, she felt differently about both.

Her spine was stiff, and she couldn't feel her feet. Her nose, irreparably frozen, *felt* blue. Her mind was stuck on a word: "drunk." Synonym to the one she wouldn't accept.

Alcoholic.

She'd been telling herself it wasn't true. She'd tried hard to believe the lie that she was fine. Under control. She couldn't do that anymore. Her present need for whiskey was overwhelming—a desperation to wash away growing fears with an antiseptic burn.

But the flask was empty. Relief wasn't coming. Left defenseless, those undeniable fears crawled into Eileen—spiders seeking a shadowy home in her heart. She thought of the letters in the linen closet. Of a bloodied piano, a lifeless body at the base of the stairs. Of painted canvases and a scribbled-on notecard reading, *Eileen paints like a total psychopath.*

"Shut up," she told the arachnid thoughts.

She lifted her eyes from the sheets, only to meet a lifeless pair of baby blues.

The doll.

Why had she chosen the room with the doll?

It stood on the dresser directly across from Eileen. One white hand was raised, fingers sealed and thumb apart, like it was pleading with Eileen, begging for spare change. Or it was reaching for her. For a grip. On her neck.

"Fuck that," Eileen said, throwing off the sheets and scrambling across the bed. To get to the door, she had to turn her back to the doll, and in that sickening moment, cold adrenaline launched through her veins. She slammed the door behind her, gripping the knob, breathing hard.

Now that she was standing, Eileen could feel an urgent pressure from her bladder. She decided to head downstairs and use the bathroom there, then settle by the fireside, next to Murphy.

Guilt dug its finely sharpened talons into Eileen.

Murph, for the love of God, not now.

She'd seen hurt swell in Murphy, drawing down the angles of her face. She hadn't meant to be cruel. She'd had another sister on her mind, and Murphy could be so infuriatingly naive, a believer only in magic and made-up royal titles.

Still, Eileen shouldn't have yelled. She'd apologize when Murphy woke up, and then they'd leave this house. They'd drive the Caravan home, and Eileen would face whatever wrath Claire had stored up for her in Emmet. That's the way it would go. The inheritance and Mark Enright—she'd think about those ugly things at a later date. After Christmas.

Eileen descended the grand staircase, shivering as she went. Her leather jacket was no match for the winter cold in the parlor. The fire had gone out, or maybe Murphy hadn't lit it. Eileen noted her on the couch, covered completely by blankets. She passed by, turning into the foyer and the adjacent bathroom.

When she was through and washing her hands, she looked

to the bathroom mirror. Past her back, through the open door, she saw the ruins of Cayenne Castle in the sitting room. Eileen shut off the tap, wiping her hands on her jeans and turning to the blanket-strewn mess. She walked into the room, and as she did, she entered the past. December twenty-firsts from years ago were present here, circling Eileen's memory in a carousel mist: Murphy's bad quarter tricks and ginger ale tea parties, and the grand fanfare her sisters had made when Eileen had hung her painting on the mantle. The memories came to life in the light of a half moon.

Eileen's gaze roved the torn castle walls and pillow thrones until her eye caught on something—a manila folder, half-obscured beneath the leg of the open storage couch. Eileen could guess what had happened: In Murphy's construction process, pulling sheets from the chest, the folder had slipped out from inside. Or maybe it had been on the floor to begin with and been knocked into sight. Whatever the reason, Eileen saw it now.

She crouched, claiming the folder and undoing its fastener. Then she tilted it downward, spilling its contents.

A spray of photographs fell to the floor.

Eileen picked up the topmost photo, a glossy 3x5. At first, she didn't understand what she was looking at. Once she did, she couldn't believe it.

She threw the photo down and picked up another, and another.

The shots were candids, taken some distance away from the subjects—across the street, through a window, from a modest height. The subjects were Claire, Murphy, and Eileen. Claire in line at the post office, tapping on her phone. Murphy standing in her school bus line at Emmet Middle. Eileen outside Safeway, loading groceries into a customer's trunk.

More shots, varied in angles but the same in general content: the Sullivan sisters, living their daily lives, unaware of the lens that captured them.

Eileen dropped the last of the photos. She felt exposed, stripped naked before a pair of leering eyes. She felt scared, like a child awoken at night. There was no adult here to turn on the light, open Eileen's closet, and tell her the monster wasn't inside. She was alone in these castle ruins with the reality that someone had been watching her.

What had Mr. Knutsen told her, in his office?

Do you know, he found out about you by way of private investigator.

This was how Patrick had discovered them, known they were his nieces. He'd had a stranger track them down and take photographs.

Only then did Eileen remember the nightmare, with its the walk along the coast, and the beach house turned blood red.

In an instant it became clear.

She was inside the red house.

She had been here before.

That unexplained trip to the coast, the day of flavornado. Their mother had brought them *here*. To Rockport. How had Eileen not seen that? The truth was obvious. Mom had brought them, as what? A failed attempt to explain?

As she stared at the scattered photos, Eileen noticed the clipping—a cut-out bit of newspaper. She picked it up, turning it over from a butchered article to the true piece of importance: *The*

Unholy Trinity. Her unholy trinity, paired with the caption, "Local young artist Eileen Sullivan displays work at Emmet High Arts Show."

Her painting. Her heart. Cut out.

"Leenie?"

Eileen shouted, turning so fast from her crouch that she fell to the ground. She stared at the ghostly figure standing over her.

It was Claire. She was breathing fast, and she'd brought in the cold from the open front door. A cut ran along her left cheek, ending in a deep bruise beneath the eye.

"W-what the hell?" Eileen choked out.

"I had an accident," Claire said, touching a hand to her face. "I was running back."

Eileen looked to the photographs, and this time so did Claire. She drew closer, kneeling beside Eileen and picking one up.

"Jeez," she said, three photos in.

"It's messed up," Eileen said. "Knutsen said Patrick used a PI. It makes me feel . . . naked, kind of. Unsafe."

Claire looked up and said, "Where's Murphy?"

"In the parlor, sleeping."

Casting down the photos, Claire swept out of the room. Eileen couldn't follow, though. For the moment she couldn't move.

Seconds later, Claire shouted, "EILEEN!"

That's when the feeling returned to Eileen's legs, along with a warm and nauseating fear. Using the couch, she heaved herself to her feet. When she reached the parlor, she found Claire throwing blankets and pillows aside, revealing a bare couch. No Murphy there.

"But she was . . ." Eileen shook her head. "I don't—"

"She's gone." Claire's voice was ice. "Weren't you keeping an eye on her?"

"Wasn't *I*—you're the one who left the goddamn house!"

Claire was shaking her head, fast. "Doesn't matter."

Eileen called, "Murphy? MURPH."

She looked to the grand staircase, the piano, the windows, the hearth. No sign of her sister. How long had she been gone?

And what if those photographs weren't the work of Patrick Enright's PI?

What if they'd been taken by . . . Mark?

And if he'd been able to follow them, *stalk* them, without their knowing it, then who was to say he couldn't be doing the same exact thing now?

Eileen opened the cabinet doors of the sideboard. She was in search of a hiding place, somewhere Murphy could have contorted herself. She *had* stowed away on the ride here. Maybe this was another one of her weird-humored tricks.

There was no Murphy inside.

There was, however, a scrap of paper on the floor, nearby. Eileen's gaze hooked on the name—a bold subtitle that read, JOHN ENRIGHT.

John.

Dad.

Queasily, Eileen grabbed the paper, reading the text:

John Enright, age 24, passed away on January 20, 2004, in Boston, Massachusetts. An aspiring environmental attorney and first-year law student at Suffolk University, John was an active participant

in his community, an esteemed intern at Rowe and
Lundergrun, and was training for his first Boston
Marathon at the time of his passing. He is survived
by his brothers, Mark and Patrick. Visitation to be
held at 12:00 p.m. on January 25, 2004, at Hay-
worth Memorial Home.

"What," Eileen breathed. "What the hell is *this*."

She raised the paper to an approaching Claire, who snatched
it, looked over its contents, stopped, and met Eileen's gaze with
wide eyes.

"That's not Dad," said Eileen. "That's . . . *not* Dad. He died
here. In Oregon. In 2006. He wasn't a fucking law student."

Claire licked her lips. "Leenie, there's something I found
out. Something Kerry told me."

"Kerry who?"

"The sheriff. She said . . . Leenie, Mark isn't Mark Enright.
Mark is *Dad*."

Eileen stared at Claire. "Excuse me?"

"Dad—our dad, John Sullivan—was Mark Enright. He
changed both his names."

Eileen continued to stare. "I don't . . . that doesn't . . ."

"Kerry said it was the mom who did the killings, not Mark.
She was messed up. It was her, not Dad. She said—"

Eileen raised her hands to her head. "*Stop*. Fucking *stop*."

Her brain was on fire. The photographs. This obit. The sheriff. There were too many thoughts in her head competing for
attention. And Murphy was lost. They'd *lost their sister*. They
didn't have time for this.

Eileen turned and screamed Murphy's name again—a frantic, lilting echo. She felt the dread coming on hard, jabbing into her spine from behind like a living, breathing presence.

And then she was sure of it. She *heard* breath.

Claire saw first. Her eyes caught on something behind Eileen, and she raised a hand to her mouth.

Slowly, Eileen turned to the foyer and the figure standing there: a grown adult carrying a limp, prone Murphy. Eileen was so startled, she didn't register the face, the *anything* of the figure.

Then she looked again, closer, and said, "Mom?"

TWENTY-NINE

Claire

O h my *God*," said Claire.

The words emerged as a sob, and as they did, Claire realized how much fear had been pent up in her bones, to the point of fracture. Her mind spun, dipping in and out of questions. How was her mother here? How was Leslie Sullivan not on a beach three thousand miles away?

"What . . . what . . ." The choked word wouldn't form itself into a sentence. Claire gave up the effort and, instead, cupped her hands over her mouth.

"She's all right," Mom said, nodding to the daughter in her arms. "She'd fallen asleep on the beach."

Murphy, who Claire now saw was awake, gave a groggy half nod.

"Yeah," she croaked. "I'm cool."

"She's cold, though," said Mom. "Is there something to warm her up?"

Eileen jolted to attention. "Yeah. There are lots of blankets in the other room."

"I'll get them," Claire blurted, suddenly needing this above anything else: to take action.

She propelled herself from the parlor, darting into the sitting room, where Murphy had constructed Cayenne Castle. She grabbed blankets and sheets with abandon, decimating Murphy's construction and turning the castle to ruins. Then, with the blankets piled high, she returned to the parlor.

Eileen was crouched by the hearth, crumpling the contents of an open filing box and throwing the papers under new logs, striking a match. Soon, the kindling was alight, and the fire grew. Leslie had laid out Murphy on the couch, and Claire made quick work of burying her in blankets, encasing her ribs, ankles, thighs.

"There's a kettle in the kitchen," Claire said, remembering. "I'll heat up water."

She dashed from the room again, because it was better to keep moving than to sit with panic-stricken thoughts.

Mom was here. She was *here*. She'd found out their secret, and she'd found *them* at the worst possible time, with Murphy lost and Claire a mess. And what came next?

Claire didn't want to think. Instead, she grabbed the cast-iron kettle from the stove and filled it with water. She turned a knob on the range and then stared, nonplussed, at the cold burner.

"God," she groaned, when she realized: no electricity. If she'd stopped to think—the thing she most wanted *not* to do— she would have realized that.

Claire set down the kettle and breathed in deep. She turned

back toward the parlor, exhaled, and resolved to face what awaited her in there.

"No power," she mumbled, as she returned to the couch.

"I'm o-okay," said Murphy, peeking her face over the mountainous pile of quilts. Her chattering teeth told a different story. Murphy's neck was stark white and her nose and cheeks flushed red. How long had she been out on the coast? Had it been since Claire had abandoned her?

"I'm so sorry." Claire barely got out the whisper, and she couldn't look at Murphy as she said it. She definitely couldn't look at Mom, who was sitting by the couch, one hand resting at Murphy's side.

"For what?" asked Murphy. "Earlier? You were just being Claire."

Claire didn't think Murphy meant for the words to hurt her, but they did—more than any insult ever could.

Just being Claire. Just insisting on perfection, blowing up, running away from her sisters, her life, *herself*, for something better in the future.

Yes. That was her.

Eileen had finished stoking the fire and joined them by the couch. She stood at a distance from Mom, hands on hips, jaw firm.

"Elephant in the room," she said. "Mom, what the hell are you doing here?"

Eileen was trying to sound unaffected, sure of herself. Claire knew, though: Eileen was at as much of a loss as Claire was. This was too surreal.

"I'm . . . sure you didn't expect me."

As Mom spoke, Claire studied her mother. She seemed small sitting there, cross-legged on the carpet, with her fine blond hair shrouding her face and her shoulders carved into a slump. Claire had never thought of her mother as a commanding presence, but she hadn't thought of her as small, either. Small, or scared, or uncertain, or—at one time—young.

Kerry's words were in Claire's ears: *Leslie, she stuck to that boy through thick and thin.*

Leslie.

Mom.

Who had once been seventeen and overwhelmed.

Claire knew a startling truth about Mark Enright. She'd been working it out on her run back to Laramie Court. Now, though, staring the truth in the face, Claire was breathless with inaction, incapable of reconciling any of it with *this* woman.

"Mom," said Claire, "why aren't you in the Bahamas?"

Mom stared at her folded legs, tucking her stringy hair behind both ears. "When we got to Florida," she said, "I changed my mind. Actually, when we got to the *dock*. Melodie wasn't happy, but I made her go on without me."

"I don't understand," Eileen said tonelessly. "Did you forget sunscreen?"

Mom sucked in her lower lip. It was chapped, Claire noticed, and unpainted. In fact, Mom wasn't wearing a dab of makeup.

"I think," she said slowly, as though testing the weight of each word, "it took getting there, being in a different place—or maybe it was the heat. It felt like . . . I don't know, waking up from a hard sleep. I saw things clearly: I shouldn't have convinced myself the trip was something I needed. I was wrong to pretend you girls

302

were okay with it. And . . ." Mom looked up, locking her eyes on Claire and, in the process, nearly knocking the breath out of her. "I was wrong to drive off when you told me how you felt. I'd been telling myself for so long that I deserved that trip. That Murphy was in high school, and old enough that this one Christmas wouldn't matter. And that the same held especially true for you girls." She nodded to Claire, and then to Eileen.

"Well," mumbled Murphy, "we told you it was okay."

"I didn't give you a choice." Mom's voice had grown firm. "I asked you, but I didn't listen. I . . . don't think I've been listening for a while. I guess you'd call it an epiphany, whatever happened in Florida. And then I knew I couldn't live with myself if I got on that ship. It wouldn't be vacation, it'd be torture. So, I came home."

"But," said Claire, "that had to cost so much money."

"Southwest." Mom smiled wanly. "No change fees. Only had to wait on standby for three different flights."

"And then we weren't home." Claire snapped the next piece of the puzzle into place. Her legs felt strained—a delayed reaction to the running before. She sank to the ground, sitting only a foot off from Mom.

"I tried calling," Mom began.

"I broke my phone," Claire replied.

"I went searching your rooms for some kind of clue. I thought—my *God*, I thought someone had taken you." Mom dropped her head in her hands. On its face the move seemed melodramatic, but Claire could see: This was true emotion. Her mom had been scared. Her mom had *cared*.

"You found Knutsen's letter?" Eileen was still standing, arms crossed, face devoid of feeling.

Mom raised her head, revealing two splotchy pink patches around her eyes. "I can't tell you how angry I am at that man. Just because you're eighteen, Eileen, that doesn't mean he shouldn't have contacted me. That he'd go behind my back— well, I gave him a piece of my mind. I called the police, too, but all they did was ask about how we got along, and how likely it was that you three had simply run away, and—I guess I had a second epiphany then. Really, you had plenty of reasons to run. You ticked every box. And I had a pretty good idea of where you'd gone to. I came here, and the headlights caught Murphy on the beach. I thought . . ." Mom unfolded the fists in her lap, a helpless motion. "God, I don't know what I thought. But you're here. And you're okay. Aren't you?"

Claire was attempting to take it in: Mom being here, worried, flying back from Florida. It was so much, and when combined with everything Claire had understood from Kerry, from what she'd seen in those PI's photographs and read in John Enright's obituary, the questions bubbled up in a rush, like soda fizz. Claire had to hiccup at least one of them out:

"It was you, wasn't it? You were the girlfriend who got Mark Enright off on the murder charge. Mark was Dad."

Mom blinked at Claire, wearing a hollowed-out expression. It was answer enough.

"When you moved away from here," said Claire, "he changed his name to John. I guess it was . . . a tribute?"

She looked to Mom for confirmation.

"I . . . ," Mom said. "He looked up to John. And John hadn't betrayed him the way Patrick had. That was his word: 'betrayed.' I think Pat was . . . very confused. He'd seen what had happened, when John had left the family for Boston. He'd gone against Mrs. Enright's wishes, and she'd disinherited him. Pat was young, sixteen. I can only guess what she threatened to convince him to testify.

"Sophia, his mother, was at the root of it. I saw the way she behaved for myself plenty of times, but the stories Mark told . . . She wasn't well. I just didn't understand, when he talked about her, how serious it was."

Mom grimaced, swatting at her face as though a fly had flown too close. Then Claire realized, she'd been wiping away a tear. Mom cleared her throat and went on:

"Mark could have left the day he turned eighteen. Should have. He'd decided to stay through the summer for Pat, though. He didn't want to leave him alone. So he still lived here in June, when it happened. Sophia went into one of her rages, only it didn't end like the ones before. Mark thought—he really did— that she hadn't meant to kill his father. Had he fallen down those stairs a different way, hit his head in another place . . . there's no knowing. Mr. Enright did die, though, and by the time the police arrived, Sophia had a story. I still don't know how she could've done that: tried to destroy Mark, turn Pat against him. Like I said, she wasn't *well*."

As Mom spoke, Claire glanced at a saucer-eyed Murphy, and then to Eileen, whose crossed arms had slackened. These were, Claire knew, truths none of them would quickly recover from.

"John didn't come back from Boston—not for the trial, or the funerals. Your father didn't blame him, though. He never blamed John for anything, up to the day we found out he had died in a car crash." Mom shook her head. "Your father used to joke there

305

was a curse on this house, that it followed him and his brothers wherever they went. I got angry when he said that. Maybe because I believed there was truth in it. We tried to escape the scandal. Went to a town off the map, where he could get work. It didn't matter that he'd been acquitted; by then, the university had dropped its scholarship offer. So we both worked, and we thought we'd gotten far enough away from this place. I guess we didn't escape the curse, though. Nothing went according to plan."

Claire was remembering the day her mother had, inexplicably, piled her and her sisters into the car and driven them to the coast. How could Claire have not seen it then? Mom had been trying to tell them. Maybe she'd meant to say everything and had lost the nerve. Maybe, as she'd said, she'd wanted them to see Rockport once, not knowing what it had meant to her, only digging their feet into the sand.

And then there was Claire's father: John, who wasn't John, who'd died before his daughters got to know his real name.

"Sophia killed herself after the trial," Mom said, the words gone low. "But not before she'd changed her will and cut Mark out. She knew this town would talk, regardless of what the coroner said. If Mark had stayed here, he would've been harassed till his dying day. Pat got a guardian, the house, and everything in it, but that poor boy had lost his whole family in the process. So . . . you see, it's difficult to blame him. All these years he must've felt ashamed about what he'd done. Too ashamed to reach out, until it was too late. I wish, when he'd found us, he would've called me. I guess he did what he thought was right. He must've thought that by leaving the house to you, he was making amends. And maybe he was. It's a beautiful place."

Claire got the impression that Mom was beginning to ramble, unsure of what to say next, or how to make anything right. How could you, after that speech? What could anyone say?

"We thought we'd made the right decision," Mom said. "We decided it'd be better not to tell you. Better *for* you. Less confusing. Or, if we did tell you, it'd be once you were old enough to understand. Then your father got sick and died. Life kept going on, and you kept growing up. The older you got, the more difficult it became. Knowing what I had to tell you, unable to do it alone. Soon it was hard to tell you anything. It was easier to take the extra shifts. At least then I knew I was doing something right as your mother: providing for you. But I wasn't *there*. God knows what could've happened to you girls, traveling up here, with this weather and this town, and . . . all of that's my fault."

No one told Mom it wasn't her fault. No one said anything. The parlor was so deathly still that the pounding on the front door seemed amplified ten times, and terror shot through Claire's veins when she heard a voice call out, "ROCKPORT POLICE."

THIRTY

Murphy

Murphy sat up straight on the couch, in spite of her frozen joints. She'd been cold before, when she'd woken on the beach with her face pressed into sand and her mother's arms unexpectedly wrapped around her middle. Now, a different coldness filled Murphy, whooshing down her spine.

"Rockport police!" the voice called again.

They'd been caught. The jig was up.

The voice was a woman's, and it sounded weirdly familiar, like that of a teacher who'd taught Murphy way back in primary school, or a grocer she saw a lot at Fred Meyer, or—

"Kerry?"

Mom was looking to the threshold of the parlor, where a woman stood wearing a tan uniform. Her black hair was braided, and her face was more familiar than her voice. In another second, Murphy had it: This was the woman from Ramsey's Diner. The Rockport sheriff. *Kerry.*

But why had Mom said her name? Even weirder, why was Kerry staring at Mom as though she knew her right back?

"Leslie?" she asked, sounding less ferocious than she had when she'd announced herself.

"I don't understand," Kerry went on, approaching them cautiously, as though the Sullivans were a pack of wildcats that might pounce. "Leslie . . . what the hell are you doing here?"

Mom was gaping at Kerry, a mirror image of shock.

This wasn't going anywhere. Murphy was going to have to speak up.

"She's our mom." Murphy pointed to herself, then an immobile Eileen and Claire. "We, uh, kind of lied about who we were in the diner. Sorry. It's not a crime to lie to a police officer, right? Not technically?"

Murphy had no clue what she was saying. Why was she asking about lying, when they'd been caught, red-handed, breaking into a house? Had her brain stopped working? Had she gotten hypothermia out there on the shore?

Kerry didn't answer Murphy's question. Her eyes stayed locked on Mom as she asked, "These . . . are your kids?"

"M-my daughters, yes," stammered Mom. "They received a letter from Pat's attorney. God knows if it's even true. It told them they'd inherited the house."

Kerry gave a slow blink. "I don't understand."

"Welcome to the club," muttered Eileen.

"According to the letter," said Mom, "Patrick willed the house to the girls. I was out of town, and they left home to come here and investigate on their own. I'm sorry if they've caused any trouble."

Kerry shook her head, pointing to Claire. "After I dropped you off, something didn't feel right. I went home, tried to sleep it off. I couldn't shake the feeling, though, after what you'd said in the diner about Patrick's house. And your face reminded me . . . That's why I came. Bonnie thought I was crazy. Turns out, I wasn't."

Kerry was still shaking her head, but she seemed looser, like someone recovering during the credits of a horror show. "I'm trying to wrap my mind around this," she said.

Me too, thought Murphy. She was pretty sure everyone was: her sisters, Mom, and the sheriff Mom mysteriously knew. Murphy's brain was pulsing with everything Mom had told them about the Enright brothers and the murders. The true story—the one she'd never been told.

"I really am sorry, Kerry," Mom repeated. "I know this is serious, and it's my fault. I left the girls unsupervised. If I were at home, if I'd paid attention to what was going on . . ."

"Enough of that." Kerry waved a hand at Mom, looking almost angry. "We're not talking about breaking and entering. There's heavier stuff on the table here; don't pretend there's not. I mean, Leslie. God. It's *you*."

"Me," said Mom, hiking her shoulders, and she suddenly looked so young to Murphy—as young as Eileen.

"I'm sorry I didn't write." Mom pushed off the couch to her feet. "Mark and I agreed, better to have a clean break. It's not that we didn't think it through, or that it wasn't hard for us. It was hell, Kerry. And I could've used a friend."

"Where?" Kerry asked.

"Three hours south. Mark got a lead, found an opening at a library. We figured it'd be a transition, a way to get on our feet before heading out farther—Sacramento, maybe, or LA. Then . . . well, life happened."

Murphy's mind was reeling, but she understood at least what "life happened" meant: Eileen, Claire, and Murphy, and then their dad's death. That was a lot of life to happen in a few years.

"Mark?" Kerry whispered, like she already knew.

"Leukemia." Mom's jawline was stiff. She didn't talk much about Dad at home, but when she did, her jaw always locked into place, metal bar shut across a door, keeping bad things inside. "The medical bills were bad. There was no leaving after that."

"You could've written or called."

"I was . . . ashamed." Mom broke then—voice and body, her neck bending sharply.

"My God." Kerry pinched the bridge of her nose. "This is a Christmas punch dream."

The parlor got quiet, and Murphy glanced around—first to Eileen, with her dark eyes and folded arms, then to Claire, sitting cross-legged by the couch, gaze vacant. She returned to Mom and Kerry, who were looking anywhere but at each other. They'd been friends, once upon a time. That's what was going on here: Years ago, Mom and Kerry had lived in Rockport, teenagers together.

Then the murders had happened.

And now the past and present were colliding, *exploding*. Had Uncle Patrick known this would happen when he left his house to the sisters? Murphy wondered. It could be this was Patrick Enright's own "ta-da" moment. That he, like Murphy, was a true magician.

Because here were all four Sullivan girls together, and here were two old friends reunited. That was magical, wasn't it? The good kind of magic. The Cayenne Castle kind. And even though Murphy was cold down to her muscles, and so confused her mind was whirling like a spinning top, she felt a sureness and safeness she hadn't known before.

"So," she said, cracking the silence in two. "You're not going to arrest us?"

She smiled guiltily at Kerry, raising bent arms as though to say, *It's the holiday season, am I right?*

Kerry did something unexpected: She laughed. There were tears beaded in the corners of her eyes, and her laughing sent them streaming down her cheeks.

"God," she gasped. "*God.*"

"Kerry," said Mom, "we'll clear out of here, I swear. If what this attorney says is true, the girls will go about things the proper way from here on out. No trespassing whatsoever."

Kerry wiped at the tears, her chest heaving. "It's Christmas Day, Leslie. I'm not going to arrest you. I'm going to invite you to my home."

Murphy blinked, dumbfounded for the hundredth time that day.

"I couldn't impose," said Mom. "This was a misunderstanding. We didn't—"

"You're not arguing." Kerry cut Mom off. "I always win an argument, remember? You called it my special skill."

"Is that why you went into law enforcement?"

A funny, not-entirely-good look flitted across Kerry's face. "Something like that. Now come on, the four of you. Bonnie's cooking a massive Christmas brunch."

Brunch. The word elicited a ravenous screech from Murphy's gut. When had she eaten last? She could remember *what* she'd eaten: live, wriggling maggots. Christmas brunch was the exact opposite of that. Christmas brunch was *everything.*

"Please," she said to Kerry. "We'd love that."

What else were they going to do, when the sheriff of Rockport made a demand? They simply had to obey.

"It's settled, then," said Kerry. "Leslie, I'm guessing the Subaru is yours?"

"It is."

"And . . ." Kerry tapped her thigh, surveying the sisters. "That abandoned Caravan that was called in yesterday belongs to you girls?"

"Guilty as charged," said Eileen, who hadn't uncrossed her arms.

Kerry nodded, businesslike. "We'll take care of that later. For the time being, out we go. No arrests, but I won't be facilitating a *technical* crime."

Kerry motioned for them to head out the door.

"Murphy?" Claire was kneeling at her side. "You okay to walk?"

Murphy rolled her eyes. "I'm just a little cold."

That didn't wipe off the worry on Claire's face.

She feels bad, Murphy realized, as she got up under Claire's watchful eye. *She left, and now she feels guilty.*

There were two ways Murphy could use this information: She could make Claire feel worse, limp a little and chatter her teeth for dramatic effect. Or, she could make Claire feel better. Because maybe, when Claire had run off, she hadn't really been thinking. Like the many times Murphy hadn't thought to feed Siegfried.

As they walked out of the house, Murphy took Claire's hand in hers and squeezed, and she said, "I'm glad you came back."

Claire looked at her, startled, hot light in her eyes. By the time they had climbed into the back seat of the Subaru, she was wearing a small smile.

Murphy put on her seat belt as Mom started the car and, waving to Kerry through the windshield, began to follow the sheriff's SUV down the bluff. On instinct, Murphy pulled out the rope from her puffer coat pocket.

Over, under, tug through and out.

There was a lot to think about. So much to figure out. But for now, the rope would do the trick.

THIRTY-ONE

Eileen

She'd been wrong.

For two years Eileen had been wrong about everything.

But she'd also been right.

She *was* the daughter of Mark Enright, and she *had* been lied to. Those two truths remained unchanged. The details, though — she'd gotten those catastrophically wrong.

As she sat at the dinner table, nodding along to Kerry and Bonnie's small talk, every one of those details went off like tiny fireworks in her brain: Mark Enright's name change, the truth about the murders, Sophia Eschenburg's rages, Eileen's parentage.

The letters she'd found in the linen closet hadn't been sent to a woman who'd had a fraternal affair, but to a girl who'd defended her innocent boyfriend in court. A teenager who'd left Rockport and gone to a place far enough away where she and Mark Enright could start again as Sullivans.

An emancipated foster kid and a wrongfully judged high school graduate—*those* were Eileen's parents. That was the story, monumentally different from the one she'd been telling herself over swigs of Jack Daniel's.

How could she have gotten it this twisted?

"Leenie."

Murphy kicked Eileen's boot under the table, returning her attention to brunch and the fact that Bonnie was asking Eileen a question, Pyrex dish in hand:

"Sweet-potato casserole?"

"Uh," Eileen rasped. "No. Thanks."

The scents wafting down the birchwood table were unreal: honey ham, green beans, parmesan mashed potatoes, candied pecans. Kerry's wife, Bonnie, was on MasterChef level, and Eileen was hungry enough after skipping out on two meals. Hunger and appetite were two different things, though. Eileen's body was too busy pumping all its energy to her brain; there was no room left for digestion.

Eileen looked across the table to her mother. She was wearing sweatpants and an oversize tee, her face unmade, and disheveled hair pushed behind her ears. She really must have booked it back to Oregon from Florida, not giving a damn about appearance.

Mom had been asked a barrage of polite questions by Bonnie, and not-so-polite ones by Kerry, including "What the hell do you do?" and "You're saying you visited once and never told me?"

Mom had asked her own questions too, like "The two of you met in Portland?" and "What would bring you back here?"

When Bonnie asked Mom about the sweet-potato casserole,

she flinched. Was she always this jumpy? Eileen had stopped paying attention long ago to the little things Mom did. For one thing, she hadn't been around the house much to be observed. For another, Eileen hadn't wanted to look at her closely since the letters. Now, she was taking in everything: the creases around Mom's mouth, the freckles on her hands, the chapped state of her lips. Here was her own mother, yet she felt so much like a stranger.

Kerry and Bonnie had also asked the sisters questions—little inquiries about life in Emmet, which they had answered with vague, distant answers. Eileen knew Murphy and Claire were as dazed as she was, processing in the face of sudden news. There was no denying it: This was the most awkward Christmas brunch in the history of Christmas brunches. Eileen would stake her life on that. Sure, she didn't have an experience to compare it to; "brunch" wasn't in the Sullivan's vocabulary. But what could be weirder than eating the food of the sheriff of a tiny town you'd only discovered a few days ago, courtesy of a letter from your heretofore unknown dead uncle's attorney?

And to top it off, Eileen had been wrong.

How the hell could she be capable of small talk?

All she was able to offer, when Bonnie asked if Eileen had enjoyed high school was, "Not really, but that's kind of the norm, huh?" And then, "Could you tell me where your bathroom is?"

An obliging Bonnie pointed down the hallway, telling Eileen it was two doors to the left.

Eileen escaped and did her business. When she was through, though, she didn't leave. She stood facing the oval mirror, studying herself as hard as she'd been studying Mom.

Dark hair. Dark eyes. Tall frame. Different from her sisters and her mother, from the memories and the photos of her father. She'd first thought they were unique parts of herself. Then she'd thought they were signs of a murderer's blood in her veins. The pieces seemed to have fit, so she'd insisted they would, ramming them together to support her truth.

Now who was facing her in the glass? Her parents' eldest daughter. Probably a surprise to them both, but not in the way she'd believed. She was just her parents' kid. She was *herself*: Eileen Sullivan, who once upon a time had loved to make art.

She needed a drink. She craved fire in her belly, fuel that could lift her brain above reality. She eyed the mouthwash sitting on the counter: LISTERINE FRESH BURST.

What she'd give for a fresh burst of anything.

She caught her reflection again, desperation etched on her bony face.

God, Eileen, she thought. *You've had a fucking revelation, and you remain goddamn predictable.*

She could say the word with more resigned conviction than she had this morning.

"Alcoholic," accused the girl in the mirror.

She'd finally admitted the truth.

The knock on the bathroom door sent Eileen stumbling away from the counter.

"Occupied!" she called, reaching over to flush the already flushed toilet.

"Eileen?"

The door cracked open, and Mom's face appeared, nose first. Aquiline, like Eileen's. They shared that in common, at least.

"Jesus, *shit*," said Eileen.

Mom opened the door wider, then stepped inside and closed it behind her.

She said, "I wanted to be sure you're okay."

"What, *now* you do?"

The words came out involuntarily, and the moment they did, Eileen threw a hand over her mouth, cementing her lips. Like she was a little girl who'd said a bad word. She *felt* like a child, suddenly.

If Mom was hurt by the words, she didn't show it. She looked reflective, and then said, "No, actually. That's not why I came. I thought, maybe, we need to talk."

"Do we?"

"Eileen."

"What?"

"You haven't been doing well. I think . . . I've known. You haven't been doing well for a while."

Did she know about the alcohol?

Eileen could study Mom, but she couldn't *read* her. And she didn't want to talk about whiskey or wine right now. Instead, she blurted, "I read the letters. The ones you kept in the closet."

Mom's eyes were unblinking. She didn't look startled, and to her credit she didn't say something banal, like, "Oh, sweetie, I'm sorry."

She said, "I shouldn't have kept them there. To be honest, I'd forgotten."

"Why did you keep them in the first place?"

Mom lowered her gaze to the pink bathroom tile. "I don't know. Maybe I wanted evidence, if some vigilante tracked us to

Emmet. Maybe a part of me wanted a reminder of Rockport—of what it had been, or a reason to stay away. I don't know, Eileen. I don't have a good answer."

"I didn't know Mark Enright was Dad. I thought he was someone else. *My* dad."

Mom got it then. She parted her flaky lips.

"I thought he'd committed the murders," Eileen went on, and then, to her horror, she began to cry.

"Leenie." Mom's arms were around Eileen. They didn't squeeze hard—only a tentative hug. "There's a lot I should have told you. There are so many things I could've done differently."

"Yeah," Eileen agreed.

Because this wasn't the time to make Mom feel okay. This needed to happen. It had been building in Eileen for two years, fueled by liquor and uneasy silence and a locked bedroom door.

"I got it wrong," Eileen said, wiping a hand beneath her nose, catching snot on her knuckles. "I guess it's not surprising, though. Like, I totally bombed the genetics exam in biology."

Mom clasped Eileen's elbows, looking her up and down. "Dad was *your* dad, Eileen. And he loved you beyond belief."

"I'm the reason you had to stay in Emmet, though, huh? Because you had a kid."

Mom said, "You came when we needed you most."

There was a blockage the size of a football in Eileen's throat. She couldn't swallow it down.

She really needed a drink.

But she needed this more.

"Did you know?" she rasped around the lump.

Mom's brows contracted. "Know what?"

That's when Eileen understood that she didn't. Mom had been *that* disconnected. And Eileen had done as good a job of hiding the drinking as she'd thought—not from Claire, maybe, but from her mom.

That was a feat, though not one to be proud of.

Eileen didn't press the question. She hugged back. She placed her arms around Mom's body-odor-stenched tee, and pulled close. This time, the hug wasn't tentative.

"Yoo-hoo!" called a voice down the hall. Murphy. "Mom! Leenie! You guys *have* to see the cake Bonnie made!"

Neither of them moved just yet.

THIRTY-TWO

Claire

Claire couldn't keep her eyes off them: Kerry and Bonnie, and the looks and words they exchanged over Bonnie's pistachio chocolate sponge cake, and then over the table as Claire helped them clear away the dishes, and then over the kitchen sink, as they loaded the dishwasher and dropped platters into sudsy water.

She knew it was creepy, paying this much attention to practical strangers. Claire was careful about it, though, never allowing her gaze to linger too long. Meantime, she hung on every innocuous word the women spoke, from talk of cable bills to New Year's plans to Bonnie's work at Rockport's bakery, the Rosy Warbler. Claire was riveted. Mystified.

Because how could it work?

How could two smart, accomplished women in love with each other be living in Nowheresville, Oregon? And, more important, how could they be *happy* about it?

They seemed happy, even though their bungalow was small, and the kitchen was outdated. Even though they lived in a tiny town without even a Walmart to its name—a town full of close-minded people who had, at one time, practically banished Claire's parents.

Her parents.

Leslie Clark.

Mark Enright.

Teenagers with a sordid story Claire had known nothing about.

She should have been processing *that*: murder, scandal, a hidden history. The fact that Mom, who'd been distant for years, was suddenly back in Claire's life, acting close and caring, the way she once had. And maybe that was the way she'd *always* been—it was just the merciless grind of life that had gotten in the way.

Claire wasn't thinking that through, though. Instead she was watching Kerry and Bonnie, leaving her mom to talk to Eileen in the hallway, as they had been doing for over an hour. Clearly, those two had their own issues to resolve. Murphy, meantime, had asked permission to turn on the TV and had settled herself in front of the TBS marathon of *A Christmas Story*. The world-weary narration of Ralphie Parker floated into the kitchen, where Claire was towel-drying the last of the serving dishes. Bonnie had left the room to take a phone call from her father, and Kerry had pulled the drain stopper from the sink. She rubbed her pruned hands against her jeans and gave an accomplished sigh.

"Well," she said, "that's that."

"I'm . . . sorry," Claire wheezed. For all her observation in the past hour, she hadn't done much talking. Now her voice was dusty and uncertain.

"What're you sorry for?" Kerry asked, surprised.

Dish towel in hand, Claire motioned in a wide arc, as though to say, *for everything*. "Lying to you about the house and who I was. Ruining your Christmas brunch. I'm sure it was going to be special, and you would've had leftovers. You could've—"

Kerry interrupted Claire with a throaty blast of laughter. "You're worried about *leftovers*?"

"Among other things," Claire mumbled.

"Trust me," said Kerry, "Bonnie and I are happy to have you. You don't know what it means to me to have Leslie here. And you girls turning out to be her and Mark's kids—well, it's a lot. Not exactly a Christmas miracle, but a Christmas . . . something."

"Shock?" Claire offered.

"Understatement," Kerry replied.

"We must've thrown things off-kilter," Claire persisted, unable to bat off the need to have her apology heard. "I'm sure you had plans, and you didn't know you'd have to, like, stop us from breaking into Uncle Patrick's house. I should have been honest when you picked me up last night. I feel really bad about that."

"Why?" Kerry asked. "If I were in your shoes, I would've lied too. Anyway, you girls were on an adventure. You didn't know who to trust."

"I guess that's true," Claire said weakly. "I just feel . . . silly. There was nothing in that house for us. It was only a house. I got caught up in the drama, you know? It's not every day you find out you've got a mysterious uncle who left you his fortune."

"Very Charles Dickens," Kerry agreed.

Claire turned her attention to the dish towel, folding its terry cloth edges together, hanging it on the oven. She didn't want to stop talking to Kerry, but she wasn't sure she could ask what she wanted. She wasn't even sure she knew what the question was.

"Claire. You okay?"

Claire continued to look at the towel, tracing its yellow floral pattern and damp green fringe. "You said something last night. That it was hard to live in Rockport. Do you still think that? I mean, why wouldn't you stay in Portland?"

"I told you," said Kerry, "Bonnie likes the coast."

Claire looked up. "Simple as that?"

"I didn't say it was simple. You're going to find intolerant people anywhere, though. Bigots, homophobes—they don't have a monopoly on small towns. It isn't fair, dealing with people's bad behavior, but you also can't let it stop you from living your life. So you choose the place you like best, and with any luck, you thrive. That looks different for everyone, and it can change. I needed to live in Portland in my twenties. These days, I enjoy Rockport. There are people here who knew me as a little girl, others who grew up with me. It's not for everyone, but I find some satisfaction in being neighbors with people who know my dirt."

"People who know you're not perfect," Claire murmured.

"Who said I'm not perfect?" Kerry deadpanned.

Then a smile burst across her face, and Claire laughed.

"Look," Kerry said. "There's no one way to do life right. That's the one thing I can tell you for sure. Anyone who says different? Well, they're full of shit."

Claire nodded unwillingly. Because this meant destruction. Walls she had built high in her head and heart—smooth, pristine—were showing their cracks. And the words *Don't plan for failure* seemed so trite.

It wasn't Settlers versus Excellers. Who could be the judge of that?

Claire thought of a girl her age named Leslie, with no parents and with a boyfriend on trial, scared out of her mind. She thought of the guts it would take to get on a witness stand and tell the truth, to leave for God knew where and start a new life.

That wasn't settling, even though anyone on the outside— Harper Everly, especially—would call her mom a settler, through and through.

Claire had done that, hadn't she?

"Oh, gosh. Anything I can do to help?"

Claire looked up, startled by the sight of Mom herself in the doorway. Though she was smiling, her eyes were rimmed red.

"Uh-uh, good timing," Kerry said, winking at Mom.

"We finished everything up," said Claire.

When Mom's eyes met hers, Claire had a sudden, reckless thought: What if there had been a spell over that house in Emmet? A curse, like the one Mom had said was on 2270 Laramie—one that drove apart the Sullivan girls, banishing them into dark, lonely corners.

A curse that had lifted, because Mom was *looking* at her.

"You and Kerry probably have a lot more to catch up on, huh?" Claire spoke nervously, stepping away from the counter and heading for the door.

As Claire passed over the threshold, Mom grabbed her hand. She gave it a single pulse and said, "Merry Christmas."

"Merry Christmas, Mom," Claire said back, and she escaped

to the den with tears gathered in her eyes. She remained in the hallway, out of sight, listening as Leslie and Kerry spoke in familiar tones, warm and worn. Standing there, Claire considered her life.

Yale.

Ainsley St. John.

Her mom, and the Bahamian cruise.

Shattered phones and broken dreams.

The Enright brothers, the Sullivan sisters.

She considered all the things she couldn't control.

Exceller status seemed out of reach in the face of all that. Maybe it always had been.

Murphy was sprawled on the sofa in the den, hand in a candy dish filled with M&M's. On television, a kid wailed in agony, tongue stuck to an icy pole.

"Hey," Claire said, taking a seat beside her, and for a moment they quietly watched *A Christmas Story*, the light of each shifting scene flashing on their faces. There was strange comfort in this, just watching TV with her sister. Claire couldn't remember when they'd last seen a movie together.

She wondered how many movies Murphy had watched on her own.

"Want some?" Murphy surprised Claire by lifting the candy dish. "No maggots. I checked."

"I'm fine," said Claire.

Then she saw a flash of hurt in Murphy's eyes. Like this question wasn't about chocolate; it was a test. A turning point, a line between past and future.

Murphy had asked all those questions over the years — questions Claire had found annoying. Claire had kept saying no to them, again and again. And at some point Murphy had stopped asking. She'd given up.

Now, here was a simple offer of Christmas chocolate.

Was Claire really going to say no again?

She knew what she had to do. Before Murphy could pull the dish away, Claire plunged her hand into the candies, took a fistful, and crammed the chocolate into her mouth. It was the most un-Claire thing she'd done in over two years. It was the most un-*Harper* thing. And what Claire did next was even worse: She chewed for a moment, then opened her mouth wide, producing a chocolate-stained smile.

Murphy looked at her, stunned. "*Nice.* I didn't think you had it in you."

"Me neither," said Claire, licking her teeth free of sugar coating.

She felt alive, untethered from a weight that had been keeping her no more than an inch off the ground.

"What, there's a party in here and I wasn't invited?"

Eileen had come into the room with eyes similar to Mom's: damp and pinked. She didn't ask her question in anger, though. Claire knew Eileen's voices. This was the one she used when she was sorry but couldn't say it out loud.

Claire scooted over, motioning for Eileen to join them on the couch, and when she did, Claire made the move: She rested her head on Eileen's shoulder. Which was how Claire said she was sorry, but not out loud. Sorry for being a Harper Everly asshole. For deciding Eileen was a Settler and cutting her out of her life. For focusing on Ivy Leagues and mythical Ainsley St. John for so long, she'd forgotten about her real-life sisters in very real Oregon.

328

She and Eileen had been close once—bound together by blood and love.

Two years ago they'd broken apart.

Now, on Christmas Day . . . maybe they could begin to mend.

As the Sullivan sisters silently watched TV, Claire felt an emptying sensation, as though the blood and viscous fluids in her had been poured out and her organs had been swept clean. That nagging sensation she had to say sorry again was gone. She felt new, like a clear blue sky.

DECEMBER
TWENTY-SIXTH

THIRTY-THREE

Murphy

Home looked smaller than Murphy remembered. There was green mold on the vinyl siding, and paint was peeling from the shutters. The driveway was cracked in a hundred places, and the spruce in the front lawn looked malnourished. Murphy had known these things about her house; she'd seen them every day. Only now, in the hard light of December twenty-sixth, they were depressing.

Had 2270 Laramie ruined her forever? A badly built starter home in Emmet couldn't aspire to be a seaside Victorian mansion. Definitely not. But . . . it was home, and it was the only home Murphy had known. Before the closed bedroom doors, and in spite of the fights and silences, the sickness and death it had witnessed, this home had also seen good times.

Like the days of Cayenne Castle.

Mom pulled the Subaru into the carport, glancing in the rearview mirror for the umpteenth time to be sure Eileen's Caravan was behind them. That morning Kerry had driven them to the towing lot where the van had been deposited. Eileen had asked what she'd owed for the fee, and Kerry had given her a lengthy once-over before saying, "What I want is for you to take a minute to think how lucky you are." She'd pointed at Claire and Murphy. "The three of you. Merry Christmas."

And that had been that. Eileen had gotten the Caravan back, and the four Sullivans, rested from a night at Kerry and Bonnie's, had nothing left to do save drive home.

Kerry and Mom had hugged good-bye for a long time, and they'd told each other they'd keep in touch; Kerry and Bonnie were going to come down for a visit soon. Murphy was cool with that idea: Bonnie's cooking was killer, and Kerry had been a pretty chill sheriff about this whole mess.

As they'd driven away from Rockport, Murphy had done the best mental penance she could muster. She *did* think of how lucky she was to not be arrested and locked in a jail cell for Christmas. She was lucky, too, that Mark Enright hadn't returned to Rockport for vengeance, and that he hadn't been the one to find her dead asleep on the beach. As it turned out, there hadn't been a real Mark Enright. Not a murdering, malevolent one, anyway. Mark had been her dad.

John Sullivan had been a name and a face in photographs that Murphy had no real-life memories of. He'd been a sadness on late nights when she got to thinking too hard, and he'd been an awkwardness when she'd explained to every stranger who'd asked that she didn't have a dad, actually, that he'd died of cancer before she was born. John Sullivan had been a blank spot in Murphy's world. Now, he was Mark Enright, and she knew

334

more about Mark than she ever had about John. How weird.

Wasn't *everything* weird now?

Like the fact that Mom saw Murphy.

Even in the driveway, hours away from the coast, Murphy could taste the sea salt on her lips and feel every grain of sand on her cheek, remembering her mother's shakes and shouts. She saw with rainbow-bright vividness the relief that had filled Mom's face when Murphy had opened her eyes.

Mom had said, "Hey, hey. You're okay. Thank God you're okay."

She'd *seen* Murphy, and then she'd held her, carrying her up the bluff. And for the first time, Murphy hadn't minded being treated like a kid.

Mom cut the engine of the Subaru. Eileen had parked behind her, and she and Claire were climbing out of the van. Murphy wondered how *that* trip had been. Clearly, her sisters hadn't fought too hard, because they were both alive, no signs of claw marks. A lot had changed since that fight on the porch, when Claire had stormed away and both she and Eileen had shouted Murphy down.

Murphy, shut up.

Murph, for the love of God, not now.

She looked down, idly counting the knuckles of her right hand.

One, two, three —

"Murphy?"

Mom was out of the car, looking in from the driver's side.

They hadn't talked much on the drive down. Mom had played soft rock radio and Murphy had nodded off, head against the window. When they had spoken, Mom had asked about school, and Murphy had told her about drama club.

She hadn't told Mom about Siegfried. It didn't seem right yet. Still, it had been an okay talk. *Weird*, but okay.

"Murphy, is something wrong?" Sudden concern was stitched into Mom's face.

How did Murphy answer that? How did she explain her greatest fear, when it was something other magicians worked years to achieve, on purpose: a disappearing act. How did she express that she was afraid if she walked into this house, everything would go back to normal, and everyone—Eileen and Claire and Mom— would lose their ability to see her?

How could you say a thing like that?

So Murphy said, "I'm sorry you missed your cruise."

Mom was quiet. Then she got back in the car, shutting the door. Eileen and Claire were walking ahead, almost to the carport. Eileen peered toward the windshield with a confused expression, but a moment later Claire had opened the kitchen door, and the two of them disappeared into the house.

"I'm not sorry I missed it," said Mom. "I'm sorry I agreed to go in the first place."

"You work hard, though," said Murphy, pressing her sneakers into the floorboard. "You were right: A sweepstakes is a once-in-a-lifetime chance. You deserved a break."

"Maybe," said Mom, "but not that way."

At last Murphy felt she could say it.

"Sometimes," she said, "I think no one can see me. Does that make sense?"

Mom gripped the edge of the console, letting out a weird

cough. "Oh, Murphy. That was my life as a kid. I spent my whole damn childhood trying to be seen. Did you know I tracked down my mother?" The cough again. "No, you don't. I never told you. That's how I got to Rockport at seventeen: I tracked down my mother in Portland—my father was already dead—and I got her to sign the paper I needed to be emancipated. Even at family court, she wasn't looking at me. Could be she was so strung out she couldn't focus on anything."

Mom still held on to the console, not looking at Murphy. "I rode out with an old foster sister to Astoria. That's where we were headed, and we got car trouble in Rockport, and . . . God, I fell in love with the place. It was June, and it was the coast, and the weather was perfect, and I could picture myself living there forever, and that was the first time I was okay with being unseen. You know? I finally wanted to be *unnoticed* and live out the rest of my days in Rockport. No stand-in parents or social worker to perform for. And then I met your dad, and we both got seen. I got what I'd wanted when I was a kid, and it turned out to be hell."

Murphy's heart was unsteady, beating too soft one second, too hard the next. She hadn't ever pictured her mom as a teenager, because Mom didn't talk about that time, and there were no photos, and why would Murphy ask about it? That was the past. Only, it turned out the past was here, in the Subaru. Mom had been Murphy's age once, and scared and unseen too. And that teenager was part of Mom, still present, like the freckles on her hands.

Mom hadn't been seen either. That is, until she'd been seen in the worst possible way. Maybe it sucked a little to be Murphy Sullivan. But maybe it had sucked a lot more to be Leslie Clark.

"This isn't easy for me." Mom's voice bent on the words. "Maybe I'm sharing too much, or I told you girls too little. I don't know what I'm supposed to do, or if this is right. I just figured it out in Florida. I've been doing it wrong, you know?"

Murphy didn't know, exactly. Mom may have once been like Murphy, but Murphy had no idea what it was to be Mom: to get married, lose a husband, raise three children on your own. The endless work, the bills, the insurance calls . . .

Murphy saw that it wasn't that Mom cared too little.

It was that the world was too much.

It's not about me, she thought, looking into her mother's eyes. *It's about the Enrights and Rockport and a hundred things that happened before I was born. Behind the scenes. Out of sight. This show started a long time ago. I'm showing up after intermission.*

Murphy's lungs felt elastic, swelling out and taking in truckloads of air. She was thinking about Siegfried, and about how easy it was to get distracted with the *too muchness* of life.

Mom reached across the console, and Murphy took her hand.

"What I can promise you," said Mom, "is that I'll try to do better, okay?"

"Yeah," said Murphy, letting out the air in her stretchy lungs. "We'll all be better."

That night Murphy woke to a knock on her door and a flashlight beam in her eyes.

"Sup, Murph. Get your ass out of bed."

"Leenie, seriously," whispered another voice.

Then Claire was at Murphy's bedside, poking gently at her shoulder. "Sorry to wake you up, but we weren't going to leave you behind this time."

"W-where are you going?" Murphy's words slurred from sleepiness as she propped herself up in bed.

"Straight to hell," said Eileen, matter-of-factly.

Claire rolled her eyes. "It's a surprise, okay? Put on your coat, and we'll go."

Murphy did as Claire asked, though with confusion. She followed her sisters into the kitchen and out the carport door.

"Does Mom know about this?" she whispered after she'd climbed into the Caravan.

"Don't worry," said Claire, at a normal volume now they were safely outside the house. "It'll be a short trip. She won't even know we're gone."

"Where have I heard *that* before," Murphy groused, while her insides danced a tango. Her sisters were going someplace secretly, in the middle of the night. And this time, they'd invited her—no stowing away required.

Eileen placed the key in the van's ignition and turned. The Caravan started up, and Claire looked back from the passenger seat to say, "Seat belt."

Murphy was ahead of the game. Her seat belt was already fastened, and her hand had wandered into her puffer coat's right pocket, taking hold of the rope trick there. She held the rope in her lap, beginning the process:

Over, under, tug through and out.

The van rumbled forward through winter drizzle, wipers squeaking against glass. Streetlights caught on Murphy's face, then flitted away. Eileen was keeping the van on town streets, no highways. Claire had said it would be a short trip.

It was. Minutes later the van stopped at the curb of a shadow-filled field. Murphy peered through the rain-speckled window, making out shapes of jutting stones that rose from the earth.

They were at a cemetery.

Claire got out of the van and opened the sliding door.

"What're we doing here?" Murphy asked, clutching the rope.

Eileen appeared at the door. "Didn't you say you wanted to see Dad's grave?"

Dad.

John Sullivan.

Mark Enright.

Murphy *had* said that. She just hadn't thought they'd noticed.

Murphy got out of the van, following her sisters up a dirt path edged by overgrown grass and fronds. Mist gathered on her coat, and the earth gave way easily beneath her Uggs. Ahead, Eileen's flashlight cut through the night. Then, sooner than Murphy had expected, Eileen turned off the path, walking into the field—the graveyard.

Claire followed, Murphy keeping close behind.

They walked on for a while longer, passing through the ankle-high grass until, again, Eileen stopped, shining her light on a tombstone that rose from the earth in a perfect arc, like a well-filed fingernail.

For some strange reason, Murphy thought of A Christmas Carol, and the inscription EBENEZER SCROOGE. Of course, that's not what was written on this stone. It was her dad's name. His *not*-name: John Sullivan, a life with a starting date in 1982 and an end date before Murphy's birth.

"You were technically here, at the funeral," Eileen nudged Murphy. "I don't remember much about it, but I do remember Mom being pregnant with you. She wore this long, billowy black dress."

"And I was here?" Claire asked in a whisper.

"Yeah," said Eileen. "Mom held both our hands."

"Oh," Claire said vaguely. Her eyes were stuck on the tombstone.

"So, we're here," Eileen announced. "We came to see you, Dad. Mark. John. Whatever you want to be called. And I wanted you to know, I get that you had a shitty life, and I hope there were good parts too. I hope Mom was one of those good parts, and me and Claire. And Murphy, even though you didn't get to know her. And if there's any afterlife? I hope you're happy there, and you can see we're getting it together on our end. Like, we're family, and we'll try to be better about sticking together. Because you didn't really get that chance, huh?"

"Leenie," said Claire, "you're being bleak."

Eileen swept the flashlight beam across the graveyard. "Uh, bleak's the operative word here. What else do you want?"

"I don't know. Just, I wanted to see it. To be here. We don't have to make a speech."

"Sure," Eileen said. "No speech."

Murphy studied the grave, turning her thumb over the rope trick. Claire could say what she wanted; Murphy had liked Eileen's speech. She hoped that she had been, in fact, a really good thing in her dad's life. The promise, at least, of a good thing.

She didn't want to speak, but she was feeling an urge—an irresistible need to *show* him who she was. She walked closer to the grave, and she knelt into the wet, high grass. It felt only natural, what she did next: She set the rope on the grave, as she would a bouquet of flowers, and backed away.

The sisters were silent for a moment, and then Claire reached for something in her own coat pocket. She took Murphy's former place, kneeling to set her object alongside the rope. Eileen's flashlight revealed what it was: an iPhone, its screen shattered to smithereens.

"Well, damn," Eileen said grittily, and then she was also at the grave, setting down a very small something: a wrapped piece of bubble gum.

Murphy felt like crying, and somehow Claire—*Claire* of all people—seemed to know, because she put a hand on Murphy's shoulder and said, "Hey, we're going to be fine."

Murphy looked up. "You don't know that for sure."

"Nope," said Eileen, slapping a hand on Murphy's other shoulder. "We don't know shit."

"Anyway," said Murphy, "you guys will leave soon. No one needs a spare tire."

The air was damp, and the silence intense.

"Wait, what?" Claire asked.

Murphy toed the soft ground. "I'm the spare tire of the family. Everyone knows."

The flashlight's beam went askance. Eileen was crouching, meeting Murphy's eyes. "Hey. Listen the hell to me. You're not the spare tire, Murph. You're the goddamn engine."

Murphy opened her mouth to talk back, but Eileen didn't

allow it. She threw her arms around Murphy, dragging her into a hug. Then Claire was holding them, squeezing tight, and though it was impossible, Murphy was sure: She could feel their two hearts beating in time with hers.

She knew her house was small. She knew Mom was trying her best and might still fail. She knew Dad would always be dead. She knew Eileen and Claire would leave her one day. But tonight, in a graveyard, Murphy stayed in her sisters' arms.

The core of their embrace. The engine.

Even when it was over, Eileen kept a hand on Murphy's arm.

"Hey," she said. "If you want to be noticed, Murph, if you need help . . . it's okay to ask. Say it straight out. I mean, I can be dense. Wrapped up in my brain. Sometimes you need to give me a wake-up call. Just ask."

Murphy was thinking of Siegfried. She couldn't talk, because a cry was waiting in her throat. She nodded, and Eileen nodded back, and they hugged again.

This embrace was magic. Not the kind Murphy studied and practiced, but magic just the same. It was real-life magic, because it was made by real people, living real lives, with no illusion or sequins or sleight of hand. With seams showing and rough edges, with curses and scrapes and mess.

Plain, real magic.

The kind that could change everything.

TWENTY-EIGHT
YEARS BEFORE

THE TRIO'S TOWER

The tower was Mark's idea, to begin with.

That summer the Enrights had moved from San Francisco to Rockport, and one of Mark's first orders of business in their new town was to buy *The Three Musketeers* by Alexandre Dumas from the Sandpiper Bookshop on Main.

Ms. Haynes from his old school had recommended the book.

"It might be a tad old for you," she'd said, "but I think you'll have fun."

Which, of course, had only made Mark want to read it more. Sure, there were words he didn't understand and long, winding passages he skipped, but the real meat of the story, and the illustration of three brave men declaring "One for all, and all for one!"—*that* had kept him riveted. It had first made him realize that he, John, and Pat could form their own brigade.

"We're the trio," he told John. "The three of us can face whatever missions come our way."

Mark was full of vision—a painter of colors, words, and adventures alike.

"What missions are coming our way?" John asked, skeptical.

"We'll make them up," said Mark. "We can hold meetings in the tower. It can be *our* place, just ours."

This part, at least, John understood. Their parents didn't go up those spiral stairs—neither their silent, stolid father, nor their constantly angered mother. They remained below, brewing arguments and resentment. Things were especially bad in the summer, when the winds stilled and the house overheated. The summer made their father quieter and their mother angrier. Downstairs were shouts and scoldings, unpredictable outbursts.

The tower, though? It was untouchable.

"It *could* be our place," John said, thinking it over. "Not a lot of made-up adventures, though, huh? We could do practical things."

"Like what?"

"Study for tests."

Mark made a face. "It's summer."

"Well, you can work on your paintings, and I can study."

"But . . . it's *summer*."

"I'm studying ahead."

John was full of plans—plenty of which he hadn't shared with his brothers. Plans for how he would study so hard that one day he'd get out of this house, away from Mom's raging and Dad's indifference, away from the too-tiny streets and chattering mouths at Ramsey's Diner. He'd leave here for the east coast, where he'd get into a prestigious Boston school. That's why he studied, even though it was summer, and even though he was "only" twelve.

You could never study too much, or too early. Not when you had a goal in mind.

When the brothers told Patrick about the plan, his eyes got wide as full moons.

"The tower's creepy," he said.

"We'll make it nice," said Mark, coaxingly. "It won't be creepy if the three of us are there. Anyway, there are all those old books, from the last owner. Could be money hidden in some of them."

Patrick considered before saying, "It *would* be a good place to spy. From the window, way up high?"

"Spy?" John scoffed. "There's nothing to spy on in Rockport, Pat."

"How would you know if you haven't tried?"

With that challenge, Patrick took off from the hallway, ascending the spiral stairs in an all-stops-out run.

Mark and John shared a look, shaking their heads.

"Weird kid," said John.

Mark agreed. Patrick was full of energy—often frenetic, zipping from one interest to the next. He had strange ideas and so much life, Mark sometimes worried there was too much of it, and that it would get him into trouble one day.

For now, though, he was just a kid. He deserved the chance to run upstairs, especially when that meant the Enright brothers would be together. They *had* to stick together, like Athos, Porthos, and Aramis. No one else in this town, parents included, were on their side. They were the trio, and if they had each other's backs, they'd be okay.

"YOU GUYS!" Patrick called. "It's still creepy, but . . . it's kind of cool up here too."

349

Mark and John exchanged a smirk and then they, too, set up the spiral stairs.

So the Trio's Tower was occupied for the first time. It was an auspicious beginning for the Enright brothers. But, like many youthful beginnings, it reached a less optimistic end.

If, twenty-eight years later, you were to ask *why* . . .

You might not get any real answers.

JANUARY
TWENTY-FIRST

THIRTY-FOUR

Eileen

The sun was shining.

Emmet wasn't known for clear winter skies—for clear skies, period—and until now, the new year had been gray. This morning, though, the clouds had cleared, and a strong sun beamed down from a crystalline sky. If Eileen believed in good omens, she'd take this to be one: hopeful weather on her first day of AA.

The meeting had been everything she'd expected. The introductory "Hi, Insert-Name-Here." The linoleum in a church basement. The awkwardness. The bad and/or sad stories. The sobriety chips.

The meeting had also been nothing like she'd expected. For instance, there was Finny, her sponsor, who was a gray-haired, flannel-wearing ex–rock climber who told Eileen she was "rad" for showing up. There was the tray of homemade green tea mochi, brought in by a two-year-sober chef. There was the fact that, when

Eileen had introduced herself, no one had judgmentally asked her how old she was. And how, after the meeting, when Eileen had walked out of Prince of Peace Lutheran's basement and into the sun, she got an urge she thought had died two years ago.

She wanted to paint this shockingly sunny day.

Eileen drove home in the Caravan, thinking about something she'd told Murphy in the graveyard the day after Christmas: "If you need help, it's okay to ask."

It was simple advice.

So how had Eileen not taken it herself, until today?

Maybe because asking for help felt like extracting her own teeth, Novocain-free.

She was doing it, though. New year, new Eileen.

She snorted to herself, making a turn at a four-way stop. She was beginning to sound like Claire's patron saint, Harper Everly.

Only, no. Because, unlike Harper, Eileen planned for failure. In fact, she guessed she probably would fail a *lot* this year. The only difference from last year was that she wouldn't fail alone.

A lot of things had changed since Rockport. For one, Eileen knew the whole story. Mom had told the truth.

Knowing that truth didn't instantly heal the sore spot under Eileen's skin—the one that had formed years ago. It had carved out a space in her heart, though. Because teenage Leslie Clark hadn't asked for any of this. Life had happened to her, *at* her, in a bad way. She hadn't had a family to make it better. She hadn't had sisters, the way Eileen did.

Eileen was beginning to see that Mom had been doing the best she could. A young single mother, raising three kids on minimum wage, paying off her dead husband's medical bills. A mom with a dark secret, but not the secret Eileen had assumed. She'd done the best she could with what life had given her. And really, wasn't that all any person could do?

Including Eileen.

It wasn't that Eileen was well now, or cured. When it came to the Jack Daniel's and her darkest thoughts, Eileen wasn't sure there was a "cure," in the real sense of the word. Amelioration, maybe. That was AA. That was the prospect of the Myrtle Waugh Fellowship.

Eileen wasn't well, but for the first time in a long time, she thought that maybe, one day, she might be. For today, the thought was enough. As was this fact: She was Mark Enright's daughter, and he hadn't been a killer. He'd been the father of her memories. He'd been the one with the citrusy scent and swishy bangs. *He'd* been the artist, the same one who had sat with her at a kitchen table and made finger-painted animals.

She had Mark Enright's blood in her veins. It was the blood of brothers, some broken, some reclusive, some beaten down. It was the blood of mothers, some absent and some monstrous. The blood of fathers, some quiet and some dead. The blood of sisters, running hot and contentious, warm and loving. Enrights, Clarks, Sullivans, and other ancestors with stories Eileen would never know—they were part of her, but none of them determined who she was.

And now art wasn't something to be feared. Art could be a *way out*.

Claire had made that possible, and while Eileen hadn't decided about the fellowship yet, she did mean to drive to Eugene in two weeks' time, for the interview.

She was doing the best she could.

Eileen pulled the Caravan into the carport and parked. When she came around to the house, she found Claire sitting on the front porch, wearing her peacoat and messy hair bun. Sun slanted across her face, drawing thick shadows of evergreen branches on her cheeks.

Eileen stopped for a moment, watching her. She and Claire, they'd been close. They'd shared secrets and fought battles, side by side. Then they'd lost the threads that had been holding them together. Maybe those threads were ripped out for good.

Maybe, too, there was another pattern to be stitched.

Claire was a living portrait in the sun and shadows—someone Eileen wanted to paint. She'd call the piece *Exceller*, and she'd mean it in the most unironic way.

Eileen breathed in deep and walked forward.

"Hey," she said, reaching the porch. "Weird weather, huh?"

THIRTY-FIVE

Claire

At the same time Eileen was driving home from AA, Claire was composing a text to Ainsley St. John.

She used a phone she'd bought from a woman on Craigslist two weeks ago. It was nowhere near as nice as her last one, but these days Claire cared less about battery life and video quality.

Ainsley had written plenty of times since her YALE, BABY! text.

Once to say, Hey, you alive?

Another to say, Happy New Year, hope you're well.

A third to say, Worried about you, girl. I've decided on Yale, hope I'll see you there.

Claire knew she'd been a bad friend. At first she hadn't responded because she hadn't known how. Then she hadn't because she no longer had a working phone. And *then* she hadn't because there'd been too much happening: school starting back up, and a return to the jewelry business, and—the biggest change—spending time with her sisters at night.

Claire didn't shut her bedroom door that often these days. Instead, after school and on the weekends, the sisters gathered in the den to watch an awful reality show, or—Claire's choice—*Jeopardy!*

Sometimes, they just talked.

It was new, and it was nice. It was also another poor excuse for why Claire hadn't found the chance to write Ainsley back.

Now, on the twenty-first of January, she knew it was time. She'd spent a full month in silence. That had to end.

And oh, the possible texts she could send:

I inherited a house from my long-lost uncle.

Or,

I uncovered way more family secrets than any seventeen-year-old has a right to know.

Or,

I was busy having a crisis about my identity.

Or,

I've become disillusioned by the college application process.

Or,

The truth is, I've fantasized about meeting you for months, and I know it sounds crazy, and you have a girlfriend, but I thought you could be my first kiss.

Instead, Claire wrote, Turns out I didn't get in. I'm so happy for you, though. Best wishes, girl. <3

It felt disingenuous. It even felt a little cold. It also felt right. Claire sent the text while sitting on the porch, warming her face in the rare January sun. Then she shut off the phone—a symbolic move.

She closed her eyes, listening to the rustle of wind in the

358

evergreens, breathing in the scent of grass and sunbathed concrete. She listened as a juddering vehicle pulled up the driveway. Then the engine cut. Claire only opened her eyes when a voice said, "Hey. Weird weather, huh?"

"Weird weather," Claire agreed. She motioned across the porch to a white-and-green-checkered lawn chair.

Eileen sat, stretching out her spider-long legs and knocking together the heels of her combat boots.

"Where were you?" Claire asked.

"AA."

Claire thought at first that she was joking. Eileen did have a sick sense of humor.

Then she saw it in Eileen's eyes: the light.

"Oh," she said. "Wow. That's . . . Leenie, that's . . . Good for you."

"Turns out I should tell people. You know, accountability. That's pretty big there."

Claire was remembering two years' worth of Eileen shutting herself in that garage, the late-night passes in the hallway and the biting sweet stench of Eileen's breath. The dull eyes, the monosyllabism. She was especially remembering a sentence that could not be unyelled: *Better to be a bitch than a burned-out drunk like you.*

For all their recent nights of TV-watching and talking, Claire hadn't addressed that.

"I'm sorry," she murmured, when the memories had ceased their parade. "Leenie, what I said at the house, on Christmas Eve? I'm sorry."

"Well. You weren't wrong."

Claire studied her sister's sharp-cheeked profile. With every passing day they'd spent together, Claire had better understood a truth: You couldn't easily make up two lost years, and the words, both spoken and unspoken, contained therein.

She wondered if it was a good time to bring up the news. Eileen didn't seem upset, so Claire decided she might as well.

"Mr. Knutsen called the house. He left a message about you missing an appointment?"

Claire braced herself, waiting for Eileen to lose her temper and call Claire a goddamn snoop.

Instead she said, "Yeah, I've been trying to figure that shit out. I know Mom said it was our decision, that we didn't need to consult her, or whatever. But I don't want to deal yet."

"Deal with what?"

Eileen shrugged. "The paperwork, I guess. The legal stuff. Like, what's the point? Until you and Murph inherit, we can't sell."

Claire studied her hands. "Maybe there's a loophole or something."

"Well, if there were, would you want to sell it?"

Claire considered before saying, "I'm not sure. It's a house, it's not Dad. Knowing everything we do, though . . . selling seems wrong. Like maybe it's something Dad wouldn't want. Him, or Patrick, or John."

Dad. To Claire he was only a fuzzy memory of broad shoulders and a deep laugh. Of a chocolatey cure to a scraped knee. The stories that Cathy, Kerry, and Mom had told seemed foreign to Claire, distant from the dead father and absent mother she'd known. Leslie and Mark may as well have been Wendy and Peter Pan—fairy-tale characters.

"Whoa," said Eileen. "So, really? No sale? What about the money?"

Claire realized that Eileen was trying to be funny. She'd missed this side of her sister, however infuriating it could be. She'd missed Eileen's humor, even her jabs.

"I guess money's not as important anymore," Claire said. "No college education to fund."

"Bullshit," said Eileen, humor suddenly gone. "You're college material, Claire. Just not for those snobby-ass institutions. You apply next year to colleges you'll get into. Hell, you'll get *scholarships*. U of O would probably offer a full ride."

Claire looked out on their neighborhood, a stretch of vinyl-sided ranches and crumbling, weed-choked sidewalks. She'd been so singularly focused on getting off this street, she wondered if she'd lost sight of the good on the periphery. Like state schools. Like sisters.

Lately, she'd been trying to focus on what she'd blurred out before. Hard as it was, she hadn't been making plans. Hadn't been looking for golden moments. Hadn't been watching Harper Everly. She'd just been *living*, taking it in.

"Leenie," she said, softly. "Are you going to the interview?"

She'd given Eileen everything when they'd returned to Emmet: the artwork she'd submitted, the application, the letter with the interview information.

"Yeah," said Eileen. "I think so."

"Then you'll do the program?"

"I don't know. I might try. I think I need it."

Claire's intestines knotted into a bow. "Well, that's good."

Eileen eyed her, saying nothing.

361

"What?" Claire asked, at last.

"You know, the thing about Eugene . . . I couldn't afford the room and board. It'd be a lot easier with a roommate. A rich one, with her own business."

Claire exhaled. "Not funny."

"I'm not being funny. I'm saying you should come. What else are you going to do when you graduate? And you can do your business anywhere, right?"

"Murphy, though."

"We'll talk to her. It's, like, an hour away. We can visit her easy. Anyway, she marches to the beat of her own drum, you know?"

Claire laughed shortly. "I know."

"And Mom, she's . . ."

"More *here*," said Claire. "Yeah."

It was true. Mom's shifts weren't any shorter, and a tension remained between her and her daughters—syllables that died on the tongue and hugs not quite seen through. But this past week she'd woken the sisters up with breakfast. No gourmet feast, just toasted Pop-Tarts for Eileen and Murphy and a cup of yogurt, no gluten, for Claire. That was something.

"There's one condition," Eileen said abruptly.

"Huh?"

"On moving to Eugene. You can't be whining about how it's not the Ivy League."

Claire laughed a little—at the Ivy League, at herself. "I'm not obsessed anymore, believe it or not."

Eileen looked doubtful.

"I mean it. I know it sounds cheesy, but . . . I've been think-

362

ing maybe you can find happiness anywhere. Doesn't have to be Yale."

Kerry and Bonnie were on her mind, though she didn't say that aloud. She felt, instinctively, that Eileen knew.

"You're right," said Eileen. "Sounds cheesy as hell."

There was Eileen's smirk again, and the sight of it filled Claire with warmth. She could go to Eugene. She could start a new life. She could even, maybe, find an Ainsley St. John who wasn't an Internet pipe dream.

Claire could do that in the future.

It wasn't excelling by Harper Everly standards, but it might be perfection, all the same.

THIRTY-SIX

Murphy

A t the same time Claire was texting Ainsley, Murphy was preparing the trick.

Eileen and Claire didn't know about it . . . yet. That would defeat the purpose of a surprise magic show.

Murphy had special-ordered this trick and, after almost twenty practices, she had decided she was ready for a debut.

She looked out the window, noting Claire and Eileen on the porch. They were talking, but seemed chill enough. Neither of them was shut in their bedroom, so they couldn't accuse her of bothering them. In fact, they hadn't done that since their return from Rockport.

Murphy set the plastic tumblers in a straight line on the coffee table.

She breathed in deep, pep-talking herself as she went into the kitchen. There, she prepared the show's refreshments: three coffee mugs of ginger ale, for old time's sake. These would be the celebratory drinks once the trick was through.

As she poured the last of the fizzing sodas, her eyes strayed to the kitchen's back door and the emptied, cleaned-out tank resting there. Siegfried's tank. His final home, but not his final resting place.

Since her seaside farewell, Murphy had looked up the way tides worked. She was pretty positive that Siegfried had washed up on the shore of Rockport and maybe even scarred some poor runner out for a morning jog. She felt bad about that, but she no longer felt guilty.

Murphy took the drinks into the den, where she stopped and stared at a new picture over the mantle: three kid brothers, arms slung over shoulders. Eileen had stolen this one item — just one — from the house on Laramie. A final crime.

Looking at it, Murphy considered that maybe there was an Enright curse, like Mom had said. If there was, Murphy liked to hope she and her sisters were in the business of curse breaking.

Even weeks after she'd said them, Eileen's words echoed in Murphy's heart: *You're the engine.*

She was starting to believe it.

Drinks prepared, show at the ready, Murphy went out to the porch.

"You two busy?"

Her sisters looked at her. There was light in Eileen's eyes. There was no phone in Claire's hands.

Eileen said, "What you got cooking?"

"It's a surprise."

Claire raised a brow. "Surprise, huh? Then I guess we'd better go see."

They followed her into the den, to the site of Cayenne Castles past. There were no parapets raised, no blanket walls or pillow thrones. The memories were there, though—the words the Sullivan sisters had spoken, and the promises they'd made, drenched deep in carpet fibers and painted into the walls. Murphy could sense the past Sir Sages, Princess Paprikas, and Prince Peppers watching them, an invisible audience.

The pressure was on.

"Okay," said Murphy, as Eileen and Claire took their seats on the couch. "Behold, before you, three cups."

Eileen said, "Beheld."

"Pick them up, check them out. Make sure there's nothing weird about them."

"Weird, how?" asked Claire.

"You know, false bottoms, et cetera."

Eileen rapped one cup with her knuckles. Claire turned over another, running her thumb along its seam. When the inspection was complete, they set the cups on the table and Murphy sorted them back in their straight line.

"Now!" she said, with practiced dramatic flourish. "Look at this ring."

From her flannel shirt pocket, Murphy produced a smooth metal ring, small enough to fit any of their fingers.

Claire took it first, looked it over, and handed it to Eileen, who, after further examination, poked out her tongue and licked it.

"Leenie," Claire said, aghast.

"I'm being thorough," Eileen replied. "You want thoroughness, right, Murph?"

Murphy nodded earnestly. "As thorough as you want."

Thoroughness through, the ring was returned to Murphy's keeping.

"Now comes the moment of truth," she announced.

Kneeling before the coffee table, Murphy dragged out the centermost cup and placed the ring beneath it. Then the magic began. Murphy moved the cups. She swept them across the table, orchestrating a dance—curves and spirals and pirouettes, changing hands from the first cup to second to third. She carried on a minute, so long that Eileen began to chuckle.

Finally, she brought the cups to a resting position, forming their perfect line.

"All right," she said. "Where's the ring?"

Eileen leaned forward and, with boundless confidence, picked up the centermost cup.

There was no ring underneath.

"Shit," she said. "Really thought I had it."

Murphy turned to Claire with a solemn, professional air. "Did you have a different cup in mind?"

Claire licked her pink-stained lips. After deliberation, she pointed at the left-hand tumbler.

Murphy raised it.

The ring wasn't there.

Then Murphy made the first of her "ta-da" moves: She lifted the right-hand cup.

There was no ring.

Claire gasped, and Murphy's heart filled with joy. She didn't let on, though. The trick wasn't over.

"Huh!" she said, maintaining the act. "How strange. It's seems the ring has *disappeared*."

She placed the three cups back in position.

"Let me try one last thing," she said.

She began the dance again: carving, whirling, circling. She drew the cups around the table with fluid finesse.

Then she brought them to a stop.

"Leenie," she said. "Check your cup again."

Eileen did. She grabbed it with the fervor of a little kid, and there, on the table, was the ring.

"Knew it," she said, scooping it up. With satisfaction, she slid it on her finger. "Perfect fit."

"Is that the ring you handled before?" Murphy asked, still all business.

Eileen held her hand close to her face and darted her tongue out. "Sure tastes the same."

"Claire," Murphy said. "Check the left cup."

Claire lifted it from the table as though afraid she might be letting out a monster.

There was no monster, though. There was another ring.

"Whoa," said Eileen, while Claire picked up the ring, mystification on her face.

"Is *that* the ring you handled before?"

"It . . . sure looks like it."

Grinning triumphantly, Murphy removed the last tumbler from the table, revealing a third ring. She picked it up, face aglow.

"Three rings for the three of us," she announced.

"Damn, Murph," said Eileen. "You've gotten good."

Claire was still studying her ring, and for a moment, Murphy felt uncertain. "I know it's not nice jewelry. Not the kind you make. But it's for you to keep. For us to remember each other by."

"You make it sound like we're going off to war," snorted Eileen.

"Well, okay." Murphy shrugged. "Make it morbid, if you want."

Claire's eyes met Murphy's, holding them in a solemn stare. "It's perfect, Murph," she said. "I've never made anything this good."

Murphy couldn't keep down her grin any longer. She'd done it. She'd finished the act, and she hadn't made a mistake. What's more, she'd had a willing audience.

"Three rings," Eileen mused. "You know, this is probably going to turn our skin green."

Murphy kept grinning. "I thought it'd be a nice magic start to the year."

"Damn straight." Eileen flashed her hand. "This thing's not coming off. I mean, not if it's *magical*."

"Three rings for the three of us," Claire said, softly.

"Sullivan sisters forever," Murphy added.

The days of Operation Memory Making were over. The days of Simply Being Together were here.

So the memory of Cayenne Castle remained, kept alive by a planner, a visionary, and a performer.

It was an auspicious beginning, and as for its end . . .

Well, you'd have to ask the Sullivan sisters themselves.

ACKNOWLEDGMENTS

Thank you, Beth Phelan, for cheering on Eileen, Claire, and Murphy from the very beginning, and thank you to everyone at Gallt & Zacker for the ongoing support. Thank you, Zareen Jaffery, for seeing me through our fourth novel together and for believing in the Sullivan sisters' story in all its zany iterations. My thanks to Alexa Pastor, Andre Wheeler, and Dainese Santos for your behind-the-scenes help and e-mailed assistance. Thank you, Heather McLeod, for your incisive copyedits. Thank you to Chloë Foglia for the stunning cover design, to Danielle Davis for the rockin' lettering, and to Pedro Tapa for an illustration that captures the sisters so perfectly. And big thanks to everyone else at Simon & Schuster Books for Young Readers who made this novel's publication possible.

The usual suspects, you know who you are, and I'm so grateful for you. It's been ten years since we met across the pond, Shelly, and you're still the best Little Miss Twin around. Destiny, you're the Louise to my Tina. Nicole, stay fabulous and give Harmony a treat from me. Mai, my fellow Marco Polo-er, by the time you read this we WILL have conquered *The Brothers Karamazov*. Kayla, thanks for keeping our kitchen twatwaffle-free. Shannon, my witchy friend, I can't wait to see what adventures await you in

New England. Hilary, you're the bee's knees, the giraffe's neck, the anteater's tongue! Sasha, you're the coolest gal I know, and you make it Clown But Fashion every day. Libby, thanks for being such a rad college-but-not-college friend. Lastly, all my literary love to the ladies of Phoebe's Book Club.

Thank you to Jen at Pop! Goes the Reader for being a fearless, indefatigable book blogger from the day I e-met you. Thank you to Kristen, librarian extraordinaire, and to Seoling, publishing wonder, for your friendship and care packages and general brilliance. Thank you, too, to teachers, librarians, and bloggers—those I have and have not met—for all you do for young readers and the YA community. You have my eternal gratitude.

Thank you, Mom and Dad, for always supporting my writing, and my thanks to the extended family for your love and encouragement. Thank you, Annie and Matt, for first introducing me to the state that would one day become my home and the inspiration for this novel. It's the best thing, being neighbors with you. Thank you to Bob, Vicki, and Megan for accepting me into your magnificent family.

Alli, thank you for loving me; for moving cross-country in only a car, with a dog; and for making this new home with me in Oregon. Thank you for cherishing my stories from the day we met. The story I cherish most is the one we share.

And thank you, dear reader, for journeying to the coast and back with me. May you never be afraid to build and rebuild Cayenne Castles of your own.